Kelly found herself unable to look away from the slender, dark-haired boy.

He had to be Alex's son. He looked just like him.

"Hello," she said, offering him a gentle smile. Hoping to coax one from him. But he just continued watching her, and she found herself wondering if he knew how to smile at all. "What are you reading?"

"An encyclopedia. I wanted to see where Arabia is. It's in a book I'm reading. About a boy and a horse."

"I remember a book like that," Kelly said. "It was my favorite when I was about your age. Except for the first part. It was kind of scary. The boy is all alone at first. And being alone…well it…"

"Stinks," he mumbled.

In that second, Kelly knew this little boy might have everything money could buy…but he didn't have what mattered most of all—love.

Dear Reader,

Silhouette **Special Edition** welcomes you to romance...
and to summer! June is sure to be the start of a great season,
beginning, of course, with THAT SPECIAL WOMAN!
This month, bestselling author Sherryl Woods takes you
on a journey like you've never experienced...and neither
has her heroine, who gets into more trouble than she can
handle—but she *does* have a sexy adventurer by her side in
Riley's Sleeping Beauty.

June also marks the beginning of a wonderful new trilogy,
MAN, WOMAN AND CHILD, from veteran authors
Christine Flynn, Robin Elliott and Pat Warren. It all begins
this month with *A Father's Wish,* Christine Flynn's story of
a man searching for his lost love and child. Reader favorite
Marie Ferrarella is also back with a poignant story in
Brooding Angel. And a mother's determination not only
reunites her with her child but finds her a ready-made family
in Arlene James's *Child of Her Heart.*

In Trisha Alexander's latest, *The Girl Next Door* decides her
best friend, a freewheeling bachelor and sexy confidant, is the
man she's been looking for all her life. Now she just has to
convince him that they're falling in love. And we wrap up the
month of June by welcoming a new author to **Special Edition.**
A Family for Ronnie by Julie Caille is a touching story sure to
warm your hearts.

So don't miss a moment of these wonderful books. It's just
the beginning of a summer filled with love and romance from
Special Edition!

Sincerely,

Tara Gavin
Senior Editor

Please address questions and book requests to:
Silhouette Reader Service
U.S.: 3010 Walden Ave., P.O. Box 1325, Buffalo, NY 14269
Canadian: P.O. Box 609, Fort Erie, Ont. L2A 5X3

CHRISTINE FLYNN

A FATHER'S WISH

Silhouette®

SPECIAL EDITION®

Published by Silhouette Books
America's Publisher of Contemporary Romance

SILHOUETTE BOOKS

ISBN 0-373-09962-2

A FATHER'S WISH

CHRISTINE FLYNN

admits to being interested in just about everything, which is why she considers herself fortunate to have turned her interest in writing into a career. She feels that a writer gets to explore it all and, to her, exploring relationships—especially the intense, bittersweet or even lighthearted relationships between men and women—is fascinating.

She has a grown daughter and lives in the Southwest with her husband and two shamelessly spoiled dogs.

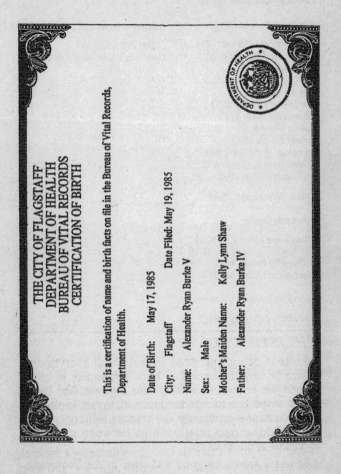

THE CITY OF FLAGSTAFF
DEPARTMENT OF HEALTH
BUREAU OF VITAL RECORDS
CERTIFICATION OF BIRTH

This is a certification of name and birth facts on file in the Bureau of Vital Records, Department of Health.

Date of Birth: May 17, 1985

City: Flagstaff   Date Filed: May 19, 1985

Name: Alexander Ryan Burke V

Sex: Male

Mother's Maiden Name: Kelly Lynn Shaw

Father: Alexander Ryan Burke IV

Prologue

Abby Thatcher laid her head on her folded arms and tried not to cry. Winthrop hated tears, though God knew he'd handled enough weeping women during the forty years he'd practiced law in this small office in downtown Phoenix.

Exhaustion, combined with sorrow, had her feeling numb. But the numbness didn't make the ache in her heart go away. She raised her head and, taking a deep breath, straightened her thin shoulders and patted her salt-and-pepper hair. Indulging her grief wouldn't get the work done, and now, on top of everything else, she had to deal with the ineptitude of the temporary help she'd just dismissed. In two days, the silly girl hadn't been able to follow the simplest directions.

It had been only three days since Winthrop's funeral, but with all Abby had had to cope with since his fatal heart attack last week, it seemed more like three years.

She opened a file on her always-organized desk, wishing instead she could give way to her grief for the man she had loved for over four decades; the man who'd seen her only as his dedicated, organized and ever-so-dependable secretary. There had never been any hope for her. Winthrop Ames, Esq., had been married to the law.

Her last official duty would be to close his office. Before she could, she had to make arrangements for his pending cases and dispose of a lifetime's accumulation of files, since he had no partners.

The half-dozen cartons along the oak-paneled wall of the small study would be picked up this afternoon by a messenger from the law firm the client had asked to have assume the case. Yesterday, she'd directed the temporary girl to mail several files. Abby was still waiting to hear from other people she'd spoken with regarding their cases, and had letters to write to Winthrop's remaining clients.

But before another sheet of paper left the office, she needed to tend to the special files; those that had been so dear to Winthrop's heart.

With a sense of purpose, she crossed the room to the cartons she'd filled herself. Large manila envelopes, along with a stack of typing paper the temporary had failed to put away after mailing the real-estate files, were on the desk next to them.

Abby stopped in front of a yellow carton. A small smile touched her lips as she looked fondly at the folders inside.

The babies, she thought, a rush of warmth suffusing her.

Winthrop's practice had been varied, but his favorite cases were the adoptions. He loved little children. Three cases in particular had been special to Winthrop: Shaw, Russell and Parker.

It was with that thought that she noticed the first folder wasn't the one she'd placed there yesterday. She was certain she'd left the Shaw file in front. She specifically remembered putting it there after instructing the temporary to mail everything in the carton next to it.

Perplexed, she removed the box of stationery and mailing labels the temporary had left on the box and searched through the remaining folders. The Parker and Russell files were there, but where was Shaw?

Ten years earlier

Three o'clock in the morning was not an unusual time for a baby to waken, wanting to be fed. At least, that was what the matronly woman in the rocking chair told Alex when, unable to sleep, he found himself standing in the doorway of the softly lit nursery.

The woman, a retired nurse recommended to the Burkes by a friend of the family, lifted her robe-clad bulk to stand by the frilled and canopied bassinet. Averting her eyes from Alex's bare chest and the silk pajama bottoms clinging to his lean hips, she beckoned him into the room.

"He's full now, and dry. He'll be sleeping in no time." She held the tiny bundle out to him. "Would you like to hold him while I take his bottle down to the kitchen?"

Alex hesitated. Then, he gave her a nod. At least, he thought he did, for the woman finally smiled at him. Since Winthrop Ames and his secretary had brought the baby to the house this afternoon, Alex hadn't gotten close enough to do much more than stare at the impossibly tiny infant. Alex's mother had started fussing over the child the moment Ames walked through the door with him, and Alex had been more than happy to let her take over. Even his father, who guarded his emotions with the same zeal he did his company's assets, had seemed taken with the sudden addition to the family. Only Alex had hung back.

Now, without his parents around to witness his apprehension, Alex let the kindly older woman settle the baby in his arms.

His first thought when the woman stepped back, leaving him holding the child on his own, was that the infant didn't seem to weigh much more than the soft blue blanket he was wrapped in.

"Is he supposed to be this light?" he asked, only to have the nanny assure him that seven pounds, nine ounces was a good weight and that as healthy as his son was, he would grow in no time.

His son.

Alexander Ryan Burke V, to be exact.

Alex looked down at the doll-like child nestled against his chest, and drew in a deep, shuddering breath. He was twenty years old. He was single. And he had a son. He knew nothing about children, and even less about babies. But the child resting so trustingly in his arms was his; his own flesh and blood. The awe filling Alex at that thought was almost as overpowering as the helplessness he felt. And the hurt.

The nanny was watching him.

Uncomfortable with her scrutiny, he turned to the nursery window and faced his own reflection. The baby's head lay just below his shoulder, the child's incredibly soft cheek resting against his bare skin. With a small squeak, the baby snuggled into him, his little mouth puckering and his tiny button-of-a-nose wrinkling as his daddy's chest hair tickled it. Shifting the baby higher so the hair wouldn't bother him, Alex cupped his hand protectively over the round little head.

Amazingly, the small show of annoyance left the perfect little features. A moment later, the baby let out a sigh as soft as his breath, and relaxed in Alex's arms. His father hadn't a clue what he was doing, but little Ryan seemed to trust that he was doing his best.

With a fervor that wasn't at all familiar, Alex could only hope it would be enough.

What the child needed was its mother.

At the thought, Alex closed his eyes on the reflection in the window.

He couldn't believe what Kelly had done. He would have taken care of her, if she'd just given him time to figure out what would have been best for all of them. Kelly had refused him that time, though. She'd let her aunt send her away, and her aunt had refused to tell him where she'd gone. If it hadn't been for Mr. Ames approaching him about a "small legal technicality" concerning his relationship with Kelly, he'd never have known that she had given the baby up for adoption. His three-day-old son could have wound up with strangers.

From what he understood, Kelly didn't know that the baby hadn't. Mr. Ames had told him only that Kelly had left the state shortly after signing over her own rights to the child two days ago. Since he'd been named the father, Alex had to sign away his rights, too, to allow an adoption to take place.

"No way in hell am I signing you away," Alex whispered against the soft little head, repeating basically what he'd said to Mr. Ames. "We don't need her."

In the years that would pass, Alex would often remember that first night he'd stood in the nursery with Ryan sleeping against his chest. He'd remember how overwhelmed he'd been, and how intimidated he'd felt by the tiny child. He'd even be able to recall the words he'd spoken. What he would forget was how he missed his son's mother, and how missing her had made his throat so thick that those words had been little more than a whisper. All he would remember was the hurt, and the anger he'd felt that she could walk away from a helpless child. But even those feelings would fade after a while. By the time Ryan turned nine, then ten, and Alex had stopped being intimidated by much of anything, all that would remain on those rare occasions when he thought of Kelly, was the disappointment he'd felt in her, and the knowledge that she'd wanted neither him nor his son.

Chapter One

Nerves knotted Kelly Shaw's stomach as the cab pulled to a stop by the tiered fountain gracing the mansion's entry. The Burkes' palatial home with its multileveled red-tile roof and high, arched windows appeared every bit as imposing to her as she'd remembered—though, to be honest, she'd tried very hard over the past eleven years not to think of it at all. She'd been only seventeen when she'd left and, when she had, she'd had no intention of ever coming back.

"So much for my intentions," she gamely muttered to herself, and tried not to dwell too much on why she'd never returned. Even after all this time, the memories could be so very painful. So she allowed herself to think only of the obligation she had to her Aunt Audrey. Once that obligation had been met, she'd head straight back to Colorado and her quiet, and decidedly unsophisticated, life. She already had a reservation on a seven o'clock flight this evening.

Feeling anything but the calm she tried to pretend, she picked up her jacket—the loose-fitting white one she'd made with fabric one of the pregnant teenage girls she occasionally sheltered had helped her weave on her rickety old loom—and tightened her grip on her blue denim shoulder bag. She could do this. After all, she'd done things that were so very much harder. Or so she coached herself as she prepared to face the old ghosts that hovered like the heat waves rising from the pavement when she stepped from the cab.

It was searing hot. One hundred and ten degrees, according to the pilot who'd announced the temperature when her plane had landed less than an hour ago. But Kelly didn't give more than passing notice to the bone-melting heat so typical for the Phoenix area in August. Approaching the sprawling house's massive oak doors and a past that demanded to be acknowledged, she was thinking only that she felt every bit as intimidated as she had as a child.

Hating that feeling, wanting desperately to keep the memories at bay, she reached toward the polished brass plate and pushed the bell. Even as she did, it occurred to her that, while she'd been raised in this house, she'd never entered or departed through this entrance. As the niece of the Burkes's cook, she had been relegated to the service entrance near the servants' quarters around back. Listening to the three-toned melody of chimes echoing through the front hall beyond the doors, she wondered if she shouldn't have used that other entrance now. While she had been asked to come here—begged, actually—the invitation had been issued by her aunt.

"It is imperative that I see you," her Aunt Audrey had said when she'd called last week—after a silence of over ten

years. *"They do these bypass operations all the time, but in case something happens to me, we need to talk. Promise me you'll come."*

Kelly hadn't had the heart—or maybe it was the courage—to say no. Since the woman was facing major surgery, it was entirely possible that what Audrey wanted was to put the past to rest. All Kelly wanted to do with that past was to leave it where it was. But if seeing her was all that important to Audrey, Kelly was hard-pressed to deny her request. After all, she could appreciate how difficult it must have been for her maiden aunt to have to take her in as a child. Especially since she'd been imposing on her employer to do so. She could understand, too, why Audrey had insisted Kelly leave when Kelly had become pregnant by her employer's son and all hell had broken loose in the Burke household. What she'd never understood was why, despite all her efforts to please her, her aunt had always treated her only like the obligation she'd always been. Not that she was about to ask.

Kelly had scarcely wondered if she'd subconsciously chosen the front entrance as an act of defiance, which truly wasn't like her, when the door swung inward. Silently, of course. Even hinges behaved themselves in the home of Mr. and Mrs. A. R. Burke III.

Kelly didn't recognize the plump, slightly harried-looking woman who opened the door. Fifty-something, her short, graying brown hair suffering a tight perm, she wore the simple black dress and white apron in which Jessica Burke uniformed the female members of her staff. In the time it took Kelly to manage a smile, the frowning woman had already run a perplexed glance from the honey-colored hair brushing Kelly's shoulders to the blue chambray shirt tied at the waist of her calf-length white cotton skirt. Now her sharp glance swung back from the yellow cab leaving the circular drive.

"May I help you?" she asked, though Kelly was sure from the suspicious arch of her eyebrow that what she really wanted to know was, *How did you get onto this property?*

"Manuel let me in," Kelly offered with a smile, thinking it best to first explain how the cab had made it through the electronic gate without calling up to the house first. "He was working down by the main entrance. I'm Audrey Shaw's niece."

The gardener's name, and Kelly's obvious familiarity with the elderly gentleman, had the woman's frown evaporating even before she mentioned her aunt.

"Why, you must be Kelly," the woman clucked, suspicion giving way to hospitality as she motioned her into the welcome coolness of the spacious foyer. "Audrey told me you were coming.

"It's so nice for you to be here for her," she went on, closing Kelly inside the airy, white-tiled space with its twenty-foot-high stark-white walls and arched windows of beveled glass. "Your aunt never said she was nervous about that surgery—I mean, you know what a private person she is," the woman added, lowering her voice to a more confidential tone. "But you know she had to be scared to death. When she told me she'd asked you to come, it relieved me greatly to know she'd have someone with her. I've been working here for a couple of years now and I wasn't even aware she had any family. Not until she mentioned you last week, that is."

Speculation fairly danced behind the silver rims of the woman's glasses. But, to her credit, and Kelly's relief, she immediately banked her curiosity about her co-worker's failure to previously acknowledge the only family she had left. "I don't mean to go on," she chided herself, waving off her own verbosity with her pudgy hand. "Everything has just been so upended around here this past week. I'm Edna, the Burkes's housekeeper." Her brow lowered in concern. "How *is* your aunt?"

The question, like the woman's friendliness, threw Kelly completely.

Scarcely aware of the anxiety in her expression, though it was relieved somewhat by this woman's obvious ignorance of her history with this family, she met Edna's kind hazel eyes. "Excuse me?"

"Your aunt," Edna repeated, her brow lowering farther. "Is she any better? They did let you in to see her, didn't they?"

They? "She's not here?"

"Well, no. She's... Oh, dear," the housekeeper muttered. "The hospital didn't contact you?"

Seeing the tension in Kelly's face when she slowly, warily, shook her head, Edna knotted her hands against her apron and took a deep breath.

"Audrey had a heart attack yesterday. She wasn't doing very well last night. But I do understand she's no worse." She added the latter quickly, wanting to soften the news she was clearly distressed to deliver. "At least, she wasn't any worse when I called to check on her this morning. I thought perhaps you'd been there and were coming by to pick up some of her things to take to her."

"Which hospital is she in?"

"Memorial. That's the one the senior Mr. Burke was in before he passed on, so I'm sure Audrey is getting excellent care. People like the Burkes want only the best, you know," she added in the secretive tone domestic help reserved for others of their ilk. "I overheard Mrs. Burke say any number of times how grateful she was for the marvelous staff over there.''

The faint riffle of shuffling papers drifted toward them. Kelly scarcely noticed it over the regret she felt at the news of Al Burke's death. "I'm sorry to hear about Mr. Burke. He was a nice man.''

The fluttering sound Kelly ignored had made Edna's expression fade to the slightly harried look she'd been wearing when she'd opened the door a few moments ago. Now, her eyebrows lifted in surprise.

"You knew him?''

Kelly hesitated. "I used to live here. With Audrey.''

"You did?''

"A long time ago. When I was a girl," she added, rather wishing she'd kept her regrets to herself.

"Oh. Well, in that case you probably know that Mrs. Burke has been on the auxiliary at Memorial for years. It's a pity she's gone for the month," she added, as if the woman's presence could somehow make a difference in the quality of the care her cook received. "Escaping the heat, you know." Glancing toward the nearest of the three archways leading from the foyer, the woman wrinkled her nose. "What on earth . . . ?''

The fluttering noise that had drawn the housekeeper's attention suddenly stopped, only to be replaced a moment later by the ominous sound of something quite heavy hitting something very solid. Now looking far more annoyed than harried, she muttered an exasperated, "Excuse me," and strode toward the set of double doors halfway down the hall.

The soft squeak of rubber-soled orthopedic shoes on the shining tiles was joined by Kelly's shaky sigh when she let out a long, low breath. The woman would never know how grateful Kelly was to learn she wouldn't be running into

Jessica Burke. Or any other Burke, for that matter. With Mr. Burke gone, and Alex undoubtedly having moved out long ago, she felt some of the tension leave her shoulders. What she felt now had more to do with concern for her aunt.

She shouldn't have let the cab go, she thought, wondering how long it would take to get another one out here, or if, perhaps, the bus still ran nearby. She wondered, too, if she should call the hospital first, or just head straight to it. Unlike the housekeeper, she didn't assume that no one had tried to reach her to tell her about Audrey. It was entirely possible that the attempt had been made. But she'd been out in her workshop until well after ten o'clock last night filling orders for the herbed oils and vinegars she made from the herbs she grew, and she didn't have an answering machine in her decidedly modest little house.

At that thought, Kelly allowed herself to glance around the atrium-like foyer. But instead of considering how most of her home, the attached greenhouse excluded, would probably fit into the airy and open space, she found herself staring at the massive curved staircase she and Alex had so often dared each other to slide down when they were children.

How many times had they nearly been caught doing that? she wondered, only to immediately catch herself and look away before the memory became too clear.

From behind her, she could hear voices. One was the housekeeper's. The other, far too faint to identify. Not wanting to eavesdrop, Kelly let her glance move through the opposite archway where the space opened into the sweep of white-carpeted living room. The cream-colored furniture had all been rearranged since she'd last seen it, but the room, with its long wall of windows looking out over the city, still looked as perfect and pristine as it had when Alex had snuck her into this part of the house so many years ago. Children had never been allowed in the living room. Not even Alex, except on special occasions, until he'd become a teenager.

Rules. Kelly tightened her arms around herself. There had been so many rules in this place that she had always thought it something of a miracle Alex hadn't found them more repressive than he had.

Not wanting to think of the person who had been her soul mate, her protector and, finally, her lover—not knowing how it would be possible not to think of him when everything her glance touched reminded her of him—she gave up on propriety and deliberately concentrated on the muffled voices drifting through the otherwise-quiet house. It wasn't polite to eavesdrop. But she was desperate for distraction. The news of her aunt was unsettling. The reminders of Alex, however, encroached too near the void in her heart.

Though Kelly couldn't quite make out what was being said, the housekeeper's voice sounded impatient. The other voice, sounding far younger and much more subdued, was nearly impossible to hear at all.

At least it was until the housekeeper, her arms crossed over the bib of her white apron and her mouth as pinched and puckered as a prune, escorted a young boy into the hallway.

The breath Kelly had just taken seemed to catch in her throat. As impossible at it was, she could have sworn she was staring backward twenty years. At least, that was how it felt to her when she found herself unable to look away from the slender, dark-haired child in the red rugby shirt and navy shorts.

He was the mirror image of Alex as a boy.

"Then take it to your room to look it up," the house-keeper insisted as the child who appeared to be about nine or ten stared down at the book he held. "Just don't go in there until I've finished cleaning. You know your grand-mother doesn't want you in the study unless there's an adult in there with you, anyway." The woman's tone wasn't unkind, but it did bear a lot of frustration. "I'm the one who has to answer for anything in that room that is disturbed or damaged. With all my cleaning supplies in there, it would be all too easy for you to knock a bucket over or get oil all over something it doesn't belong on. Don't you remember what happened yesterday?"

"Yes, ma'am," came the dejected reply. "But I didn't break anything this time."

"Only because you were lucky."

"Yes, ma'am," he repeated with his chin tucked to his chest. "May I go now?"

Edna opened her mouth, only to have whatever she was about to say interrupted by the ringing of the telephone. Looking more than a little put-upon and clearly at a loss as to what to do with the child, she headed back in the di-rection from which she'd come. Had Edna not held her hands so tightly in front of her, Kelly was under the dis-tinct impression that she'd have thrown them up in the air.

Heaving a sigh that ruffled the shining brown hair tum-bling over his forehead, the boy finally looked up. Since he'd endured the reprimand on the way back from the study by contemplating the toes of his preppy, boater-style shoes, he hadn't realized that anyone else was in the foyer.

Now that he did, Kelly watched the tips of his ears turn pink. Seeing him so obviously embarrassed that a stranger had witnessed his scolding, she added a soft smile and a shrug to her quiet, "Hi."

He looked back toward the floor. "Hello," he returned, ever so politely.

The boy could only be Alex's son. He had to be. Alex had been an only child. So only his child could be Jessica Burke's grandson, and Kelly knew she'd heard Edna refer to the boy's grandmother a few moments ago. Even if it hadn't been for that reference, the similarities between what she saw and what she remembered were too startling for the little boy to belong to anyone else. The child had the same dimple in his chin that would deepen into the cleft that Alex had inherited from his own father. And while the lean, angular jaw and that beautiful, chiseled mouth looked so much softer in the younger version, the thick dark lashes Kelly had always thought it so unfair for a male to possess were very much the same. Only the eyes were different. Not their shape. Their color. Instead of the deep, moody, indigo blue of his father's eyes, the child's were the softer, clearer hue of a summer sky.

Vaguely, she wondered if that gentler color, along with the hint of freckles dotting his nose and smooth cheeks, had been passed on by his mother. She wondered, too, what kind of woman Alex had chosen for his wife. Without knowing a thing about her, she'd have been willing to bet her mother's high school ring—the only item she possessed that had belonged to the woman—that his bride had come from Burke-approved stock. Judging from the child's age, it was obvious that Alex had found the "right kind of girl" not very long after their own relationship had ended, too.

Amazed by the hurt that realization caused, not wanting to believe such a thing could matter after so long, she focused on the child standing so rigidly still. The look in his eyes now seemed more sad than embarrassed. She offered him a gentle smile, hoping to coax one from him. But when he just continued watching her and his beautiful little mouth didn't move, she found herself wondering if he knew how to smile at all.

Wondering at the odd thought, and touched far more than she wanted to be by the child's dejection, she motioned to the heavy volume he held.

"What book do you have?"

"Just an encyclopedia."

"Looking up anything in particular?"

He didn't seem to trust her interest. But he didn't seem especially eager to escape her company, either. "I wanted to see where Arabia is."

Pausing, he waited to see if he was expected to continue. Apparently seeing that she wanted very much for him to do so, he added, "It's in a book I'm reading." He gave a small one-shouldered shrug, then added, "About a boy and a horse."

"I remember a book like that. It was my favorite when I was about your age." A frown touched her forehead. "Except for the first part. It was kind of scary."

Reticence vied with curiosity. "How come?"

"Because the boy is all alone at first. And being alone...well, it..."

"Sucks," he mumbled under his breath, then darted a quick glance in her direction.

"Yeah," she agreed, wondering if he didn't look a little relieved that she didn't question his description. "In a lot of ways, it sure does."

Again, he didn't return her smile, but either her agreement or her grin finally allowed him to fully meet her eyes, his guard falling enough for them to figure out that the book he was reading just happened to be Kelly's childhood favorite. But for Kelly, it wasn't the interest they shared in a fictional horse and his young companion that drew her. It was the very real feeling of isolation she sensed in the quiet, almost-shy little boy. He seemed positively starved for company.

Hurting for him because, after the Burkes had started sending Alex away to school, she'd so often experienced that kind of loneliness herself growing up in this house, she found herself standing protectively beside him when Edna came bustling back into the foyer.

With her arms crossed over her ample chest, she stopped in front of her charge. "I trust you've introduced yourself, Ryan."

He hadn't, but Kelly immediately drew the housekeeper's attention from his look of chagrin. "Ryan has been keeping me company," she told the woman, using his name since the housekeeper had just supplied it. She wondered if, like Alex, the boy bore the full formal name of his father, complete with ascending roman numeral at the end.

"Well, that's good." The woman sighed. "There are a few of Audrey's shortbreads in the cookie jar," she told him. "You can have one if you keep the crumbs off the floor. I've just waxed it."

Ryan didn't say a word. He merely tucked the heavy volume he held in his arms against his chest and, glancing once over his shoulder at Kelly, disappeared through the middle archway behind the stairs.

"He's Alex's son, isn't he?"

"That he is," the woman replied with a rueful shake of her tight curls. "I swear, he's always underfoot. Not that Mr. Alex is, you understand. Why, I hardly ever see him at all. And it's not that I mind the boy. It's just that he's bored to death here in the summer, and I haven't got the faintest idea what to do with him. I'm a housekeeper. Not a nanny. The only reason I'm watching him now is because there's no one else to do it. Audrey tended to him when he was around before, and I offered to stay when she found out she had to have surgery until someone else could come in. But to my knowledge no one's called any of the agencies yet and my sister's waiting on me."

The woman was clearly perplexed.

Kelly was just as clearly confused. "Your sister?" she repeated, not sure what the woman had to do with anything, but trying to following along anyway.

"She's expecting me in Florida. I was supposed to leave on vacation last week, you see. With Mrs. Burke away, we don't have houseguests and there's no entertaining being done. So it's a perfect time for me to go. Of course, there's Mr. Alex to tend along with boy, but even when he is in town he slips in and out and a body hardly knows he's around. Which is why someone from an agency could easily fill in—"

Kelly's heart gave a decidedly unhealthy jerk. "Alex?" she interrupted, before the woman could move on to yet another subject. "Alex *lives* here?"

"Well, yes. He has ever since right after his father died. He's in Europe right now, though. London, I think. But I'd have to check his itinerary to be sure."

"I see." And where was his wife? she couldn't help but wonder, only to assure herself that Edna wouldn't have been going on so about Ryan, had the woman been in town. "May I use a telephone, Edna? I'd really like to call the hospital, and a cab."

"Oh, of course. I can't believe I'm standing here rattling on like I am. Must be that I haven't had any adult company all day." She smiled—half in apology, half in chagrin. "Tell you what," she went on, leading the way to the kitchen and the telephone, "don't you worry about what time you come back. You spend as much time with

Audrey as you need to, and be sure and tell her I'm thinking of her."

Kelly hesitated. "I wasn't planning on coming back here."

Undaunted, reminding Kelly of a barge with a full head of steam as she forged through a swing door, Edna waved her off. "There's absolutely no sense spending your money on a hotel while your aunt's recovering. It's just me and the boy in the house. With everyone away, I see no harm in you spending the night in your aunt's room. I'm sure the Burkes wouldn't mind. Mr. Alex isn't due back until the first of next week. Not that he'd mind, anyway. Like I said, he's hardly ever around even when he is in town."

Chapter Two

Except for the exterior lights, the house was dark when Kelly returned at ten o'clock that evening. Edna, anticipating her late return, had given her the code to the security gate and the spare house key from the pantry so she could let herself in without having to wake anyone. Kelly did so as quietly as she could. Not that any sound she made in the foyer could possibly be heard in the back of the house. Or in the upstairs wings. The place was huge.

And silent.

And filled with shadows.

She closed the door without a sound, and frowned into the darkness. Edna had said she'd leave the light on, but she must have forgotten. Not that it mattered. Moonlight streamed through the tall, arched windows, making it easy enough for Kelly to find her way, even if she hadn't known exactly where she was going. The single door leading to the back of the house, where her aunt had her room, was just beyond the wide archway to her left.

She hadn't eaten since breakfast, but she was too tired to do anything about it now. Wanting nothing more at that moment than the oblivion of sleep, and praying this wouldn't be one of those nights when she'd find herself pacing a rut in the rug at 3:00 a.m., Kelly moved through the shadows slanted across the floor. It felt so odd to be in this house again. Odd, and as unreal as the fact that her Aunt Audrey was now lying unconscious in a hospital bed, lines and tubes running every which way. Audrey had always been such a stalwart woman, as strong in her body as she was unyielding in her stoicism. According to her, there wasn't any situation that couldn't be handled simply by straightening one's backbone. Life was not something a person spent her time daydreaming away, complaining about, or dwelling on. It was simply to be dealt with.

At least, that had been the philosophy of the woman Kelly had known. What changes her beliefs might have undergone, Kelly couldn't begin to imagine. The woman she had seen lying in that bed scarcely resembled the woman who had raised her. Audrey had aged more in the last eleven years than she had in the previous forty-five. Those changes hadn't just come in the twenty-four hours since her heart attack, either. The furrows in her brow had been etched there by years of unhappiness.

Wishing she hadn't been so willing to accept the distance Audrey had put between them, unable to imagine how she could have forced the woman to remain in touch with her, Kelly let out an uneasy sigh as she passed the arched opening of the hallway. As she did, she noticed a shaft of light slanting across the wide, tiled hall, and heard the soft rustle of pages being turned.

The double doors of the study were partially open.

The image of a lonely little boy with sky blue eyes whispered through her consciousness. Wondering if Ryan had snuck down to look something up again, Kelly found herself moving into the hall rather than through the narrow door beneath the stairs. She really hoped it was Ryan, and not Edna finishing her cleaning, which was really rather doubtful given the hour. She wouldn't consider why she wanted to see him, though. To do so would be to risk comparisons to another child; one whose memory she held so closely to her heart.

Thinking only that helping ease someone else's loneliness was infinitely preferable to dwelling on her own situation, she stopped by the partially open door and glanced into the formal, book-lined room.

Only one lamp was on; the one on the corner of the large desk facing out from beneath the portraits of the Alexander Ryan Burkes, Senior, Junior and numbers two and three. But it wasn't the youngest Burke heir behind that desk.

Kelly's heart jerked against her ribs. For a split second, she could have sworn she was looking at Mr. Burke. But the decidedly attractive man sitting with his brows knit in a frown as he studied the papers that spilled from the open briefcase near his elbow, hadn't yet acquired the streaks of silver that had threaded the older man's hair. Time had etched maturity into his features, but the meticulously cut hair sweeping back from his face was still as dark as midnight.

Alex.

He wasn't supposed to be here.

At the thought, her heart gave another unhealthy lurch. Whether or not he was supposed to be here, seeing him again felt like every nightmare—and every dream—she'd ever had.

He must have come straight to this room when he'd arrived. A black travel bag had been dropped near the wet bar, and a dark gray suit jacket lay over the arm of one of the leather wing chairs flanking a small table and lamp. His shirtsleeves had been rolled up, on his way to the desk, perhaps, and his tie hung loosely below his unbuttoned collar.

It didn't appear that he'd wasted any time getting down to business. Nor did it appear that whatever that business was, was going very well. With one hand kneading the muscles in the back of his neck, the motion reminding her as much of frustration as fatigue, he turned a sheet of paper over with the other. A moment later, she saw him shove the sheet aside in disgust.

She had no idea what he was working on, or what about it had caused his reaction. As she stood in the security of the shadowed hall, she knew only that she'd never seen a person look as weary, or as desolate, as he so suddenly did.

Alex had closed his eyes as he'd drawn in a deep breath. Now, his shoulders falling as he slowly released that breath, he shook his head as if he were truly at a loss. He wasn't looking toward her. He hadn't even seen her. But when he pushed the chair back and stood, raking his fingers through his hair in a gesture that seemed as much habit as statement, he seemed to bear the weight of the entire world on his broad shoulders.

Kelly took a step back. She didn't know if it was pure cowardice on her part or the knowledge that, given whatever was on his mind, her intrusion right now would be the last thing he'd need, but she didn't want him to see her. And she didn't want to see him. Not now. Not ever.

Not that she had a choice.

Alex caught her movement in the doorway.

"Edna? Is that you?"

His voice sounded deeper than she'd remembered. Richer. Certainly, it was more commanding.

Kelly took another step backward, only to immediately check herself. What did she think she was going to do? Run? And if she was, just where did she plan to go? Out into the night? Back to Colorado? To her aunt's room? That the reaction had even occurred to her unsettled her nearly as much as did so unexpectedly seeing him there. It was entirely possible that, after so long, he would scarcely even remember her. He had a wife. And a son. He could well have forgotten all about her.

She moved back to the door, and slowly pushed it open. "It's not Edna, Alex." With her heart beating in her throat, she took the step that brought her to the threshold. Watching his hand fall from where it cupped the back of his neck, she added, "It's me."

The light from the lamp illuminated the desk, but little beyond it. From where Alex stood, he could see the willowy, feminine shape in the doorway. But not until he took the three steps to the wall and turned the rheostat to bring up the lighting, was he able to clearly see the face that belonged to the hauntingly soft voice.

Alex felt himself go still. The slender young woman in the doorway could have been an apparition, standing as she was with a white jacket draped over her loosely crossed arms and her honey-colored hair hanging softly to the shoulders of her pale blue shirt. And maybe that was all she was, he thought. Nothing more than a figment of his imagination; a product of fatigue brought on by the idiotic pace he'd maintained for the past several months, three nights of little sleep, and a major case of jet lag.

The rationale was seductive. And he'd have cut a deal with the devil himself to buy it. Yet, even with her hair so much shorter than she'd once worn it, her eyes so much wiser and touched with a kind of sadness that added an indefinable fragility to her already delicate features, he knew the woman standing there was very, disturbingly, real.

"Hello, Alex."

There wasn't a shred of welcome in his expression; even less in his voice. "What in the hell are you doing here?"

He saw her open her mouth, only to close it when her glance jerked from him to the boy slipping into the room from behind her. Ryan, holding a book in one hand and pulling up the shoulder of his blue cotton pajama top with the other, stopped just ahead of her.

Ryan looked over at his dad, then quickly dropped his glance to the valise by the wet bar.

"Audrey is sick. She's her niece," the little boy said, as if this might be news to his father. "Kelly is, I mean. Edna told her she could stay in Audrey's room tonight."

The glower in Alex's eyes faded considerably as it shifted to his son. His frown, however, remained firmly in place. "What are you doing up?"

Ryan hesitated, seeming either uneasy, embarrassed or some combination of each. "I was waiting for Kelly."

Alex did not look pleased with that answer. "Why?" he wanted to know, though it was Kelly who looked surprised.

"I wanted to tell her what part I was up to."

"Part of what?"

"My book. It was her favorite."

"*The Black Stallion,*" Kelly offered, though she would have bet her next breath that Alex couldn't have cared less about the book's title. "We were talking about it earlier."

"Did you know she used to live here?"

Ryan's question made a muscle in Alex's jaw jerk. "Yes, I did. Now, please, Ryan . . ."

"She said it was a long time ago. And she knew you, too. She said you were kids."

It was impossible for Kelly to guess what Alex was thinking as he looked from his son to her. She knew only that he didn't seem to care for what he was hearing. Suspicion, protectiveness and displeasure all vied for space in Alex's expression.

Only with effort did he keep the latter from his voice when he looked back to the younger version of himself.

"Go back to bed, Ryan."

The little boy opened his mouth, then immediately closed it again. In the process, the animation in him died completely.

From where Kelly stood to the side of Ryan, she couldn't really see his face. She saw him look down, though, and caught the way he sucked in a corner of his lip to worry it for a minute before looking back up at his dad. He seemed to have something on his mind. But he seemed equally reluctant to mention it.

Finally, she heard him ask, "Are you going to be here tomorrow?"

"I'll be in town. But I've got work to do. Why?"

Ryan didn't answer. He simply shrugged.

"Ryan, if you want something, say what it is."

"Were you going to come up to my room?"

His presence upstairs wasn't what Ryan had originally wanted. Alex felt fairly sure of that. But feeling guilt pile on top of everything else he felt far too tired to handle at the moment, Alex didn't bother making the boy spit it out. As disturbing as it was to know that his son had been waiting up for Kelly, equally so was the knowledge that Ryan hadn't cared to come down to see him when he'd come in half an hour ago.

His conscience jerked a little harder. Not at all pleased with the intent way Kelly watched them both, he was nonetheless compelled to remind himself that he hadn't gone up to see Ryan, either. He'd been away for over a week and when he'd come home, his thoughts hadn't been of his son. His only concern had been how to salvage the negotiations that had fallen apart in his absence.

"I'd have come up when I got here, but I didn't know you were awake." The excuse was as lame as it sounded. Not knowing what to do about it now, he added, "I'll be there in a few minutes."

From the corner of her eye, Kelly caught the slump of Ryan's shoulders. A moment later, he gave her a quick, almost apologetic glance, then slipped out the door as quietly as he'd come in.

He must have been waiting on the stairs, she thought, offering a quiet, "Good night, Ryan," to the small shadow moving down the hall. She thought, too, that she'd have liked very much to hear about his book. She looked back to his father. "Don't let me keep you from tucking him in."

For a moment, it appeared to her as if the idea of physically tucking the child into bed hadn't occurred to Alex—though it was truly impossible for her to guess what caused his brow to pinch in the moments before his long strides carried him past her and the door.

With so little light in the hall, she couldn't see him very well, but from where she stood inside the study door, she heard his deep voice calling Ryan's name. A moment later the quiet rustle of fabric drifted toward her, along with Alex's husky, "Come here, son."

Alex had lowered himself to his haunches, a large, solid shadow that almost obliterated the smaller, much thinner one moving back toward him. She saw Ryan hesitate, as if unsure what to do, until Alex stretched out his arms. Even then, it was a moment before the child stepped into his father's embrace and hugged him back, rather fiercely.

Kelly felt something tighten in her chest. She didn't know which affected her more: seeing Alex hugging his son, or the thought that neither one of them seemed overly familiar with the gesture. Yet, as she turned back to the room, she had the strangest feeling that what she had just seen had been precipitated by her presence. On Alex's part, anyway.

The murmur of voices, one rich and deep, the other sweet and sounding almost shy, faded with the sound of footsteps. A moment later Alex was back. This time he didn't move past her, though. This time, walking back into the staidly formal room, he snagged her arm and brought her in with him.

His touch was impersonal, merely a means of getting her from one spot to the next. But she felt the heat of his big hand, and the involuntary flexing of his fingers as he drew her inside.

Letting her go as soon as he had her far enough inside to close the door, he turned to face her. "What's wrong with your aunt?"

"She had a heart attack," Kelly replied, unprepared for both the question and the demand behind it. "Edna didn't tell you?"

The question was ignored in favor of his own.

"When?"

"Last night. Edna said—"

"Is that when you got here?"

She shook her head, forcing herself to remain where she was, rather than stepping back from him. She was lousy at confrontations. She always had been. But she'd learned to defend herself. She'd had to—once she'd no longer had him to stick up for her.

"I got here this afternoon. About two." Her chin came up, the motion not so much a show of stubbornness as an attempt to get a better angle on what she was up against. She'd had no idea what his reaction would be to seeing her after all this time. But his being upset over *when* she'd arrived made no sense to her at all. "I wasn't here for more than ten minutes before I left for the hospital. And I just now got back." She held up a key. Dismayed to find her hand trembling, she set the key on the little round lamp table beside her. "Edna lent me the spare from the pantry so I could let myself in."

He actually seemed to relax a little, though for all practical purposes, the change was negligible at best. He didn't acknowledge her explanation. Or enlighten her with one of his own as to why he was acting as he was. He simply stared down at her, his jaw working and his indigo eyes as hard as the set of his beautifully molded mouth.

Kelly tightened her arms over the knot of anxiety in her stomach. He was easily as tall as she'd remembered, the top of her head barely reaching the small cleft in his chin. But he seemed so much more imposing, somehow. Maybe it was the way he was glaring at her. Or maybe it was because he'd filled out so remarkably, his lean, athletic body seeming more powerful, more overwhelmingly...male. Kelly didn't consider herself a small woman by any means. At five feet five inches, she rarely felt disadvantaged. But it wasn't just his physical size she found intimidating, though the fact that he intimidated her at all was unsettling in itself since he'd been the only Burke who, at one time, *hadn't* intimidated her. It was his relentless masculinity and the aura of absolute authority that clung to him; a kind of confidence that didn't demand deference so much as it caused it. He had become the kind of man other men would either envy or emulate; the kind of man who might never even notice a woman like her.

There had been a time when he had noticed her, though. As his glance moved over features that were seldom enhanced or camouflaged by makeup, seeming to linger on the fullness of her mouth before moving down the row of buttons on her plain cotton blouse, it seemed he remembered that as well as she did.

The tension radiating from him was almost tangible.

She supposed he picked up a few less-than-serene vibrations from her, too. Especially when she realized that he was looking at her as if he didn't know whether he wanted to reach for her and wrap her in his arms or throw her out.

Finally, deciding against either, he simply left her standing by the door.

He had his hands jammed into the pockets of his dark gray trousers as he moved back toward the desk. When he stopped, turning to face her, he'd quite deliberately put a good fifteen feet of distance between them.

It was almost as if he didn't trust himself to be anywhere near her.

"What is the proper protocol here, Kelly?"

A frown of incomprehension darted through her eyes.

"I mean, shouldn't one of us ask the other how they've been for the past—what is it? Eleven years?"

"Alex, please. I didn't plan this. Until Edna mentioned it, it never occurred to me that you'd be living here."

"I'm sure it didn't."

He might as well have said he doubted she'd given him any thought at all. There was that kind of accusation in his tone.

She flenched at his bitterness. "Is that necessary?"

"What? I'm only agreeing with you."

"That's not what you're doing."

He crossed his arms over his chest, his stance as challenging as it was defensive. But even as he did, he caught the silent plea in her eyes—and realized she was right. The moment he'd seen her, it had been like opening Pandora's box. Emotions long repressed slithered out and swirled around him. Some, all but forgotten. Others, far more familiar. He hadn't seen Kelly in eleven years. Yet, the anger and hurt had returned in a heartbeat. He'd felt something else, too: a quick insecurity with her presence that felt far more threatening when he'd realized she'd spent time with his son. She apparently hadn't been around all that long, though. And it was obvious enough from seeing her with Ryan, that she hadn't a clue the child was hers.

The weariness he'd felt before seemed to double itself when he backed down.

Closing his eyes, he pushed his fingers through his hair. Never ask what else can go wrong, he admonished himself, remembering he'd done that only moments before he'd caught the movement outside the study door.

"What have the doctors said about your aunt?" he asked, not particularly happy with himself when he realized he'd all but forgotten about the staid and somber woman who'd been the family's cook for the past twenty-nine years. "Will she be all right?"

Hugging her arms tighter, Kelly pressed a few more wrinkles into her jacket. "The doctor I spoke with said the next twenty-four hours are critical. Beyond that, all they'd tell me is that she's stable. I'm not sure she even knew I was there."

"You couldn't talk to her?"

"I tried, but she never responded."

"Where is she?"

"Memorial," Kelly told him, more conscious than she wanted to be of the weariness he did his best to ignore. In the last few moments, she'd finally noticed what his ill-concealed anger had kept her from seeing before; the hollows beneath his piercing eyes, the drawn look of his cheeks. She'd thought he looked weary when she'd first seen him. Now, she realized that the man looked worn-out.

"I understand your father was a patient there," she added, using the chance he'd given her to add something she very much needed to say. "Edna told me about him, Alex. About how sudden it was." A stroke, Edna had said. Over in a matter of days. With his father's death, Alex would have become responsible for the advertising agency his grandfather had founded half a century ago, and which had grown to have offices in major cities on both coasts and a couple of places in between. A responsibility he'd been groomed from birth to bear. She was sure he'd never expected to inherit it so soon. "I was sorry to hear that he'd passed away. I know how much he meant to you."

It was her voice that drew him; the sincerity in it, the softness. But it was the very real compassion in her eyes that caught Alex so completely off guard.

He'd been fine as long as he considered only what he'd allowed himself to remember of her these past several years; as long as he hadn't let himself recall any of the little things he'd once liked about her. Now, seeing the empathy in her lovely blue eyes, knowing that more than anyone else, she probably would have understood all he'd lost when his father had died, the darker emotions protecting him unexpectedly receded.

For that one, dangerously unguarded moment, he was actually grateful for her understanding. She had been the one person who'd known how much he had loved and admired his father. How close he had been to him. Over the years he and Kelly had spent growing up in this house, it had always been Kelly to whom he could confide his fears that he might not measure up; that he might disappoint. Like the good friend she had been, she'd listened to him drone on for hours about how he would someday take his place beside his father working with some of the most powerful companies in the country. While he'd been daunted at the thought, Kelly had never questioned that it could possibly be any other way.

He didn't mourn his father anymore. It had been nearly a year since he'd died. But he missed his presence, and his advice. At that moment, he was disconcerted to find that he had missed Kelly, too.

"Alex?"

He saw the concern enter her expression only an instant before she spoke his name. That instant was all the time he needed for most of his darker, more familiar feelings to jerk back into place. He was tired. Exhausted, actually. And clearly in no shape to be talking to her now.

She was the cook's niece. Since she needed to be there for the woman, he'd consider the implications of her presence after he'd had a few hours of badly needed sleep.

"It's late, Kelly." He stepped back, his fatigue sweeping through him at the sight of the three-inch-thick stack of memoranda he had to wade through before he could even hope to figure out how the two top ad execs in the Phoenix office had almost lost the company's oldest account. He simply couldn't tackle anything else. Not tonight. "Your aunt's room is where it always was. You're welcome to stay the night."

From the other side of the room, he heard her quiet, "Your wife won't mind?"

His dark eyebrows drew together in a single slash as he reached for the thick pile of papers. "I don't have a wife." The papers landed in the briefcase. "She divorced me last year."

Locks snapped into place.

"I'm sorry, Alex."

"Don't be. Things just don't always work out the way they're planned."

"No," she whispered. "They don't."

The fatigue in his voice was almost palpable. "Good night, Kelly."

He turned from her then, making it as clear as he knew how that he had no energy left for conversation. Every movement was an effort, every thought weighted down by the need for sleep. Yet, one thought still managed to form. Alex was a man who believed in reducing everything to its simplest terms. And to him, Kelly was simply the woman who hadn't wanted either him or his son.

Chapter Three

The digital clock on the nightstand indicated 6:03 a.m. when Kelly quietly left her aunt's bedroom and entered the back hallway leading to the kitchen. She'd heard Edna leave her room next door a while ago, so rather than remaining in her old twin bed staring at the rosebuds on the wallpaper while she worried about her aunt, she'd showered and dressed and called the hospital. Attempted to call, that was. When she'd picked up the telephone in the kitchen, she'd heard Alex's deep voice on the line and immediately hung up.

Now, thinking to give him a few more minutes before she tried again, she stood in the spacious, sunlit kitchen fortifying herself with a glass of orange juice. The high-ceilinged room, with its shining brass pots hanging from a brass rack over the cooking island and the long expanses of pink granite counters, was her aunt's domain. It was what lay beyond the large bay-type window at the sink, however, that had Kelly's attention. Her view from there was of the chef's garden—the one she'd so often helped the gardener tend so her aunt would have fresh herbs for cooking. Manuel still kept it as beautifully groomed as ever, his skilled hands maintaining the curved and intersecting rows of parsley, basil, thyme, mint and savory in a perfect lover's knot.

The thought of the man who'd let her in through the gate yesterday brought far better memories than those she'd wrestled with most of the night. Memories that could easily make her smile. The flinty old Hispanic gentleman, bent and gnarled as an old rosebush even then, used to call her *sombra*. Shadow. And she supposed she had been. From the time she'd been six years old and had come to live with Audrey after her mother had died, she'd followed that poor man all over the Burkes's impeccably manicured grounds, pestering him endlessly about the identity of every bug and plant she encountered.

"It hasn't changed."

Juice sloshed precariously close to the rim of her glass as Kelly turned her back to the sunlight. Alex, his dark, damp hair combed straight back from his face and a burgundy paisley necktie draped around the collar of his fresh white shirt, stood just inside the doorway on the far side of the room. Even as his eyes held hers, he slipped a gold cuff link into place.

Forcing herself to ease her double-fisted grip on her glass, she watched him over the surface of the cooking island centered between them. "What hasn't?"

"Your garden. That's what you were looking at, isn't it?" With a cursory glance at his cuff, he fastened the other link into place. "Manuel keeps it the same way you and he planted it. I still don't think Mom knows it was your idea to do it that way."

"Meaning she'd make him change it if she did?"

There was no challenge in the question. Only honest curiosity, and an unwitting hint of how aware she was of the trouble everyone thought she'd caused.

Alex caught that hint, and hesitated. A moment later, he'd apparently decided against any pretense. "Mom was never angry with you, Kelly. Only with me. Even if she'd hated the sight of you, I doubt she'd change the garden. She's not likely to deprive herself of the comments she gets on it just to get rid of a reminder."

His tone was utterly matter-of-fact; his expression no less unremarkable when he gave his cuff a final, distracted tug. "What are you doing up so early?"

Alex's cynicism jarred Kelly. Yet, it didn't catch her nearly as unprepared as the way he'd so subtly, so honestly, let her know that she hadn't borne blame alone with his family. Uncertain why he'd been so generous, and now even more unsure about how he regarded her presence this morning, she found herself fumbling uncomfortably to mimic his unaffected attitude.

"I wanted to call the hospital before I go. To see how Audrey is doing," she added, caught between concern for her aunt and unease with Alex.

"I just did. She's still the same."

He'd called? Surprised, and not sure why, Kelly watched the play of muscles in his powerful thighs while he headed across the room. Seconds later, hoping the unexpected heat she'd felt in her midsection hadn't suffused her cheeks, she forced her glance to the middle of his broad back. "Did they say anything else?"

"Not really. The nurse I spoke with said she had an uneventful night, and called her condition critical."

"Then she still hasn't come around?"

"Not yet."

But she would, Kelly thought. She couldn't imagine her aunt *not* recovering. Audrey was a strong woman. Determined. Surely that determination had survived.

"It was nice of you to call."

Looking as if "nice" had nothing to do with it, he opened the cabinet above the coffeemaker. "I just wanted to get visiting times for the ICU," he told her, his innocent-sounding intentions bringing an inexplicable note of defense to his tone. "I was going to take you to see her, but the first scheduled time isn't until eight o'clock and I have a seven-thirty meeting."

The mug he took from the collection on the bottom shelf hit the counter. But it wasn't the sharp, almost-impatient sound that caused Kelly to frown at his broad back. It was the fact that Alex had considered taking her to the hospital himself. That, and the tension lurking beneath his deceptively casual motions. Something about him reminded her of a watch spring that had been wound just a little too tightly.

For some reason she couldn't begin to explain, she felt sure that at least some of that tension had to do with Audrey.

She couldn't see what he was doing. She could hear the sound of coffee being poured, though, and the clink of the glass carafe as it was slipped back into place. Caffeine wasn't going to do his nerves any good, she thought, even as it occurred to her that she'd never seen Al or Jessica Burke get their own morning coffee. Her aunt had always served it from the sideboard in the dining room.

She rather liked that Alex knew where to find the coffee cups.

"Since I can't go," he said, sounding as if he wanted to minimize the import of his request, "I'd appreciate it if you'd call my office and let me know how she's doing after you see her. Will you do that?''

"I'd be glad to. I'll get the office number from Edna.''

"Fine.''

"Alex?''

"What?''

Drawing a breath filled with the rich scent of fresh coffee, Kelly looked from the sharp crease in the sleeve of his white shirt to the bits of orange pulp clinging to the inside of her glass. "Thank you for letting me stay here last night.''

"I couldn't exactly turn you out in the street.''

"But you thought about it, didn't you?''

She saw him pause, his hesitation as palpable to her as the heavy beating of her heart. Then, with a casualness that totally belied the tension stretching across the ten feet separating them, he turned and leaned against the counter.

His eyes, cool and blue as a bottomless lake, held hers just long enough to let her know he'd have preferred that she hadn't asked.

"Yes, Kelly," he finally said, the hint of weariness in his tone making her think he'd found little rest in his sleep. "I thought about it. I thought about a lot of things when I first saw you. But that was all in the past, and I'm sure you're no more interested in dragging it up than I am. We both have more immediate matters to contend with.''

She should have felt relieved. He wanted to leave the past where it was. Which was fine with her. Yet, she felt no relief at all. If anything, the way he studied her, as if looking for the answer to a question he refused to ask, made her horribly aware of how that past was coloring every word they spoke.

Still, he was right about having more pertinent matters to take care of. She had the situation with her aunt to deal with, and he obviously had other obligations weighing on his mind—though she could only guess what concerns etched the lines of stress in his brow. The problem was that, despite the distance he obviously wanted between the two of them, despite the past each would be content to ignore, the memories, the hurts and the questions were still there, hanging like a pall between them.

Why did you go?

I had no choice!

Why didn't you wait for me?

His eyes remained steady on hers as he reached to tie his necktie. His hands moved deftly, the motions automatic as his glance skimmed her face, the look in his eyes as indecipherable to her as Sanskrit. Even when his scrutiny wandered to the skin exposed by the open collar of her chambray shirt, halting to linger on the gentle swells of her breasts, his expression betrayed no discernible emotion. It was only when his glance moved down to where she'd tucked her shirt into the waist of her white skirt, then slid over the flatness of her belly, that she knew he wasn't as unaffected by her presence as he wanted to be.

The breath he drew was slow and deep, the expression on his face becoming dark and a little forbidding before control flickered over it and he jerked his eyes back to hers.

In the space of a heartbeat, the muscle in his jaw jerked and he'd turned back to the counter. "Call me about your aunt," he said, and picked up his mug to take with him just as a load of laundry with legs appeared in the doorway.

Edna's salt-and-pepper curls were barely visible over the armload of navy blue sheets and towels she'd stripped from one of the upstairs bedrooms. Fearing the woman would run into something with her vision blocked as it was, wondering how she'd avoided mishap already, Kelly left her juice on the counter and met the housekeeper in the center of the room.

"Why didn't you just shove these down the laundry chute?" she asked, pushing down the top of the load to see the woman's face. She started to take the bundle from the woman. Edna didn't seem to want her help, though. Not that she didn't appreciate it.

"Thank you, dear, but I can manage. And I would have used the chute, had a certain young man not stuffed a pillow in it. The thing's stuck halfway down. Oh, Mr. Alex," she went on, seeming to forget her minor annoyance when she saw him pass by her. "I'm so glad you haven't left yet. I need to speak with you."

Alex came to a halt. "I'm running a little late, Edna."

"It'll just take a minute."

"Can you call me at the office?"

Edna couldn't hear him. She'd already headed for the laundry room off the back hall and disappeared through the door.

Alex frowned after her. Two seconds later, he turned his frustrated expression to his watch. He was anxious to leave. That was apparent enough. Equally apparent was the way he deliberately curbed his impatience as he raised his cup and, still frowning, took a sip of the steaming brew.

The frown promptly turned into a grimace.

The oath he muttered was short and to the point. Looking as if he were about to repeat it, he glanced from his mug to the pot sitting innocently on the counter across the room. "What did Edna do to the coffee?"

The question was rhetorical. Still, Kelly felt somewhat compelled to supply an answer. Warily eyeing the pot herself, she cleared her throat.

"Edna didn't do anything to it. Since she wanted to get started on the laundry, I told her I'd put it on. Which is it?" she ventured, knowing there could only be one of two problems, even though she never drank the stuff herself. "Too weak, or too strong?"

"Any stronger, it could pump iron."

"You could dilute it with water," she said helpfully.

For half a dozen seconds, Alex said nothing. He simply stared at her, slowly shaking his head as if glitches in his life were becoming the norm rather than the exception, and started toward the sink.

Remembering how much space he'd so deliberately put between them last night, she stepped to one side to make room for him. Or, perhaps, she did it to keep from being too close to his tension. She didn't like that she could feel it so easily.

"It could have been worse."

"How?" he muttered, looking as if he couldn't fathom such a possibility while he turned on the water.

"I could have fixed your breakfast."

She stood an arm's length away from him. Maybe more. But Alex could easily see the anxiety beneath her tentative smile. With the sun pouring through the window, he could see, too, the fine grain of her skin and the threads of silver the golden light shot through her honey-colored hair. She had it pulled back into some sort of scrunched-up blue thing at the nape of her neck, the style much more confined than the loose way she'd worn it last night. He'd always liked her hair down. But he couldn't help thinking that the restrained style seemed much more suited to the woman she was, though beyond her seeming reserve he really didn't know her well enough anymore to draw such a conclusion.

For years, he'd seen her face in his mind every time he'd caught a glimpse of hair the color of spun gold, or breathed in the springlike scent of citrus blossoms. But the soft-spoken woman now watching him so guardedly bore little resemblance to the exuberant and spirited young girl he'd once known.

Yet, it was the girl he remembered when he saw her uncertain smile slip from her mouth.

"I take it your cooking hasn't improved all that much."

"My cooking hasn't improved at all," she corrected with apology. "If it doesn't come in a box or a can, I'm hopeless. But don't tell Aunt Audrey. Okay?"

The fragile smile returned to her eyes. A peace offering, the cynic in him supposed, even as that smile made him feel as if she had just made him privy to some closely guarded truth. Not that her lack of culinary skills had been any secret. He couldn't count the number of times he'd come into the kitchen to find her struggling with some inevitably inedible creation, and looking utterly miserable while she attempted the impossible. To please her aunt.

He was surprised he still possessed that memory, and a little uneasy with the recollection when that memory nudged another. Or, maybe, it was being close enough to breathe in the scent of spring clinging to her, that jerked him back to a time when he would find her outside under one of the citrus trees or in the flower gardens. That was where she would inevitably go, following one of her aunt's terse lectures about how she would never amount to anything if she didn't try harder. *You don't have to like to cook,* he could almost hear Audrey assert. *You simply* do *it.*

He remembered that he would take off after her, expecting to find her either mad at herself for not being able to get it right, or in tears because she couldn't make her aunt happy with her. And he had. At first. The last couple of years before she'd left, more often than not, she would see him coming and greet him with a smile, eager to talk about anything other than what had just happened in the kitchen. If he'd thought about it at all, he would probably have figured she just wasn't letting her aunt get to her anymore.

Watching her now, the intervening years having added a touch of the wisdom he'd most definitely lacked then, he had to concede that the smile he remembered was gone. Or, quite possibly, it had never existed. What he remembered had been a bright, easy curve of her lips, an infectious grin that had softened so beautifully beneath his mouth when he'd finally gotten her alone that last summer he'd come home. She'd been fifteen when he'd first gone away to college; all lanky limbs and impish blue eyes. Yet, each time another holiday or vacation had brought him home, her slenderness had become that much softer, her developing body more enticingly feminine. When he'd come home that last summer, the summer she'd turned seventeen, she'd scarcely resembled the girl he'd thought of only as his buddy, his soul mate. And that smile, so full of eagerness and relief at seeing him again, had nearly undone him.

He looked from the lovely shape of her mouth to the hesitation in her eyes. What he remembered was a product of a selective memory. The smile he'd seen moments ago had possessed a sad, almost-haunted quality; a sort of emptiness that could well have been there all along.

Alex gave himself a mental jerk. Thinking of Kelly with any compassion at all felt foreign, threatening and more than a little dangerous. Almost as dangerous as thoughts about that summer.

"Tell Edna I'll talk to her tonight. I've got to go."

The words were no sooner out of his mouth than Edna, smoothing her uniform, reemerged from the back hall. She didn't even look up before she started in.

"I don't know if Mrs. Burke mentioned it to you," she began, too preoccupied with picking towel lint from her apron to notice the tension coiled in Alex's body, "but I was supposed to leave yesterday. I only stayed on because there was no one to watch Ryan, what with Audrey being ill. Since you're back early..."

"You're leaving?"

"Only on vacation," she explained.

"Now?"

"Well," she said, suddenly hesitant in the face of his less-than-receptive attitude. "I did make the arrangements with Mrs. Burke last month. And your mother arranged for a temporary to come in next week to cover for both Audrey and me. Of course, your mother assumed Audrey would be here to familiarize the girl with everything before she went into the hospital, but we didn't know her heart was so bad. But as I said," she went on in her usual, rambling way, "I stayed on so Ryan wouldn't be alone. Now that you're back, I'd like to leave as soon as you can get someone else to come in."

Caught completely unprepared for this particular complication, all Alex could do was sift through the small mountain of information Edna had just dumped on him to get to the heart of the matter. Though he had no less than a half-dozen questions, the most pressing at the moment was, "Who?"

Edna didn't seem to see this as the problem Alex apparently did. "If you like, I can call the employment agency and have them set up interviews for you. I'm sure they can find you a temporary housekeeper who will also prepare meals. I suggest that you get a companion for Ryan, too.

He's too old for a nanny, but he does need someone to keep an eye on him. And to keep him entertained," she added, since she apparently regarded this as a problem. "Most housekeepers don't consider child care part of their duties."

Alex appeared to miss Edna's implication that she was going above and beyond the call of duty in caring for the child. Kelly caught it, though, along with Alex's unnatural stillness in the moments before he closed his eyes and pushed his hand through his hair. She'd seen him do the same thing last night, right after he'd given up on whatever it was he'd been working on.

"Edna," Alex began, speaking in the patient, precise way of a man determined to remain in control. "I believe you said my mother arranged for a temporary housekeeper. Where is she?"

"Back in Mexico. Audrey called her last week to see if she could start a day early, but the girl had apparently gone home."

Confusion momentarily overtook defeat. "Why was a temporary coming to begin with?"

"To take care of the house and the meals while I was on vacation and Audrey was having her surgery," Edna explained in the deliberate tones one might use with a small child.

"What surgery?"

"On her heart. That's why she called Kelly."

Alex possessed an analytical mind. Normally, he had no trouble following even Edna's sometimes-baffling train of thought. There was something important here he wasn't getting, though. He knew Audrey had had a heart attack, but he was positive no one had mentioned a previously scheduled surgery. Not having the time or the patience to figure out what clue he was missing in this little puzzle, he focused only on what he knew for fact. And the fact of the matter was that he couldn't cope with anything else.

"I can't possibly interview housekeepers right now. Can't you stay until my mother gets back?"

"She's not due back until the first of next month."

"That's only a couple of weeks."

"I'm leaving on a cruise in four days. It's my first ever and my ticket's already—"

"Just stay until Ryan goes back to school," he cut in, latching on to the compromise. "He goes back to Tucson next week."

"I don't know. I wanted to spend some time with my sister, Mr. Alex. I appreciate your position, but I really don't even know what to do with him. A companion, perhaps a nice high school girl—"

"I'll pay you double," he offered, seeming oblivious to both the woman's desire to get on with her own life and the fact that the housekeeper was more aware of Ryan's needs than was his own father. "I can't be worrying about Ryan, right now. He goes back to Tucson in a few days," he repeated, hoping he didn't sound as desperate as he felt. "Just stay until then."

Losing a housekeeper would be an inconvenience—especially with Audrey out of commission. But Alex didn't care if he had anyone to pick up after him or his son. Or even to feed them, for that matter. Restaurants delivered. And there was always takeout. For the first couple of weeks after Diane had left them, he and Ryan had become true connoisseurs of meals out of cartons and paper bags.

That was before his father had died, though, and Alex had had time to spend with his son. Now, he just wanted to be sure the child would be safe while he wasn't around—which wasn't going to be very often, given the demands of the agency. Not to mention the upheaval. But he couldn't think about the agency, or let himself succumb to the fear clawing at him when he thought of losing everything his father and grandfather had worked so hard to build. Not until he got this settled. Right now, he had to think about Ryan.

Looking up from yet another check of his watch, he caught Kelly intently watching him. She had moved to the small bay-windowed eating area off the kitchen when Edna had started talking, tactfully removing herself from the discussion. But he could see the curiosity in her expression, and something else that made him a little uneasy. Something that looked suspiciously like disappointment.

"Through Monday," he heard Edna agree, and told himself to forget about the woman whose reactions shouldn't matter to him, anyway. "But I have to leave then."

With everything else on his mind, relief was something he simply couldn't feel. So he settled for gratitude. "That'll be perfect." Ryan left for school on Monday. "You're a good woman, Edna."

"The boy's going to end up just like his father," the woman muttered, shaking her head at him when he disappeared through the arched doorway. She turned to the sink. Frowning at the mug of coffee Alex had abandoned, she picked it up and dumped it. "Just like his father," she repeated, and stuffed the mug in the dishwasher.

Kelly didn't ask the disgruntled housekeeper which Burke she was referring to—the one who'd just left, looking as if he were about to face the Inquisition instead of the work he'd once anticipated with such impatience; or the one who'd just called "Dad?" and could now be heard upstairs, bare feet running down the long hall.

"'Bye, Ryan," she heard Alex call an instant before the front door closed.

As if the volume on a television had just been turned off, the sound of running feet came to an abrupt halt.

Kelly joined Edna at the sink. Rinsing out her glass, she asked the woman if she had a bus schedule—and tried very hard not to let on how badly she felt for the little boy whose father couldn't wait for a hug, or whatever it was that Ryan had wanted. She didn't know what to make of Alex's attitude toward his little boy. But it was none of her business. Given the distance he so clearly wanted to keep between her and himself, she was sure he'd be the first person to tell her that, too.

The walk to the bus stop that morning was far more pleasant than Kelly had anticipated. Ryan met her at the door after hearing her promise Edna she would call with news of her aunt, and shyly asked if he could walk to the bus stop with her.

As hopeful as he looked, it would have broken her heart to tell him no. As it was, she felt an odd little ache in the center of her chest when, after telling him she'd like his company, his smile finally broke free.

He was quiet at first, content to walk along with his hands in the pockets of his neatly pressed shorts. But he began to open up once they passed through the gates at the end of the drive, his reticence slowly dissolving as he asked her about where she lived and what she did, and she told him of the little town nestled in the mountains of southern Colorado and the herbs and plants she grew there. Because he was reading *The Black Stallion,* he was particularly interested in the horses she told him about— the stallions and mares that grazed in the vast green meadows adjacent to the twelve-acre herb farm she ran for a gentleman who owned plant nurseries.

She thought Ryan might be interested, too, in the bonsai her neighbor, Mr. Yakamura, had taught her to train, and would have told him about the perfect, miniature trees she loved to work with, had he not so suddenly fallen silent. All she'd done was ask if he'd ever been to Colorado. When he'd told her he hadn't, she'd simply suggested that he ask his dad to take him there sometime.

"I don't get to go anywhere with my dad," he said, scuffing his toes in the gravel and dust alongside the road. "I really don't get to see him much since we came to live with Grandma. But that's okay. When I grow up and go to work with him, I'll get to go places, then. Like he did with Grandpa. Dad does important stuff," he went on, innocently bragging about his father the way young boys have done for centuries. "He makes up ads for television and magazines. At least the people that work for him do. Did you know that?"

Kelly smiled at Ryan, telling him that, yes, she knew what Burke & Co. did and that it was indeed "important stuff"—to the companies who hired the agency, anyway. But when Ryan made a point of mentioning again that it didn't matter that his dad was gone most of the time, she knew his father's absences from his life mattered very much. Especially when he added that his dad's busy schedule wasn't important because he was being sent back to boarding school soon, and though he hated boarding school, it was better than being home with no one to talk to.

Because of the conversation between Alex and Edna, Kelly already knew Ryan was leaving next week. She'd assumed, obviously in error, that when Alex said Ryan was going back to Tucson, he'd meant that the child was going back to his mother's home; that perhaps Ryan was only with his dad during the summer. She didn't ask about his mom, though. Or let herself wonder why the child was opening up to her as he was. She didn't want to feel this child's hurts, or care about how he seemed to be coping all alone.

She cared anyway.

Kelly had learned long ago that she seldom got what she wanted when it came to protecting her heart. Though she tried to keep an objective distance, she ached for the girls who came to her, young, pregnant and scared to death by the enormity of the decisions they faced for themselves and their unborn children. She agonized with them, sometimes cried with them, and always supported and defended them, no matter what they ultimately decided to do. But most of all she hurt for them, because, if the crisis house had sent them to her, that meant they had no support network of their own.

What she felt for Ryan was different, but it seemed to be rooted in that same empathy. There was something else there, too—a kind of protectiveness she wasn't sure she understood, and didn't care to analyze. It didn't matter, anyway. By the time they'd captured the little green lizard sunning itself on the kiosk at the bus stop and she'd shown Ryan how to hold it so he could get it home and into a jar, all she was thinking about was how she wished she'd been able to say or do something to make him feel better. The lizard helped, but watching him walk back up the hill to the house after she'd boarded the bus, she could still see the dispirited slump in his shoulders.

She'd never had much to do with children. Perhaps if she had, she'd have known what to say to the little boy. He'd said he was going to be in the fifth grade—which she assumed made him the same age as her neighbor's nine-year-old daughter, since she would be in that grade, too, come September. Still, she knew little about the age, so she'd been unable to offer any brilliant turn of phrase for him to cling to while the adults in his young life went on ignoring his needs. She wished she could have explained how just because a parent wasn't around, didn't meant he or she didn't care. But the finer points of that argument would be lost on a child who knew only that his father was simply too busy to be there for him.

Her child would be only a little older than Ryan. If he'd been hers—

Kelly cut off the thought before it could go any further. Taking a deep breath, she forced herself to concentrate on her surroundings; on the sound of the bus's air brakes being pressed and released, the rustle of newspaper as pages were turned by passengers catching up on the news on their way to work. She no longer allowed herself to think about having a child of her own. It was a dream that had died a long time ago.

The thunderstorm that rolled into the valley shortly before five o'clock didn't depart until after it had created utter chaos by flooding just about any street on the east side of town that didn't happen to run uphill. The monsoons, as the locals called the storms that brewed nearly every afternoon in August, could typically dump three inches of rain in one part of town and barely dampen the ground in another. When that three inches landed on soil with the absorbency of cement, traffic became a nightmare.

It was because so many of the streets in Scottsdale were flooded that what should have been a twenty-minute ride for Kelly back from the hospital, took just under two hours. On the plus side, it had stopped raining just before she'd boarded the bus at seven o'clock. It wasn't quite dark yet, either, though there wasn't much light left where the clouds had finally lifted from the horizon. Another advantage was that the rain had pulled the temperature down from the hundreds into the nineties. The fact that it was now as humid as the inside of her greenhouse was something Kelly tried to overlook.

Telling herself to be grateful for the small stuff, since she could find precious little else to consider positive at the moment, she let herself through the gate at the end of the Burkes's long drive. Audrey's doctor had told Kelly that morning that her aunt's prognosis wasn't getting any better, but not to give up hope. Anything was possible. She could wake up at any moment, or in a day or a week.

Or, maybe, not at all.

When the doctor had left, Kelly's only thought had been the same one on her mind now—that she wished she knew who her aunt wanted at her bedside, for surely there had to be someone other than a person she'd kept away for over ten years. Kelly had even called Edna earlier to ask who her aunt's friends were, in case there was someone whose presence her aunt might somehow find more comforting than that of the niece who could only sit at her side and wonder why it had been so hard for them to get along. Edna hadn't known of anyone Audrey was particularly close to. But she did mention that Audrey met with a group of women to play cards every other week, and that she thought she was pretty well acquainted with the butcher and the checkers at a nearby supermarket.

As for relatives, there was only Kelly.

Even if she hadn't been the only remaining family Audrey had, Kelly would have stayed with her. She owed her that much. She wasn't going to stay at the Burkes's, however. Though she'd spoken with Alex, no invitation had been extended beyond last night.

As he'd asked her to do, she'd called him after talking to the doctor. Her call had been put through immediately, too, making her think he'd been more than a little anxious for whatever news she had. But when she'd told him what the doctor had said, Alex only replied that he was sorry the prognosis hadn't been better, then asked her to let his secretary know if there were any changes. The entire conversation had lasted a grand total of fifteen seconds—and left Kelly with the same feeling she'd had when he'd left this morning: that he'd be forever grateful if she'd simply disappear from his life—for good, this time.

Being the cooperative sort, and also possessing a fairly healthy aversion to conflict, she'd do her level best to accommodate him. As soon as she retrieved the jacket she'd left in her aunt's room and borrowed a nightgown from her dresser, she'd find an inexpensive hotel near the hospital.

The entryway lights burned brightly, illuminating the high, arched windows and the fountain in front of the massive double doors. Kelly didn't use the front door, though. When she reached the split in the blacktopped driveway, rather than taking the curve that circled around to the front, she kept walking the more familiar route toward the back.

The kitchen lights were on, but she couldn't see anyone inside as she peered through the window's open shutters. Not having a key, since she'd left the one Edna had loaned her last night on a table in the study, Kelly started to ring the doorbell, thinking that, if Edna was in her room watching television, she wouldn't hear anyone knocking on the door. But just as she reached for the bell, Edna, looking none to pleased, came bustling into the kitchen from the main part of the house and saw her through the glass.

"Is something wrong?" Kelly asked, the moment the disgruntled-looking housekeeper opened the door.

"Nothing that won't be solved by a certain young man going back to school," Edna muttered as Kelly closed the door behind herself. "Or a certain older one hiring the proper help. Ryan was told he had to go to bed early, but that's twice now he's come down wanting a drink of water. And here it is after nine o'clock. He was sent up there over an hour ago."

The woman's overpermed curls barely moved as she shook her head at the inconvenience of it all. A moment later, she replaced her mutterings with a tsking sound as a look of chagrin heightened the color in her rounded face. "Listen to me go on," she chided herself, "and with you having more important troubles on your mind. Can I get you anything, dear?"

The woman looked truly frazzled. She also appeared to be trying her darnedest to overlook her inability to cope with a person half her size while she asked about Audrey, then inquired as to whether or not Kelly had eaten anything other than the apple she'd made her take with her for breakfast.

"There's some leftover pasta and some of Audrey's marinara sauce in the refrigerator," she went on before Kelly could admit that she hadn't had much of an appetite today—or that the apple was still in her purse. "That was what Ryan wanted for dinner. That and chocolate-chip cookies," she added in a way that made it obvious she did what she could to make the boy's sentence here a little easier, despite her lack of natural affinity for children.

"Thanks, Edna. But I won't be here long. I just want to pick up a couple of things from Audrey's room."

That wasn't all she wanted at the moment. She wanted to know what the problem was with Ryan. She also knew she should just let it go.

She asked anyway. "Why did Ryan have to go to bed early?"

A look of discomfort clouded the woman's hazel eyes. Or maybe it was disapproval. Whichever, the normally chatty woman suddenly became uncharacteristically quiet, and very preoccupied with untying her apron.

"Edna?"

It was apparently physically impossible for the housekeeper to keep anything to herself, though, in this instance, it wasn't for lack of trying. Her lips were pressed together so firmly that they had all but disappeared.

"His father told him he had to," she finally muttered.

"Why?"

"Because he walked you to the bus this morning."

Chapter Four

"May I come in?"

At the sound of Kelly's voice, Alex looked up from the exit interviews he'd kept his secretary overtime to transcribe. In the aftermath of losing the company's oldest client, the two men who'd worked the account had quit.

"It looks like you already are in," he said, the range of his frustrations broadening as he watched her lean her slender frame against the study door to close it.

He had one hip on the edge of his desk. Glancing across the clutter, he found an empty spot near a glass of bourbon and melting ice cubes and dropped the memos onto it. Damage control. He'd been dancing like a fool all day in an attempt to mitigate losses.

It hadn't left him in the best frame of mind. "How's Audrey?"

"The same." From speakers built into the floor-to-ceiling bookshelves, came the faint strains of a Mozart concerto. The adage about music soothing the savage beast entered Kelly's mind. It was hard to tell if the concept was working. "But that's not what I want to talk to you about."

"Then I can't imagine what else it would be."

Alex straightened, his motions as dismissive as his words when he picked up his glass and started toward the wet bar.

"Please don't do that."

"Do what?" he returned, thinking to dump the diluted contents of his drink and start over—which was exactly what he had to do with Warner-Pico Communications. Start courting them from scratch.

Kelly was a different story. He wasn't at all sure what to do about her.

"Try to punish me."

Slowly, deliberately, he placed the heavy glass on the mosaic of blue tiles by the small blue ceramic sink. Not entirely sure he wasn't attempting to do exactly what she'd just said, he glanced toward where she stood with her hands behind her, still leaning against the closed double doors.

She was a lovely woman. He couldn't deny that, any more than he could deny the very real physical effect she had on his body. He liked to think the reaction was simply because he'd once been so intimately familiar with her; because it had been he who had taught her how to make love. Better yet, he could blame the reaction on the fact that he hadn't been to bed with a woman since the last time he and Diane had slept together, and that had been weeks before their marriage finally ended. Not that there weren't women available. He just wasn't into one-night stands. And a relationship—which he wasn't particularly interested in, anyway—took time he didn't have.

Those were the arguments he'd used this morning, and every other time he'd found thoughts of Kelly interrupting his concentration today. Though his ambivalence about her made it hard to acknowledge, seeing her now, he knew his attraction went beyond memories or the physical needs of a normal, healthy male. As soft and sexy and, to him, incongruously innocent as she looked standing there with strands of her hair tugged free by the wind and her skin flushed by either the breeze or whatever it was that had brought her here, she looked terribly vulnerable.

That vulnerability had to do strictly with him. She hadn't been able to hide the hurt his manner had caused. It had been in her voice. It remained in her eyes.

"What did you want to talk about?" he asked, when what he really wanted was to ask her why she'd walked out on him so long ago. Why she hadn't given him a chance.

"Ryan."

For a fraction of a second, he hesitated. A moment later, he unceremoniously emptied his glass into the sink. "What about him?"

"I understand he got into trouble for walking me to the bus this morning. If you wouldn't mind telling me, I'd like to know why."

Alex hadn't realized he was holding his breath until he felt it leak out, slowly, like air from a punctured tire. All day long, he'd insisted to himself that he had nothing to worry about where Kelly was concerned. Even if her aunt did wake up and say something that could lead Kelly to figure out who Ryan was, legally and financially, he had her over the proverbial barrel. Still, holding the upper hand didn't feel as good as it should have.

"He knows he's not to the leave the property. He did it, anyway." Black-and-white. Right and wrong. Ryan knew the rules. "That's why he got in trouble."

Her quiet, "Oh," sounded a bit deflated, as if she'd expected there to be some other, perhaps some more personal reason. "He didn't tell me that. I'm sorry, Alex. I didn't mean to cause a problem."

"You didn't get him into trouble. He did it himself when he asked to go with you." A small refrigerator was concealed within the cabinets beneath the wet bar. Taking a handful of ice cubes from it, Alex dropped them into his glass. "I wouldn't even have known if he hadn't shown me the lizard he caught. When I asked him where he got it..."

"He told you he caught it at the bus stop," she completed when he paused.

"After he'd squirmed around about it for a minute. But, yes. That's exactly what he said. Along with the fact that he knew he wasn't supposed to go past the gate." Bourbon was poured from one of the crystal decanters. "Does that answer your question?"

Common sense told Kelly it wasn't her place to interfere. It also told her that if she had the brains God gave a guppy, she would take the hint and leave before Alex asked her to leave himself. Her sense of self-preservation resoundingly agreed. She could practically feel the tension in him, along with the effort he was making to keep everything very civil. But she liked Ryan too much not to go to bat for him, and there didn't seem anyone else around willing to take up his cause.

"Maybe he wouldn't have disobeyed if he hadn't been been so desperate for company."

Alex's eyes narrowed. "Excuse me?"

"I think he just needed someone to talk to," she offered in Ryan's defense. "Someone to pay attention to him. He needs something other than books and television to occupy his time, Alex. The walk was probably even good for him."

"I don't think I need you telling me what's good for my son."

"Someone needs to."

"Well, it sure as hell isn't you."

Had Kelly not already been flat against the door, the impact of his statement would have caused her to recoil. Though his tone had been completely matter-of-fact, pure challenge entered his eyes.

In a voice far calmer than she felt, she met that challenge. For Ryan. "You don't seem to hear what Edna has tried to tell you, so it *has* to be me. There probably isn't anyone around here who knows how hard it is growing up without friends, anyway. Damn it, Alex," she muttered, moving away from the door so her voice wouldn't carry. "You made a point of informing me this morning that the past was history. Yet, you're letting it keep you from listening to something you need to hear. What happened between us doesn't have anything to do with what's happening with Ryan."

Alex opened his mouth, then shut it again, his jaw clenching so tightly she swore his back teeth should have shattered.

Kelly ventured closer. "I know he's going back to school soon," she went on, mistaking Alex's silence for attention. "But there must be some sport or something around here he could participate in until then. The child is going stir-crazy. Can't you at least take him on a hike? Or to a ball game? He's dying to spend some time with you."

The drink Alex really didn't want was completely forgotten. He'd turned toward her, watching as she'd moved across the thick, sand-colored carpet—and wondering how in the hell he was supposed to fit a hike or a ball game into a day that couldn't even accommodate a meal not eaten at a desk or a decent night's sleep. Now, the air feeling as dangerously still as the calm before a tornado, he took a single step toward her, forcing her to back up from where she'd stopped a few feet away.

His glance swept her upturned face. He hated that it still mattered; hated that with the rest of his world falling down around him, he couldn't banish the thoughts of her that had crept into his every waking hour. He'd done his best to concentrate on the sense of betrayal he'd felt when he'd come home and found her gone all those years ago. But instead of resurrecting a little defensive anger, he'd found himself recalling how she'd looked this morning with the sunlight in her hair. He'd tried to dredge up the confusion he'd felt the day the attorney had brought Ryan to the house, wanting to remember how he'd blamed her for saddling him with the responsibility of trying to raise a son without a mother, and found himself, instead, thinking of how haunted her smile had seemed; of how much spirit had been drained from her.

Now, standing so close he could breathe the scent of rain-dampened air clinging to her skin, feeling his body tighten at the thought of once being able to so freely touch her, his sense of self-preservation finally kicked in.

"You want to tell me how to raise my kid, Kelly? Fine. Go right ahead," he urged, his voice the deadly calm of a man who knows he holds the last ace. "Just tell me first what makes you such an authority on children when you gave up your own.

"On second thought," he continued, the quick shake of his head designed to cut her off, though all she'd done was look as if she'd forgotten how to breathe, "I really don't want to talk about Ryan with you." Sharing anything about his son with her suddenly felt too risky. She'd kissed her legal rights goodbye where Ryan was concerned, but her emotional appeal to the boy was beginning to make him nervous. "So answer something else for me. Tell me why you ran. Tell me why you couldn't wait until I got back so I could work something out for us."

Kelly didn't remember wrapping her arms around herself. She must have, though, because she felt her arms tighten over the roiling sensation in her stomach.

The thought occurred to her vaguely, but she wished she'd stayed by the door. Not because she felt so totally, completely exposed standing there with Alex's eyes hard on her face, but because as weak as her knees felt, she desperately needed something to lean against.

Having learned long ago that all she had to lean on was what strength she could pull from within, she drew a deep, shuddering breath and tipped her head back to meet Alex's unflinching gaze. She'd expected to see anger, for that was what she'd heard in his voice. And it was definitely there. But what she also saw in the taut lines of his features was hurt; the betrayal he'd felt over what she'd done.

It was the pain she might have caused him that made her courage falter. "I thought you weren't interested in dragging this up."

"I'm not 'dragging it up.' I'm just not ignoring it any longer." His voice dropped. "Tell me why you didn't wait, Kelly."

At his quiet command, she turned from him. Not to pace, which she would have done, had there been more strength in her legs. But to move to the leather wing chairs flanking a reading table. She didn't sit, though. She would have felt too much like a prisoner at an inquisition with him hovering over her. She simply stood by the chair and the wall of books behind it, needing the time to gather the thoughts—the dreams—she hadn't allowed herself to fully remember in years.

"Do you remember how your parents found out I was pregnant?" she finally, quietly, asked.

Alex hadn't moved. From where he remained, six feet away, she saw the muscle in his jaw jerk.

"Mom overheard us talking about it."

"It was the day after Thanksgiving," she added, bits and pieces of the bittersweet summer before floating through her memory like frames from an old movie clip. In her mind's eye flashed pictures of Alex coming home from Harvard that June, seeking her out after everyone had gone to bed, and the two of them talking until sunrise because there had been so much stored up to share; Alex laughing at the mess she'd made of a meringue, his laughter dying when he'd finally reached for her, kissing her that first time; Alex, no longer content with the soul-stirring kisses they'd shared while he'd held her, telling her of his dreams, his doubts, and finally making love to her as she'd ached for him to do, teaching her things she'd never known about her own body, teaching her all about his.

Her fingers flexed against her arms, her chest feeling tight as she drew a deep breath. Despite the chill inside her, her skin felt warm. But that was only because Alex, too, remembered what they had shared. She felt sure of it as she watched his darkened eyes move to her mouth and down the length of her body. What she wasn't so certain of, was if he was remembering what she'd felt like beneath him back then, or if he was wondering what she'd feel like beneath him now.

"I'd become pregnant sometime before you went back to school that fall," she reminded him, more aware than she wanted to be of the rigidity in his body when he reached behind him for his drink. "You asked me for time to decide what to do. Do you remember that, Alex?"

His hand tightened around the glass. "I remember."

"Did you ever decide what that something would have been?"

He hadn't been prepared for the question. A quick frown slashed his forehead, his eyebrows drawing together in a way that made it clear he didn't appreciate the tables being turned on him.

"What difference does it make now? You didn't stick around to find out."

"What would you have done?" she pressed, just as he had pressed her only moments ago. "If we're going to talk about this, I have as much right to answers as you do. Tell me honestly, Alex. What decision had you made between the time you went back to school after Thanksgiving and when you came back home at Christmas?"

"I'd told you before I left that I'd take care of you."

"I know you did." She'd clung to that promise, weaving all manner of impossible dreams around it. "What I want to know is how you'd planned to do that. You still had two years of college left, and another after that to get your MBA—"

"I know what the situation was," he cut in.

"So what had you decided?"

Alex stared at her, hard, his stomach knotting. He hadn't decided what he would do. She hadn't given him the chance.

"That's what I thought."

The resignation in Kelly's tone, or maybe it was the hint of accusation beneath it, had Alex's eyes narrowing.

"What's that supposed to mean? I'd wanted to look at the choices we had," he defended, both his tone and his statement reminding her of how analytically he'd always approached problems. "I wanted to do what was best for both of us. You just said yourself that I had to finish school. I didn't have any money that didn't come from my parents, and I couldn't ask them to support us." Pride alone would have prevented that. *"You can't touch your trust until you're twenty-five,"* his father had reminded him. *"We'll pay your tuition, but how can you support a family and keep up your grades? If you want to work with me, you have to finish school. Don't cheat yourself, son."*

"I needed to explore our options."

"Options?" She looked at him blankly, wondering just how many he'd thought they'd had. "You told me yourself about the talks your parents had with you right here in this room," she reminded him, certain he couldn't have forgotten the concerns that had been voiced about his obligations to the family, the family business and to his own future. She certainly hadn't. She'd even understood what those obligations meant. Heaven knew, she'd been hearing about them from him most of her life. "It became clear in a hurry that it was a choice between your responsibilities to your family, or to me. My choices," she added, laying her hand on her chest, "were that I could either leave with you or without you. After you'd gone back to school, I couldn't stay."

"Why not?"

"Because Audrey didn't want me here." And neither had his mother. She'd made that clear. She didn't know what Mr. Burke thought of her. "I don't know what your mother said to her, but Audrey made it plain that I'd created a problem for her with her employer. After you went back to school, my aunt saw to it that I got a hefty dose of reality myself."

The reality Audrey had drilled into her was actually quite obvious to anyone not blinded by idealism or dreams of knights in shining armor. Alex, as her aunt had so clearly pointed out, had, since birth, been instilled with a strong sense of duty and loyalty to his family. He had been raised and was being educated to take his place at his father's side and to move among the rich and influential. Kelly was the niece of a cook; a girl who, because she had no parents and would be out on her own once she turned eighteen, might, if she was lucky, get some sort of financial aid to attend community college when she graduated from high school—provided she didn't drop out because of her pregnancy.

"I'd told Audrey you'd take care of us," she told Alex, slipping into the plural without even realizing it. At that time, she'd already thought of herself and Alex's baby as a family, with Alex at its head. Never, ever, had she wanted anything so much as she had him and his baby: a real family. "I told her you promised." She swallowed, remembering the only time her aunt had ever put her arm around her. Audrey had said Kelly was just like her mother, too trusting for her own good; and, though it was a hard lesson to learn, Kelly needed to understand that the only person she could ever really count on was herself.

"I'd thought by taking care of me, you'd meant marriage," she explained, sparing herself nothing as the old feelings of panic, confusion and hurt rose to tighten her throat. "But Audrey told me I was even more naive than she'd thought if I really believed that. She'd said that to people like you and your family, taking care my 'situation' meant sticking me and the baby in an apartment somewhere while you paid our expenses. Or just paying me off outright. I told her you weren't like that. You couldn't be."

A catch entered her voice "You'd been my friend for as long as I could remember, Alex. There wasn't much of anything I thought or did that didn't somehow include you. And that summer...that summer," she repeated, her voice dropping to nearly a whisper, "I honestly thought that you cared about me as much as I cared about you.

"I know you never said you loved me," she hurried on, sure from his silence that he hadn't found much to disagree with so far. "But I never even questioned how you might think of me until Audrey started asking questions. She wanted to know if you'd ever introduced me to any of your friends when they'd come over. And if you'd ever taken me out where you'd be seen with me...."

Her throat felt dry, raw. So she stopped, seeing no reason to belabor the point Audrey had made. Her aunt had known even as she'd asked the questions that Alex had never taken her anywhere; that he treated her differently from the "socially acceptable" young ladies in the Burkes's circle of friends. At the time Kelly had blamed that on Mrs. Burke, because Alex's mother had actively discouraged Alex's friendship with a relative of "the help" once she and Alex had entered their teens.

Yet, even though Kelly had gone to a nearby public school, never quite fitting in because she really didn't "belong" in the decidedly wealthy area, and Alex had spent most of his time away at private schools, their friendship had somehow endured, and the feelings had grown. On her part, anyway.

Alex looked down at his glass, studying it as if he found the shapes of the silvery ice-cubes in the caramel-colored liquid utterly fascinating. She had the feeling she'd struck a few rather telling chords. Instead of regarding her with accusation and anger, he no longer seemed able to meet her eyes.

Or, maybe, he was simply finding it impossible to forgive her.

"You still left without telling me," he said, his tone as tight as a bowstring.

Before, that thought had always succeeded in eliciting hurt and anger over how she'd left without allowing him to make a decision. Now, Alex felt only as if he were clinging to an argument that allowed him to justify the way he'd made himself remember her. Yet, instead of feeling secure in his memory, he felt like a climber losing his grip on a sliver of rock destined to crumble anyway.

That feeling only increased when he raised his head and met her eyes.

"I left," she admitted, "because I didn't know what else to do. I knew Audrey was disappointed in me. And I knew she was worried that your mother would decide it was too complicated having me around . . . that she'd tell her she'd have to find other employment if she wanted to keep me with her. But I know Audrey was also trying to make me see there were consequences that went beyond what was going on just then. That's why she explained that if you really did love me, you'd have to choose between me and your family. And she said that if I really cared about you, I wouldn't ask you to make that choice." She paused, hoping he understood; uncertain how to make him, if he didn't. "I left so you wouldn't have to choose. Because whichever way you did choose, I'd lose, anyway."

Had he chosen her, she knew he'd have risked alienating his family and losing the fortune that was his birthright—because it had been as clear as Mrs. Burke's collection of crystal that Kelly was not the kind of woman the Burkes had in mind for their son. And if he'd chosen his family over her . . . well, she simply wouldn't have been able to bear hearing him say the words.

She told him that, too, knowing he could fault her actions but not her reasons. Then she fell into silence.

From beyond the closed doors across the room, she heard the muffled bong of the grandfather clock at the end of the wide hall. For the space of the first two sounds, neither one of them moved. Kelly wondered if she even breathed. Then, as if pacing himself to the clock's measured beat, Alex slowly moved toward her.

She had no idea what expression his features betrayed. Wondering how much more of her soul he expected her to bare, she was staring at the nubs in the pale carpet when she saw him offer her the glass he held.

The gesture surprised her. "No, thank you," she said, when she actually would have welcomed the bourbon's numbing effects. "I have to leave in a few minutes."

The drink retreated from her view. "You're going back to the hospital tonight?"

"To a hotel. There's one a couple of blocks from the hospital. I would have been there by now, but the weather had the traffic so messed up."

"It's almost ten o'clock," she heard him say, even as the clock beyond the doors struck the last resonant chord. "Don't you think it's going to look a little odd for a single female to be checking in without luggage at this time of night?"

She shook her head, utterly amazed at how... normal... he sounded. She could have just as easily spent the last twenty minutes telling him why she'd chosen blue paint for her bedroom, for all the difference her explanations had seemed to make to him. At least that was what she thought before she looked up.

He was watching her, his expression guarded. For the first time since she'd seen him, he didn't look as if he wished she'd simply vaporize. Something almost like pain tightened his mouth as he quietly studied her face. He had been hurt, too. Though she had the feeling he either couldn't or wouldn't admit how much. It seemed, too, when he lifted his hand toward her face, her breath seeming to catch in her throat, that he just might have realized how frightening it had been for her to be seventeen and alone in this house with adults who saw her only as a roadblock to his future. Or to their own.

It must have been her need for him to understand that had caused her to see something that wasn't really there. His fingers were a whisper away from the contact she hadn't allowed herself to want, when his hand fell and the hardness she'd seen in him before crept back to shadow his features.

Unable to imagine what thought had just jerked him away from her, she did her best to pretend it didn't matter, anyway. "I thought I'd borrow a few things from Audrey's room," she told him, since his very practical mind had found her lack of luggage a concern. He'd always been so much more pragmatic than she, able to see minor pitfalls along with major potential. She simply went full speed ahead. At least, she once had. "I'm sure she has an overnight case in there somewhere. I don't want to impose on you any more than I already have."

"You're not imposing." His voice was flat, almost weary. "This was your home."

This house had never been *her* home, but Kelly saw no reason to point that out. Even if she had, she'd have been deprived of the opportunity. The telephone on the desk behind Alex interrupted with a low, electronic ring, the summons effectively stalling a conversation that seemed to be over anyway.

Alex didn't seem particularly appreciative of the intrusion. Kelly merely looked apprehensive as he turned and picked up the receiver.

He seemed to read her thoughts. He shook his head, indicating that it wasn't the hospital even as he said, "Not at all," to whoever was on the other end of the line. "I was just trying to evaluate where we'd lost you,'' he added to his caller and set his drink down near the papers he'd dropped there earlier. ''Hang on a second, though, will you?''

With his hand over the mouthpiece, he looked to where Kelly had turned to the door.

''You're not leaving are you?''

She shook her head. She really wasn't in a position to spend money on a hotel if she didn't have to. Especially when she had no idea how long she'd have to stay. ''I'm going to bed.''

She could tell little from the nod he gave her before he returned his attention to his call. Alex still had questions. She was sure of that. But his call obviously had to do with whatever it was that had him so uptight—since it was the same thick set of notes she'd seen him with last night that he now pulled from his briefcase—and she simply felt a little too raw to stick around and find out what those questions might be.

She'd said she was going to bed. She really should. But she knew she wouldn't be able to sleep.

That was why, after throwing her clothes, underwear included, into the washing machine and pulling on the nightgown she'd borrowed from her aunt's dresser last night, she slipped out the kitchen door. For now, for a while, she wouldn't let herself think how badly it hurt to know that Alex didn't even care that she'd done what she had for him; and that, at the time, it had been the only thing she could do.

The air was balmy, damp from the rain and far warmer than the air-conditioned rooms she'd left behind. A faint breeze blew, either carrying the last of the storm clouds away or bringing a new batch in. It was hard to tell. There were no stars overhead. No moon. But off to the east, an occasional flash of sheet lightning strafed the horizon.

Kelly moved past the pool, her footsteps soundless as she crossed the large expanse of cool-decking and took the steps leading from the main level of the property to the one just below the house. The Burkes's home was at the top of a small mountain. The ground beyond the front doors was a gentle uphill slope. The ground in back fell away in a breathtaking view of the city. It was at the back of the property that Kelly finally stopped; at the ornate, waist-high wrought-iron railing that separated the tiered yard from the steeply angled drop-off beyond the cascades of crimson bougainvilleas.

The nightgown she wore was white cotton, sleeveless, worn thin and soft from dozens of washings, and at least two sizes too big. It smelled of soap and fresh air, which didn't surprise Kelly at all because she'd never known Audrey to pamper herself with anything so frivolous as perfume. The gown, except for the size, could have come right off the clotheslines in Kelly's own backyard. As for perfume, hers was usually limited to whatever it was the manufacturer put in the baby powder she used.

Kelly curled her fingers over the smooth, black rail. This wasn't the first time today that she'd found herself wondering if she hadn't acquired more than a few of her simpler tastes from the woman who had raised her. Yet, it wasn't really Audrey taking precedence in her thoughts. Even though she tried not to think of him, as she stood at the railing, the breeze tangling the thin cotton around her legs and lifting her hair from her face, it was what had just happened with Alex that kept her from really seeing the endless sea of lights stretched out before her.

She wanted to understand him. Because if she did, maybe it would be easier to accept that he couldn't understand how hurting him was the last thing she'd wanted to do. That he'd become so cynical, so hard, was something she never would have expected of him. But just as she had changed, she supposed he'd had no choice but to change himself. The stress of losing his father, of taking over a company and of having his marriage end, all in such a short time, would certainly have taken their toll. Especially the divorce, she thought; because, to Kelly, the death of a marriage was something very sad. All that hope. All those dreams. Just . . . gone.

She knew exactly how that felt, too. And, though she knew it wasn't wise, she ached for Alex; for what he had lost. Not because she'd ever divorced, but because she'd once known what it was like to dream. At least she had until she'd lost the ability. She'd given it up—right along with her baby.

A knot formed beneath her heart. Alex knew she'd given up their child. She'd realized that the instant he'd left her reeling from his crack about how she could know anything about kids, since she'd given hers away. Had she thought about it, she would have realized sooner that he'd know, since he hadn't asked about the child. She supposed he'd found out from his mother. After all, it had been Mrs. Burke who'd recommended the attorney Audrey had sent her to see. But none of that mattered. What Kelly wondered about now was if Alex ever thought about the child they'd created together. If, like her, he prayed that it was healthy and safe and, most of all, that he, or she, was happy. She'd never known if she'd had a boy or a girl. She hadn't wanted to know because, at the time, she was sure she would then see her child in the face of every child of that sex. But the ploy had backfired miserably. Now, every child anywhere near the age hers would have been held the potential of being the baby she desperately wished she'd been able to find a way to keep. Even Ryan had made her think of her baby. Especially Ryan. Because he was Alex's son; his other child.

She didn't know how long she stood there, trying to make sense of why so much pain had to be resurrected; why decisions made so long ago couldn't simply be accepted as having been made and everyone gone on from there. But nothing was that tidy. It had been apparent from the moment she and Alex had found themselves in the same room together that the past had never been laid to rest. Ironic, she thought, that it should be her aunt who'd brought them together to close the final chapter.

Somewhere, off in the distance, thunder rolled out over the valley. The wind picked up, carrying the smell of rain, and a flash of lightning lit a huge thunderhead from within. Kelly stayed where she was, too agitated to go inside and wrestle with sleep.

The thunder faded out, leaving only the rustle of leaves, the drone of cicadas—and the sound of footsteps on terracotta tile.

Holding her hair back from her face as the wind pulled at it, she turned to see Alex stop a few feet behind her.

Chapter Five

Kelly had said she was going to bed. So when Alex finished setting up a breakfast meeting with the president of Warner-Pico, allowing himself to breathe a little easier because the man was at least willing to talk, he'd headed upstairs to go to bed himself. When he'd stepped out onto his balcony, though, wanting to catch a breath of air that hadn't been purified, conditioned and electronically cooled by the ever-present home, office, car, and restaurant air-conditioning systems, he'd seen Kelly on the lower terrace.

His only thought when he'd come out after her, had been to finish what had started in the library. Feeling his throat go dry when she turned to face him, he wasn't so sure finishing it tonight was such a hot idea. From his balcony, he'd noticed only that she was wearing a loose white nightgown. What he noticed now was the feminine outline of her body as the breeze tugged the thin white fabric across her breasts and twined it around her long, slender legs.

Jamming his hands in his pockets, he took another step forward. Considering the number of distractions he was dealing with already, he ought to be able to handle one more. "I thought you'd gone to bed."

"I was going to, but I didn't think I could sleep." Her hand fell, allowing the breeze to win the battle with her hair. "How did your call go?"

"Not as badly as it could have," he returned, not sure how she'd known he'd been worried about it. Not sure he wanted to know.

Her only response was a slight lift of her chin before she turned back to the railing.

Alex came up beside her, resting his elbows on the waist-high rail. The breeze blew her hair back from her face and, in the glow of the security lamps positioned around the perimeter of the yard, he could see her profile. The light was weak, though, so mostly he saw only shadows.

"Would you answer one more question for me?"

Mimicking his position, Kelly looked down at the lights scattered over the valley floor. There was a definite hesitation before her quiet, "I suppose."

Alex heard her reluctance. And promptly ignored it.

"How could you give up a baby?"

Closing her eyes, Kelly pulled in a lungful of the damp night air. If the man had learned anything at all in the past eleven years, it was how to land a gut punch.

The way he'd posed his question left no doubt in her mind that he thought she'd done something unpardonable when she'd given up her child. The way he looked at her when she finally glanced over at him, so clearly disappointed in her judgment, only confirmed the conclusion. But she saw something else in him in the moments before she turned away: a desire, maybe even a need, to understand.

She already felt bruised inside. The thought of having to defend the decisions she had made only caused the pain to go deeper. Had it not been for the hope he'd just given her that he might eventually understand, she might well not have answered.

"Have you ever been scared, Alex? I mean really, down-deep frightened to the point where you didn't know how you were ever going to resolve something?"

He could so easily have told her that he had. He was scared to death right now, because he was fighting as hard as he knew how to keep from losing what his father had entrusted to him. Instead, he looked away, uneasy with being able to so clearly relate to a feeling he hadn't real-ized she had suffered.

"It doesn't allow you to think too clearly, does it?" she asked, though there was more understanding in her tone than inquiry.

"Are you saying you don't know why you did it?"

"I had my reasons," she said softly. "I just didn't see any way around them. I wanted more for my baby than what I'd had, Alex. I never knew my father, and Audrey said my mother had to work two jobs to keep food on the table. All I remember of her... of my mother," she clari-fied, thinking of the woman who had only been seventeen herself when Kelly was born, "was that she was never there."

"Then what you did doesn't make any sense. You wanted something different, but you did the same thing. You weren't there for your child, either."

She couldn't deny his conclusion, or the knot that formed in her stomach because of it.

"That's true. I wasn't there. But someone was. Someone still is." Her child had a good mother and a good father. She had to believe that.

"But it's not you."

The knot clenched. "What kind of parent would I have been if I'd had to work two jobs, myself? I wouldn't have been around enough to provide the kind of stability a child needs." Unless she'd gone on welfare, but that was exactly the sort of existence she'd wanted to avoid for her child. "I was seventeen, Alex. I hadn't even finished high school. Any job I got wouldn't have paid more than minimum wage and that wouldn't exactly allow me to pay for music lessons or start a college fund. Those were the kinds of advantages I wanted for my baby."

Feeling as empty as she'd felt those months following the baby's birth, she watched a leaf blow past, looping once, then disappearing into the blackness below. Alex, his expression a study in stone, continued staring straight ahead.

"I also had to think about what would happen if something happened to me . . . like it did to my mother. She was just crossing the street, Alex. The driver of the car didn't even see her. I was lucky she had a sister. But I didn't have anyone to take my child in and I couldn't have stood worrying about where it might wind up."

"There was Audrey. . . ."

"Under the circumstances, accepting responsibility for another child was the last thing Audrey would want. Or need. It's all over and done with, anyway. Trying to come up with answers or arguments now is pointless."

"I would have helped."

"Alex, please."

"I would have. My family had money. They'd recognized my obligation—"

"That's just how every child wants to be thought of. As an obligation," she retorted, too upset to realize what he'd just said.

Alex realized it, though. He also realized they were getting dangerously close to something neither one of them was ready to cope with at the moment. But the feelings he'd had no luck resurrecting before seemed to have found a foothold now. No one had ever hurt him as much as she had. But then, after she'd gone, he'd never let himself care about anyone as much as he had about her, either.

The first drops of rain fell on her face as she straightened to look up at him. "I wanted a real family for my baby, Alex. One with a mother and a father who loved that child for itself and for no other reason. The only way that could happen was for me to do what I did."

"You never—"

"Don't tell me what I didn't do!" Despite the plea in her tone, her voice was barely audible over the sudden crack of thunder. "And please don't stand there telling me what you would have done. You can say anything you want right now, because we'll never have any way of knowing whether or not you would have followed through. I'm not doubting any of your intentions, Alex. It's just that you weren't here trying to deal with what I had to face.

"I was a kid," she begged him to understand, oblivious to how much faster the rain was falling. "I was going on nothing but raw emotion and whatever the adults around me said, and you were back east wanting more time than I had to figure out how involved you wanted to be. I'm not saying anyone forced me to do anything. The decision I made, I made alone, and whether you want to believe it or not, what I did was the hardest thing I've ever had to do in my life. I'd give anything to have my baby with me. I could take care of it now the way I couldn't then. But when

I think that way, I want to find my child. And that wouldn't be fair to anybody." Least of all the adoptive parents. "Please, *please,* leave it alone."

She had her arms crossed so tightly she could barely breathe. Or maybe it was the anger, the hurt that had welled up inside that left so little room for air. There had been a time when she could have told him anything and he would have at least listened. Now, he wasn't even trying to understand a thing she said.

She started past him, wanting only to escape, not knowing if she felt more chilled on the inside, or out. The rain was coming down in earnest now, the fat drops flattening her hair and soaking into her thin cotton gown.

She was even with his side when he turned, his fingers curling around her upper arm and stopping her dead in her tracks.

His hand felt hot against her cool skin; his grip, insistent. "You weren't the only one hurt, Kelly."

"Why are you doing this?" she whispered, the words a desperate plea.

In the dark, he looked forbidding. In the bright flash of lightning that arced from the heavens, he looked as tortured as anyone she'd ever seen.

His fingers flexed against her flesh. The bleakness in his eyes was echoed in his voice. Slowly, his hand slid down her arm and fell back to his side.

"I don't know," she heard him say, sounding as raw inside as she felt. His voice dropped to a whisper. "Maybe because it hurt so much."

He didn't seem to notice the rain. Or, if he did, he didn't care that they were both getting soaked. As he stood with his eyes searching hers, he looked like a man torn; a man in pain.

Kelly felt that pain join her own. But there was nothing she could do to ease the ache; nothing more she could say that would make any difference to him.

"The last thing in the world I wanted was to hurt you," she begged him to believe over the cacophony of the downpour. "That's why I left, Alex."

He couldn't seem to understand that, and she couldn't explain it all to him again. He wouldn't have heard it, anyway. She didn't know him anymore. Didn't know how to reach him.

Kelly could have walked away just then, and Alex wouldn't have stopped her. But she didn't move. And he didn't know what to say that wouldn't only make matters worse. The rain had her hair clinging to her head and plastered against her neck. One thick strand stuck to her cheek. Droplets ran from her face to her shoulders to be absorbed by the cotton gown that was now so wet he could clearly see the outline of her firm breasts and their dark nipples, tightened by the chill.

With the wet fabric sticking to her, bunched and draped as it was over the flatness of her stomach, outlining her long legs, she looked like a Grecian sculpture. Exquisitely beautiful. Innocently erotic. Alex felt his body tightening, responding, aching. But it was an entirely different kind of ache that filled him when he dragged his glance back to her face. He couldn't tell if there were tears clinging to her eyelashes and rolling from the corners of her eyes, or if it was just the rain that had her face glistening like wet marble.

Thunder cracked. Seconds later, lightning split the sky. The wind that had blown toward him only a moment ago, now seemed to come from behind. He lifted his hand, his own shirtsleeve sticking to his skin. With the tip of his finger, he caught the strand of wet hair clinging to her

cheek. His eyes on hers, he pushed it back from her face.
But when he let his hand fall to her shoulder, wanting—
needing—to pull her against him, he felt her stiffen.

"We shouldn't be out here," he heard her say as lightning streaked across the sky. Like the snap of a whip,
thunder cracked before the light had even faded. She
stepped back, deliberately breaking the contact. "It's
dangerous."

She was speaking of the storm. And she was right. They
had no business staying where they were. With the storm
on top of them, standing next to a metal rail on the top of
a mountain was pure stupidity. But it wasn't the damage
nature could wreak upon life and limb that Alex considered as he watched her gather the wet fabric from around
her knees and hurry up the steps toward the house. As he
followed a few steps behind, he considered only that there
had been a time when Kelly wouldn't have resisted him at
all. He would only have had to touch her and she would
have come to him willingly. Now, they were strangers.
Strangers who had once been intimately familiar with each
other's thoughts; each other's bodies. Strangers who had
once been young. And scared.

There had been a time, too, when he had known exactly
how he felt about Kelly and what she'd done. Now, unable to get past the anguish he'd seen in her eyes, he had no
idea how he felt about her, or anything else.

Alex didn't follow Kelly in through the kitchen. He
didn't take the pool entrance in the middle of the house,
either, or go in through any of the half-dozen other doors
leading inside. He stayed on the covered patio above the
pool, his hands on his hips and his back to the house while
he watched nature remind mortals just who was in charge
out there. At least, that was what Kelly thought he was

doing when she closed the door behind herself, after checking to make sure she wouldn't be closing it in his face.

She was shaking. Not just because she was drenched to the skin, either, though entering the air-conditioned house as wet as she was didn't help matters any. She'd bared her soul to Alex, all but begged him to understand how she'd felt about him, and all he'd done was lash out at her.

Hugging her arms across her chest, desperately in need of a towel, she dripped her way across the tile floor. She wanted to be home, back where she felt safe. There was no sense of safety here. No security. There never had been. But never, in all the years she'd lived in this house, had she felt that lack so much as she did tonight.

"Kelly?"

At the sound of Ryan's voice, Kelly turned from where she'd just started down the short hall to her aunt's room.

Ryan had been standing at the archway leading in from the dining room. Now, a look of pure puzzlement screwing up his nose, he tugged at the light blue pajama top that kept slipping off his shoulder and gingerly moved toward her.

"How come you're all wet?"

He wasn't supposed to be up. His father had sent him to his room early, after all. But when she saw his eyes widen at the boom of thunder a moment later, windows shaking in their panes from the concussion, she had the feeling she knew why he was wandering the halls.

Because I got caught outside talking to a brick wall, she felt like saying. But what she said as she wiped at the moisture on her face, hoping the child couldn't distinguish rain from tears, was, "Because I was out in the rain. It's really nasty out there."

Managing a smile, finding the expression easier than she'd have thought because he looked so brave trying to pretend he wasn't scared, she sniffed and motioned him closer. "Why don't you wait for me here?" she asked, nodding to the door leading to the hallway. "I'll get a towel and be right back."

She was back in thirty seconds, which was all the time it took to step inside the bathroom off her aunt's bedroom, drop the sodden gown into the tub, wrap her aunt's lavender chenille bathrobe around herself, and grab a towel from the rack.

"I got grounded," Ryan told her as soon as she stepped back out into the hall.

"I heard." Bending forward, she wrapped her hair in the white towel as she walked toward him. "I'm sorry that happened, Ryan. I really am." Her voice softened. "But if you knew you weren't supposed to leave the property, you really shouldn't have. You could have just walked me to the gate."

"Are you mad at me, too?"

"Oh, sweetie, no. I'm not mad." He sat on the floor where she'd left him, his eyes downcast as he toyed with the hem of his boxer-style p.j. bottoms. Crouching in front of him, she tipped up his chin. The kid had drop-dead dimples even when he didn't smile. "I don't think your dad is really mad at you, either. He just doesn't want anything to happen to you."

"He sure acted mad."

Kelly swallowed. She couldn't speak for Alex on this subject, but she certainly sympathized with his child. "Come on," she said, holding out her hand as she rose. "Let's get a glass of milk. I don't know about you," she added when another clap of thunder send a faint but discernible shudder through Ryan, "but storms make me a little nervous."

"Milk makes it better?"

"No," she replied, answering his skepticism honestly. "But sharing it with somebody does."

She barely caught the boy's smile. The boom of thunder had masked the sound of the back door opening. But the rush of warm air and the dampness that came with it, caused both her and Ryan to glance up as they turned into the kitchen.

The brass light fixture hanging over the bay-windowed eating area to Kelly's left had been turned off. The main kitchen lights were still on, though, fully illuminating the huge, high-ceilinged room—and the features of the man whose glance bounced from Kelly to his son as he closed out the storm.

For what felt like an eternity but was closer to six seconds, Alex stood with his hands on his hips, his wet hair slicked back from running his hand through it, and his expression as closed as Kelly had ever seen it.

"You're supposed to be in your room, Ryan. In bed," Alex added, because it was now way past his normal bedtime. "What are you doing out here?"

Kelly wasn't sure, but she thought she felt Ryan's fingers squeeze hers in the moment before he pulled his hand away. She was, however, quite positive that he looked both embarrassed to have been caught holding her hand to begin with, and a little uncertain about what sort of excuse he could offer the man now walking toward them.

The last thing in the world Ryan would admit was that he was afraid of the storm. As much as he admired his dad, Kelly was sure he didn't want his dad to think him a sissy.

"Ryan?" Alex prodded, stopping in front of them.

"I wanted a glass of milk," he finally said, apparently more willing to risk further punishment than risk having his dad discover why he'd been wandering around the house in search of an adult.

Kelly cinched the borrowed robe a little tighter. "I was just going to get it for him." They were so much alike, she thought. When Alex was a boy, he'd have walked over hot coals to keep his father from thinking him anything less than a man. "He's going to keep me company until the storm passes. If I remember right, they pass through pretty quickly, don't they, Alex?"

A flicker of incomprehension passed through the big man's otherwise unreadable expression—probably because he knew she'd always loved thunderstorms. "Since when do you—"

"Don't they?" she cut in, her voice a little firmer as she held his eyes.

At the interruption, the incomprehension increased, only to fade when he saw her protectively touch Ryan's shoulder.

Seeing that he'd finally gotten the hint, she didn't give him time to decide what he wanted to do about it.

"Get the glasses, will you, Ryan?"

Looking a little hesitant since his father hadn't said anything else to him, he asked her, "How many?"

Kelly looked back to Alex, more aware than she wanted to be of how his jaw clenched when she raised her eyebrow in silent question. The situation was awkward, to say the least. But as far as Kelly was concerned, at the moment, helping alleviate a child's fear, real or imagined, took precedence over escaping the tension tightening his jaw and her stomach.

Alex's only reply was a tight nod.

"Three," she replied. "But get your dad a towel first. Okay?"

"That's all right." Catching his son by the shoulder as Ryan started past, Alex gave that thin shoulder a squeeze. "I'll get it myself." Lightning flashed, illuminating the windows as if someone were rapidly flipping the patio light switch. Moments later, thunder rumbled by. "You stay here and help Kelly count the seconds between the flashes and the thunder. That way she can tell when it starts to get farther away."

Kelly didn't know if Alex caught Ryan's relieved expression before the boy assured him that he'd take care of her and he headed off to the cupboards on the opposite side of the room. She didn't know, either, if he realized how much it meant to his son that he was about to sit in the kitchen with him and do something so simple as have a glass of milk. It was apparent, though, that he truly cared a great deal for his child. Not only from the understanding he'd just exhibited, but because, for the sake of his son, he was willing to work around the bitterness he felt toward her. For a while, anyway.

"*...it hurt so much....*"

She'd never meant to hurt him. Ever. And the pain and the regret filling her at the realization that she had, was as awful as the hurt she'd suffered herself. Yet, as she watched Ryan and Alex together, she couldn't help but wonder how other hurts he'd suffered had compounded what he'd obviously seen as her betrayal; if he felt his wife, and maybe even his father, had betrayed him, too.

Kelly knew Ryan needed to spend time alone with his father. That was why, five minutes later, she vacated the stool at the end of the cooking island where she and Ryan were dipping crackers in their glasses, when she heard Alex's somber, "Where's mine?"

"I got it," said Ryan, grabbing the empty tumbler between his and Kelly's to pour it full of milk.

Reminding him to be careful, Kelly watched the procedure from behind Ryan, as much to avoid eye contact with the man looming at her shoulder as to supervise the filling of the glass. Alex had changed his clothes. Instead of a dress shirt and slacks, he now wore a pair of faded jeans and a soft gray T-shirt that faithfully delineated his beautifully muscled chest and shoulders. He was also barefoot.

Kelly had no idea why she should find his appearance disconcerting, unless it was because it was so unexpectedly casual. Not casual like tennis-club, tea-on-the-terrace casual, which was more the Burke style. But more, sit-on-the-riverbank, it's-okay-to-get-dirty casual. She might even have thought he looked more approachable dressed as he was—were it not for the distance he so deliberately put between them when he picked up the glass and pulled a stool around to keep Ryan between them.

"I think I'll go to bed now."

Kelly's quietly spoken decision made Ryan's face crumple. "You can't. The storm's not gone yet."

Cinching the belt of the lavender robe because the belt kept loosening, and aware of Alex's eyes on her, she started to tell Ryan it was okay because his dad was with him. That point wouldn't have meant anything to Ryan, however. The boy believed *she* needed the company.

Apparently, Alex was on to her thinking. "You might as well finish your milk." His shuttered glance moved from the belt of the comfortable old bathrobe to the white towel still wrapped around her head. Inexplicably, his expression softened. "It shouldn't last too much longer. What do you think, Ryan? How far away has it moved?"

"We counted to six the last time. It was five just before that. That means the thunderhead that thunder came from is about six miles away." He dunked a cracker into his milk, his expression quite serious. "But there could be a closer one in a different storm cell."

"It'll probably all be gone soon."

"Yeah, probably," Ryan agreed, giving Kelly a little nod that he no doubt meant to be encouraging.

Alex caught that gesture and the smile that followed, but she hadn't a clue what he thought about Ryan's reactions to her as she watched him concentrate on his son's expressions. She and Ryan had been talking about electrical storms just before Alex had come back, and the child's knowledge about them had both surprised and impressed her. She had the feeling his knowledge rather impressed his father, too, as a half gallon of milk slowly disappeared between the two glasses to her right.

Had it not been for the fact that the two adults weren't saying anything to each other, the conversation that centered around a field trip Ryan had taken last year to an observatory near his school in Tucson would have been quite pleasant. The rainy night, the house quiet except for a child's gentle voice, the man and woman on either side of him, each toying with their empty glasses, all might have created an almost-familial atmosphere—which was apparently how Edna thought it looked when she came wandering out of her room several minutes later to see what was going on and mentioned how cozy they all looked sitting there.

Kelly managed a weak smile at the bespectacled woman's description.

Alex looked uncomfortable.

Ryan simply did what he didn't do nearly often enough. He grinned.

In her light green wrapper and with her pincurls covered with a yellow-green semisheer scarf, the housekeeper looked like a round lump of lime sherbert. She also looked puzzled by Kelly's attire.

"She got caught in the rain," Alex said, apparently wanting to avoid the speculation going on behind the woman's glasses.

"I had no idea it was that bad out there. I had the earphones to my television on and hardly heard a thing." The quiet ring of the telephone joined Edna's last few words. "I'll get it," she muttered, just before it rang again.

"She shouldn't do that," Ryan whispered to Kelly, his eyes on the housekeeper's back as the woman ambled over to the phone at the built-in desk.

Kelly, half of her attention on Edna, leaned closer to Ryan. Puzzled, she whispered, "Do what?"

He moved his mouth to her ear again. "Watch her television with her earphones on during a storm. She could get her brain fried if lightning hit the house."

Though he had a valid point, when one considered the conductive capabilities of a house's circuitry, there was a definite hint of mischief in Ryan's eyes when she pulled back to shake her head at him. Grateful to see that animation, thinking he spent way too much time looking serious as it was, she treated him to a smile of her own.

That smile died when she caught Alex watching them.

It wasn't disapproval in his expression. Or even curiosity. Certainly, it wasn't amusement. It was something that might almost have looked like...comparison, had it not been for the hard set of his mouth.

"I think the storm's moved far enough away now." His big hand settled on his son's slender back. "It's ten-thirty, sport. You need to be in bed." Stool legs scraped against the tiles as he stood. "Say good-night."

"Kelly," Edna called as Ryan's mouth twisted in disappointment. "It's for you."

* * *

It bothered Alex a lot that Ryan had stopped smiling. What bothered him more was the reason he so abruptly returned to his normal, quiet self. It wasn't just that it was time for the child to be in bed, though that was where he went after mumbling good-night to Alex and closed himself in his room. It wasn't that the storm was still upsetting him, either. There wasn't anything left of the storm but rain, and even that was letting up now. Ryan had wanted to stay with Kelly.

Alex turned from the closed door, his hands in his pockets and his head bent as he headed down the wide, white-carpeted hallway to his own room. So many thoughts churned in his mind. All unsettling. Most having to do with Kelly. Yet of all the thoughts begging to be dealt with, the most immediate was how he seemed to be failing his little boy. He hadn't even considered that his son might have been frightened by the thunder.

But Kelly had known. And she'd known how to handle it. She'd also, somehow, made it easier for Ryan to smile. He couldn't remember the last time his son had wanted to share something he found amusing with him. Or maybe, what he couldn't remember, was the last time he'd allowed his son the opportunity.

He needs someone to pay attention to him, Alex.

He needs to spend time with you.

Giving up my child was the hardest thing I've done in my life.

I know you never said you loved me....

I made the decision alone.

Alone.

He'd just needed some time....

What would you have done, Alex?

He pressed his fingers to his temples as he passed the gilt-edged mirror his mother had brought back from Europe years ago. The gaudy old thing always reminded him of something a person would find in an old bordello, and he disliked it as much as he'd always disliked the cool formality of this house. Dropping his hands as he drew a deep breath, he caught a glimpse of lime green in the shining glass.

Edna, her faced pinched, was lumbering up the curved staircase.

"Mr. Alex," she called, approaching the landing. "You don't think your mother would mind if Kelly borrowed something to wear, do you? All her clothes are in the wash and everything Audrey or I have would be way too big for her. That was the hospital on the phone."

The indecision clouding Alex's features had nothing to do with something so mundane as borrowing clothing. In the long seconds that Edna stood looking confused by his hesitation, the thoughts pulling him in so many directions were far more complicated.

"Get her what she needs," he finally muttered. He turned to his room, the muscles in his shoulders bunched with the kind of tension that was bound to result in a headache. "And tell her I'll be right down. I'll take her."

Chapter Six

Kelly didn't argue about Alex taking her to the hospital. Having him drive was faster than waiting for a cab. That was the logical reason for her quiet acquiescence. The truth of the matter was that she simply didn't have the energy to fight with him anymore.

He was as subdued as she when she met him at the front door wearing the peach silk shell and matching linen slacks Edna had borrowed for her from his mother's closet. Subdued and disturbingly distant. The only words to break the silence that resonated between them were her thanks for the ride—which she repeated ten minutes later when he turned his black Lexus into the drive in front of the brightly lit hospital complex. Even then, Alex didn't acknowledge her comment. He didn't let her out in front of the building as she thought he'd do, either. He simply drove past the main entrance, pulled into the first available parking space and cut the engine.

"I'm coming with you."

He had his seat belt off and his door open before Kelly could draw in her breath, release it and tell him it wasn't necessary for him to do that. So she saved her breath, since he'd probably only ignore what she said anyway, and got out before he could open her door. The nurse who'd called had said that Audrey had taken a critical turn. She would add nothing beyond that, other than that Kelly should hurry.

They moved quickly across the parking lot, not running, but not wasting any time, either. The doctor had warned Kelly earlier that her aunt might not survive, but Kelly hadn't honestly believed Audrey wouldn't somehow pull through. As the electric doors parted at their approach, Alex's hand hovering at her back to guide her around two orderlies coming on shift, Kelly had to admit her convictions were being severely shaken. As convinced as she'd been that Audrey would be all right, she'd been equally certain that the past between her and Audrey was something she'd have preferred not to discuss. Now, more than anything, she wanted the opportunity to hear what her aunt had wanted to say to her, and to tell her that, whether it had seemed so or not, she was truly grateful to her aunt for having taken care of her all those years.

There was one thing more she wanted; something equally imperative, and just as unlikely to happen. She wanted to take away Alex's bitterness and resentment and make them stop hurting him.

The sounds as they entered the building were familiar: the gentle ping of the elevator when it reached the floor Audrey was on, the squeak of soft-soled shoes moving over polished floors. Familiar, too, were the omnipresent antiseptic smells permeating the endless corridors, and the feeling of apprehension that seemed to cling to the pale green walls. As Kelly hurried down the wide hallway of the intensive care unit, Alex right beside her, she felt as if she'd spent a lifetime here in the past two days.

In some ways, she had.

She was halfway down the corridor, scarcely aware of the mind-boggling array of blipping monitors and other electronic equipment jammed into the large, open space, when she noticed two nurses outside the curtain that had been pulled around her aunt's bed. She recognized the shorter of the two as the nurse who'd let her sit with Audrey long past the unit's restricted visiting times. It was that woman who, seeing Kelly, approached her now.

Seeing the sympathy in the woman's face, Kelly automatically braced herself. Even as she stopped, she felt Alex's hand at the small of her back. His touch was firm, solid, supportive.

Her aunt was failing rapidly, the woman quietly told her.

The words had scarcely left the nurse's lips when Kelly felt Alex's hand move to her shoulder. He leaned toward her, his deep voice scarcely above a whisper. "You don't have to do this alone."

Hearing what he said, Kelly thought that nothing could have mattered more.

Unless it was what he did.

He stayed at her side, a solid presence in a distressing situation, while the nurse explained that the doctor would be in to talk with her, then took her to Audrey's bedside. He said nothing as he pulled over a chair for her. He merely moved to the foot of the shiny metal bed, close enough to let her know he was there, and far enough back to remind her that the distance between them was so much more than a matter of physical space.

In spite of his silence, or maybe because of it, there was something protective about the way he watched her when the various members of the staff came and went from the confining, curtained-off area—just as there was something decidedly deferential about how the nurses and the resident on duty acknowledged him each time with a silent nod before again confirming to themselves that there was nothing more they could do for Audrey. Alex could have gone at any time, but he never left once during the long hours she sat by Audrey's bed, not doing anything so much as simply being there. And after the once-robust woman drew her last breath at a little after three o'clock in the morning, and Kelly finally let go of her hand, it was he who eventually answered the nurse's questions concerning the arrangements Kelly hadn't even thought about.

"I'll take care of this," he told her after she'd gone silent when the nurse asked which funeral home should be notified. "Why don't you go to the waiting room? I'll be there in a few minutes."

Grateful for his help, Kelly didn't question the way he so competently took over. She simply took his suggestion, finding it as easy as others no doubt did to rely on his judgment, and entered the empty waiting room to stare out the night-blackened window.

It was in that window's reflective surface that, five minutes later, not having moved, she saw Alex enter the doorway of the austere space. Passing a row of chairs and the television that had been turned down but not off, his deliberate strides slowed markedly as he neared.

Three feet behind her, he stopped and pushed his hands into the pockets of his jeans. "Are you all right?"

Her arms crossed protectively, she met his eyes in the reflection.

"I'd be better if I'd been able to talk to her." Across the roof below her, she watched a light go on in a room in the wing opposite them. "She never even knew I was here."

"No one knows for certain what an unconscious person hears or understands, Kelly. She might have been aware of you, but just couldn't let you know."

She lifted her shoulder in a weary shrug. She didn't know much of anything for certain, right now. Except that she felt wholly incapable of trusting her judgment. She could have sworn she heard concern in his voice. Sympathy she might expect, circumstances being what they were. But not the sensitivity she heard.

Or, maybe, she was only hearing what she so desperately wanted to hear.

"There was something she wanted to say to me. Now, I'll never know what it was."

He took a step closer, his reflection looming over hers. "Edna mentioned that Audrey called you last week." It was the timing of that call that had nagged at him, once he'd realized what he'd missed of his convoluted conversation with Edna yesterday morning. That timing made him more than a little uneasy. "Didn't she say anything about it then?"

"She called right after her doctor told her she needed bypass surgery. All she said was that it was important that she see me. *Imperative* was the word she used." From outside the doorway, the soft ping of the elevator sounded as its doors opened onto the floor. "She said we needed to talk . . . in case something happened to her."

Though his expression betrayed nothing, Alex didn't like the sound of that at all. "She didn't give you any hints?"

The overhead lights picked up the sun streaks in Kelly's hair when she slowly shook her head. Because her hair had still been wet when they'd left the house, she'd brushed it into a knot on top of her head. It was dry now, and little tendrils had pulled free to curl at her nape.

Alex watched those silky curls brush her shoulders, wondering what she'd do if he were to test their softness. More tellingly, he wondered what she would do, were he to turn her around and pull her into his arms. Her eyes were huge in her face, and so sad. But he doubted she'd be terribly receptive to the idea of him holding her, given the way she'd pulled back from him before.

"All I can think of," she said, concentrating on her conclusions rather than Alex's interest in the question, "is that she wanted to end the silence she'd imposed. I wrote her twice after I left, but she never answered. And the one time I called, she said she thought it best that I didn't ever call there again." Her voice grew quieter. "I'd called right after the baby was born to tell her where I was going."

Her brow furrowed. Not from the memory, but because she couldn't imagine any other reason her aunt would have tracked her down after so long. "Unless she just wanted to apologize for the way things happened. She didn't have to do that, though. Apologize, I mean. It had to be hard for her, being responsible for me. All I did was cause problems for her."

The peach silk shell Edna had borrowed for her rustled slightly as she turned from the window. Until a few hours ago, Alex would have thought her attitude far more generous than his own would have been, given the limited knowledge she possessed. And, given that knowledge, he truly did find her forgiveness extraordinary. After all, as far as Kelly was concerned, her aunt had sent her away more or less because she'd made the woman's life difficult. But after having spent much of the past few hours replaying all that Kelly had told him about the circumstances surrounding her leaving, he was beginning to discover a few alterations in his thinking—among them, that

Audrey might not have been as unfeeling as she'd always seemed.

"Is there anything else that needs to be done here?" he heard her ask.

"They need your signature on a couple of forms. Look," he said, wishing he could offer the comfort she needed. "Is there anyone I can call for you?"

Incomprehension furrowed the corners of her lovely blue eyes. "What do you mean?"

"I don't know who your friends are. Audrey never talked about you." No one had. After Ryan had been brought to the house, Kelly's name had never been mentioned again. "All I know is what Edna told me...that you manage an herb farm outside of Durango, and that you live alone."

"I do."

"Which?"

"Both. At least, I live alone most of the time."

Alex matched her puzzled expression. "Most of the time?"

"Sometimes I'll have a teenager or two living with me. I keep in touch with the people who run the crisis house I stayed in while I was pregnant," she explained, turning her attention to the tissue she'd wadded in her fist. "Every so often, they send a girl to stay with me while she decides what she's going to do."

"While she decides whether she's going keep a baby, or give it up?"

There was no accusation in his tone. Only inquiry. And, maybe, a little caution. Glancing up to make sure she wasn't missing the condemnation she'd seen and heard before, she found only a guardedness she wasn't sure she understood at all.

"That's the basic decision they all face."

"What do most of them do?"

"Of the nine girls I've had, four have kept them."

"Is there one with you now?"

"No," she returned, clearly puzzled by his interest. "The girl that was with me last, left a couple of months ago. I'm lost here, Alex. What were you getting at?"

She didn't trust his questions. Alex couldn't blame her for that, either. But just as she couldn't hide her wariness, she couldn't hide the sadness in her eyes that made them look even more haunted than usual; the sadness that had been there even before tonight.

She took in girls who were in the same position in which she'd once found herself. That admission, spoken so matter-of-factly, told Alex more than he cared to know about how deeply she'd been affected by what he'd once convinced himself she had forgotten. She hadn't forgotten, though. She'd lived with the consequences of her decision, in some form or other, every day of her life.

"I just wanted to know if there was someone you wanted here. Someone who might make all this easier for you."

"Like a boyfriend, you mean?"

His glance skimmed her face. "Yeah."

She hadn't expected that sort of compassion from him. In a way, she really wished he'd kept his concern to himself, too. She couldn't begin to explain why, but his thoughtfulness brought a quick and definite tightness to her throat—and made her all too aware of just how much she was holding back; holding in.

Had she been home right now, she would have sought refuge in her greenhouse, lost herself in clipping and tending and pruning until the fragile feeling passed, and she could once again pretend it didn't matter that there were never any arms to hold her—no one for her to lean on, even for a little while. Oh, she had friends, and she supposed she could have called Mr. Yakamura, who would have been up now because he always rose at 4:00 a.m., or her hyper friend Rosie, who never slept anyway, and they could have sipped herbal tea and talked about Rosie's soap-opera love life, her newest foal, or local politics. But Kelly wasn't at home. And even if she had been, she wouldn't have called anyone. There was no one who could have helped more than Alex already had.

For a few hours, he had again simply been her friend, for it had been that kind of unquestioning support he'd offered. As well as he'd once known her, he seemed to understand that it wasn't grief she felt over losing her aunt, so much as it was sadness that the relationship couldn't have been different, and the simple sorrow a person feels for anyone whose life has ended so unexpectedly.

"No," she finally whispered, certain it wouldn't be long before whatever obligation he'd felt to be with her had been satisfied and the friendship that had surfaced would once again be buried under the debris of the past. "There's no one."

Rolling the tissue into a ball, she turned and dropped it into the trash basket next to the window. "I'm glad you're here, though. I appreciate your help a while ago, too," she hurried on to add. "I wouldn't have known which funeral home to call. I just hope they aren't terribly expensive."

Alex saw her pulling back, pulling in. He doubted she was even aware she was doing it. But when he saw her straighten her slender shoulders he knew she was steeling herself to deal with whatever came next all on her own. Just as she'd no doubt done most of her life.

The knot in his gut felt suspiciously like guilt. "Don't worry about it."

"I have to worry about it. As her only relative, I'm responsible for her funeral expenses."

"I'll take care of them."

"Why would you do that?"

"Because she was an employee. Consider it part of her benefits." Kelly's blue denim purse lay in the chair next to her. Picking it up, Alex held it out to her. "Let's go take care of those forms, and get out of here. I could use some coffee, and you look like you're about to drop."

The inky sky was streaked with a glow of pink along the horizon when Alex unlocked the front door and held it open for Kelly to pass. It was five o'clock in the morning, and the sun would be coming up soon. But, for now, the foyer was lit only by what light leaked in from the porch lamps. When Kelly stepped inside, the curving staircase and arched doorways looked like nothing more than different shades of shadow.

Alex's face was shadowed, too, when he turned after closing out the chirps of birds rising with the sun.

"You have an early meeting, don't you?"

At Kelly's question, he cocked his head and pushed his keys into his pocket. "How did you know that?"

"I just thought you might. After that phone call earlier," she expanded, then looked up at him, hesitating. "I'm sorry you didn't get any sleep. It's going to make your day so much longer."

They were all long, he thought. "I'll manage. Will you be all right?"

Silk rustled as she slipped the strap of her purse from her shoulder. "Don't worry about me." Her voice, already quiet, dropped another notch. "You have enough on your mind."

Alex's first inclination was to ask what she was talking about. His second thought was that his first one was pretty foolish.

He didn't know how she did it, but Kelly had always been able to sense when he was having a problem. Even one he'd said nothing to anyone about. Especially then. Her powers of perception had usually proved their sharpest when he'd wanted to keep something to himself.

It seemed she still possessed that unnerving ability. And she was also correct. He had plenty on his mind—though she couldn't possibly know the half of it. At the moment, however, he actually wasn't thinking about how he was going to reschedule all the appointments he'd had to cancel in London when he'd come back early to put out the fire on the Warner-Pico account—or how he was going to resurrect that account from the ashes. He was wondering how Kelly, after the way he'd treated her before the hospital had called, could stand there feeling badly for him because he'd lost a few hours of sleep.

There was something else on his mind, too. A picture that had seared itself into his brain and refused to budge— an image of her standing in the rain, pain in her eyes and that gown clinging to her incredibly beautiful body. He'd tried all night to shake that image. Much as he'd tried to shake the need he felt to touch her.

Not sure where that need was coming from, he didn't trust it. Not sure what he'd do if he did touch her, he didn't trust himself.

The first rays of the sun had just spread over the horizon, turning the shadows lighter shades of gray. In that gathering light, Alex's eyes looked like chips of glittering coal as they moved from where her heart stammered against her breastbone and settled on her mouth.

Slowly, he raised his eyes to meet hers.

"Get some rest," he said.

The air felt heavy. Or maybe it was the quickened beating of her heart that made breathing more difficult. "You,

too. And, Alex?'' The words she had to offer were pain-
fully inadequate, but they would have to do. "Thank
you.''

"I didn't do anything.''

"Yes, you did.'' The faintest hint of a smile touched her
mouth. "You were there.''

His eyes stayed steady on hers, narrowing ever so slightly
as he slowly raised his hand toward her cheek. When she
didn't move, when she didn't pull away from him as she'd
done before, he let the pads of his fingers slip beneath her
jaw. Carefully, as if he feared she might change her mind
about allowing the contact, he brushed the side of his
thumb over the soft skin below her cheekbone.

He should have been there for other things, too, he
thought, but Alex was no longer sure if there was resentment behind the thought, or only guilt and sorrow. All he
knew for certain was that her skin felt like satin beneath his
fingers, and that she was no better now at keeping her
emotions from her eyes than she'd been as a girl.

"That's not fair,'' she said, her voice little more than a
whisper.

"What's not?''

"What you're doing.''

He wasn't sure what she meant. And he didn't ask. He
only knew that she looked very much like she could use a
pair of arms, and that he very much needed to hold her.

He drew her to him, slowly so she'd have time to pull
away if that was what she wanted to do. But she was either too tired or too drained to act on the hesitation that
flashed over her features.

His hand slipped up to cup the back of her neck. He'd
thought he meant just to hold her. The moment he felt her
body brush his, that thought vanished like woodsmoke on

a windy day. Tilting her head with his thumb, he muffled the soft intake of her breath with his mouth.

He'd needed to do this since the moment he'd seen her.

Kelly hadn't been prepared for the feel of his mouth on hers; for the slow, devastating, totally thorough way he kissed her. Not being prepared, she felt her knees go weak at the warmth that slowly balled low in her stomach. He seemed to sense her need for support as his arm locked across her back, drawing her closer. Or maybe it was she who pulled him closer when her fingers bunched in the soft fabric covering his rock-solid shoulder.

Encouraged when her lips parted on a faint moan, Alex deepened the kiss, and felt himself answer that surprised little sound with a groan from deep in his chest. He'd only wanted to taste her, to feel her against him. He hadn't expected to find himself struggling with the quick, brutal ache that had him all but gritting his teeth when he felt her pull back, moments later.

He kept her from moving away by keeping his hands on her shoulders. But, as Kelly looked up at him in the pale light, she had the feeling he was scrambling as rapidly as she to make some sense of whatever it was they were doing.

Neither one of them had forgotten the wounds that had been torn open. But the events of the night had taken over, pulling them along in the current, so their efforts had been focused. With Ryan and the storm, then with Audrey, their attention had been temporarily diverted from the maelstrom of emotions that revisiting their past had unleashed. Yet, the past was still there. The problem now was that it seemed to be getting all tangled up with the present.

As accustomed as Kelly was to denying her own needs, the need Alex had resurrected in her was simply too much for her to cope with right now.

"I'll ask Edna to make the coffee," was all she said before she slipped from his touch and left him beside the shaft of sunlight that had just begun to filter through the window.

It was after noon when Kelly awoke, and nearly six by the time she returned from the errands she'd had to run. The memorial service for Audrey would be on Monday, which, since it was Friday, left the weekend for her to pack up her aunt's room and donate to charity that which Audrey's friends couldn't use. There were papers to sort through, too; a two-drawer nightstand full of them. But Kelly couldn't bring herself to start the task when she returned from the funeral home after dropping off the blue dress Edna had told her was Audrey's favorite.

Instead, she hung up the plain beige sheath she'd bought to wear to the service and changing into the khaki shorts and camp shirt she'd also purchased. She didn't want to borrow any more of Jessica's clothes and she was sick of wearing the things she'd arrived in. Then she hauled Ryan up from where he was brooding in front of the television in the huge family room and told him to get into his bathing suit. He couldn't use the pool unless there was an adult outside with him. Since Edna insisted that she didn't have time to sit out there, and it was much too hot for her to do so anyway, the child hadn't been able to use the pool at all. So while Kelly sat on the edge, dangling her feet in the sparkling blue water, Ryan played porpoise by diving after the weighted cylinders from a pool game that she would pitch into the deep end and he would gleefully retrieve.

The kid was a fish. He was also having a ball. And for the first time in three days, Kelly felt the awful anxiety that had been her companion since the moment she'd arrived begin to melt away with the sound of a little boy's laughter.

It was that laughter, followed by a splash and Kelly's shriek, that drew Alex to the shuttered windows of the study within moments of setting his briefcase on the desk and shedding his tie.

Working at the top button of his shirt, he opened the shutters that had been closed against the sun blazing just above the tops of the palms. From this part of the house, he could see the sprawling patio and most of the pool. He could also see Kelly sitting on the edge, her face lit with a smile as she tossed something orange over Ryan's head. Ryan, in the pool just ahead of her, twisted and leapt with more enthusiasm than grace into the sloshing water, only to pop up a moment later with the neon object and stroke madly back to her, splashing all the way.

Seeing the boy coming, Kelly scrambled to her feet and backed up before he could add any more spots of water to the shorts and shirt she wore. Alex couldn't hear what she said. But he could definitely see the sunshine in her smile. And he could see her legs.

Her legs, he thought, his body hardening as he tried to remember how they must have felt wrapped around him, were incredible.

"I thought I heard you come in."

Clearing his throat, Alex swung his glance to the door. Edna stood just inside, concern etched in her already wrinkled brow. "Are you feeling all right, Mr. Alex?"

"Of course," he returned, thinking the question as odd as the combination of conflicting feelings the scene at the pool jolted through him. "Why wouldn't I be?"

"It's awfully early. For you to be home, I mean. It's barely seven o'clock. I don't know the last time I saw you much before nine when you were in town. Do you have a dinner engagement?"

"I'm home for the evening."

"Ah, you're working then."

Work was what he'd planned to do. Certainly it was what he'd intended when he'd left the deserted office and come home.

The sound of his son's laughter filtered toward him. "I don't think so."

Already puzzled by his presence at this time of day, his seeming lack of an agenda only increased Edna's confusion. Since his plans were none of her business, beyond what she might be required do because of them, she had to be satisfied with his less-than-enlightening reply.

"Is there anything you need for me to do? I could take something out of the freezer for you, if you'd like."

"Don't bother. I'll find something later. Did you by any chance call my mother about Audrey? I'm sure she'll want to know."

"I called this morning, right after Kelly went in to lie down. I didn't want to just leave word about what had happened, so I left a message at her hotel for her to call home." Her voice dropped a notch. "It's too bad about Audrey, isn't it?"

"Yes, it is," he agreed, thinking of how Kelly had sat by the woman's side. "Thanks for making the call."

He moved from the window then, only now taking a close enough look at his mother's housekeeper to realize why he thought she looked different. Instead of the black-

and-white uniform he usually saw her wearing, she had on a shapeless gray-and-pink print dress. "Are you going somewhere?"

"A friend is picking me up. We thought we'd light a candle for Audrey, then get a bite to eat. Kelly said she'd keep an eye on Ryan and see that he gets fed. They're out at the pool."

He didn't tell her he was already aware of that. Nor did he say a word about her abdicating her responsibility for Ryan to Kelly, especially since the woman was doing him a favor by staying on. All he did before the intercom beeped and her friend called up from the gate to have it opened, was tell her to have a good evening, and asked her to light a candle for him, too.

A huge blue umbrella centered in a round white table provided the only shade near the pool. So that was where Kelly was sitting, one leg drawn up on the blue seat cushion and the other stretched out in front of her, when Alex wandered outside carrying two drinks a few minutes later. Ryan, he noticed, was underwater.

Coming up behind her, Alex frowned over the top of her head. "What's he doing?"

"Trying to see how long he can stay under."

"How long has it been?"

Kelly hadn't so much as glanced at him, her focus on the dark hair waving in the water a dozen feet in front of her. From where he stood above her, Alex saw her glance at her watch. "A minute and four seconds."

Three seconds later, Ryan popped up with a splash, water spraying every which way as he shook his head. With both fists rubbing at his eyes, he called over to Kelly to tell him how long he'd been under this time.

Hearing his time, he frowned. Then, without having successfully wiped the water from his eyes and thus, not noticing his father, he demanded, "Time me again!"

After grabbing a great gulp of air, he went right back down.

"What time is he trying to beat?"

There was a faint breeze tonight. Nothing like the stiff wind that had driven in the storms last evening, but enough to make him aware of the thunderheads off to the east—and of the way Kelly's hair seemed to shimmer as that breeze lifted the soft strands at her crown.

Setting one of the frosty glasses down by her, aware of her quick and wary glance to the side to see why he'd reached over her shoulder, he heard her reply with a soft, "Yours."

"Mine?"

"You used to be able to stay under for two minutes. He wants to see if he can, too."

"I never told him that."

"I did. You used to have me time you."

For a moment, the memory refused to materialize. Then, as so many other images of Kelly had formed lately, a picture flashed in his mind of a gangly little girl holding his watch while she bounced excitedly at the edge of the pool. She'd been no more than nine or ten. Around Ryan's age. Alex had forgotten all about that.

There was a lot he'd forgotten. Had made himself forget. But there was even more that he hadn't known.

With the scrape of metal legs against terra-cotta tile, he pulled out the chair next to her. "You remembered my time?"

The one-shouldered shrug she gave him was accompanied by a faint curving of her mouth. It was just a detail, that smile seemed to say. Certainly nothing that meant anything. And it didn't mean anything to Alex, either. Except that she'd remembered it.

She'd yet to look at him, her attention moving between the wavering shape of the little boy under the water and her watch. She was intent on Ryan, making sure he didn't get himself into trouble. But Alex didn't doubt for a moment that she was also using her lifeguard duty as an excuse to avoid looking at him.

The last time he'd seen her, she'd just stepped out of his arms.

The dark head broke the surface again, water sluicing down Ryan's face as he gasped for air, then sent water flying with the shake of his head. "How long was that one?" he wanted to know, once again rubbing at his eyes.

"Get out and I'll tell you."

"Why do I have to get out?"

"Because you need to rest for a few minutes," she said, smiling at his determination. "Your times are getting worse. Besides that, your eyes are all red. You've got too much chlorine in them."

He looked as if he wanted to protest. But even before he noticed his father sitting at the table watching him, his well-schooled manners kicked in and he started toward the side. When he'd wiped enough water from his eyes to see Alex, he stopped just as he prepared to lever himself over the edge.

"How come you're here, Dad?"

Kelly finally glanced at the man who sat with one elbow on the table, his thumb under his chin and his fist pressed to his mouth. For a moment, it looked as if Alex didn't know what to say to a little boy who looked genuinely surprised to be seeing his father home three nights in a row. The dismay was gone in the next instant, though, covered by a smile that did its best to make her forget what she'd seen.

"I live here," he replied in a tone designed to be teasing.

"Did you come home to change clothes?"

The smile faded. Alex had already changed into white Burmudas and a navy polo shirt. But that wasn't what his son meant. "I'm not going anywhere tonight, Ryan. I just thought I'd come out here and watch you swim. I think Kelly's right. Your eyes are awfully red. Maybe you should get out for a while."

"Do you have any goggles?" Kelly asked.

"In my room. Should I get them?"

He asked the question of Kelly, but almost immediately looked to his dad.

Alex, in turn, looked at the woman whose eyes, minus the pink, were the identical shade of blue as those of the child waiting for his response. "How long has he been in?"

"Only about an hour."

"Sure, sport. Go ahead."

"Take the towel!" Kelly called after him, tossing the large red terry-cloth rectangle at him. "Edna will have my hide if I let you track up her floor."

"I doubt that," Alex muttered, and finally saw her turn to meet his quiet scrutiny.

The slap of small feet on the rust-colored tiles disappeared with the closing of the back door. Now all that could be heard was the singing of a lone cicada in one of the Natal plums bordering the terrace. That high-pitched buzz vibrated much like Kelly's nerves.

Needing to focus on anything other than the speculative way Alex was watching her, she touched the tall glass he'd set near her elbow. A slice of lime floated atop ice cubes and clear, brightly bubbling liquid. He'd brought an identical drink for himself.

"What's this?"

"Tonic water. As hot as it is, I thought you could use something to drink. If you don't want it, I'll get you something else."

"This is fine." Adding a quiet, "Thank you," she saw him nod.

A moment after that, conversation stalled completely.

Alex seemed no more anxious than she to let the silence magnify.

"Did you get everything taken care of today?"

Relieved by the question, she picked up the glass. Its icy chill felt good in her hand. "The service is scheduled for Monday at two o'clock." She hesitated, surreptitiously taking in the tired lines around his eyes. "How about you? How did you do today?"

"Do?"

"Without sleep."

"Better than I thought I would."

"Did you get your problem at the agency taken care of?"

Alex sat back in the blue-cushioned chair, one sockless, boater-shod foot propped on a table rung and one hand wrapped loosely around his drink. The casual position was remarkably deceptive. From a distance, a person would undoubtedly think him relaxed. But Kelly swore she could feel the tension radiating from him.

"I'm afraid it's not as simple as that," he said in a voice as cool as the ice clinking against his glass as he absently rocked it back and forth.

"I didn't mean to pry."

She started to pull back. The weight of Alex's hand clamping over her wrist as he straightened stopped her.

"You're not." She wasn't prying. The problem was with him. Her question had simply caught him wrong—because he was so tired of not having answers to problems he should be able to resolve without compromising the growth of the agency, the people who relied on him, or his own integrity. "I'm sorry. It's not you. It's just been a long week."

The bones in her wrist felt fragile beneath his fingers, and her skin as soft as silk. He could still remember how she'd felt against him this morning, how she'd tasted. The memory had been with him all day, pumping enough frustration into his system to make him forget that he hadn't gone to bed last night. But the uncertainty in her eyes now made him all too aware of how uneasy she was with him, even as the agitated beating of her pulse betrayed the unnerving physical effect they still had on each other.

Considering all that had happened between them the past couple of days, he understood completely why the uncertainty was there. "Kelly," he began, the need to erase her wariness of him jarring him with its import. "Don't be afraid of me."

"I'm not."

"Yes, you are. I can see it in your eyes." With his free hand, he nudged her chin up when she started to look away. His thumb brushed the underside of her wrist. "I can feel it."

She was afraid of him. Of what he could make her feel. Of what he could make her want. She'd had relationships. Friendships, mostly. But she'd never felt about anyone the way she'd felt about Alex. And no one had ever been able to resurrect the dreams she'd once had of a real home, a real family.

No one but Alex. The last couple of days had brought those dreams back with an intensity that scared her to death. If she wasn't careful, Alex could hurt her all over again.

He ducked his head to see her eyes, tightening his grip when she tried to pull away. "Kelly?"

"What's going on with the agency?" she asked, desperately needing to change the subject.

His breath came out in a frustrated rush. Leaning back, he told himself not to push, and let her go when she pulled on her arm again.

"Actually, it feels like it's falling apart."

Alex had scarcely admitted that fact to himself, much less mentioned it to anyone else. As far as anyone in any of his offices knew, including his managers, he was on top of everything. Even the loss of Warner-Pico and the upheaval in the Phoenix office was simply regarded as the normal course of doing business in an extremely competitive field. Only Alex knew how close he was to losing his grip because of all he was being forced to juggle.

Yet, he could no more explain why he'd just confessed that little detail to Kelly than he could explain the relief he felt when he saw her wariness fade to confusion.

The trepidation she'd felt only a moment ago all but vanished as she leaned closer. "Can you tell me what's happened?"

The look in her clear blue eyes was as guileless as a child's, her guard completely, perhaps unwisely, gone. All that was visible now was her concern and her interest. Alex couldn't remember the last time anyone had looked at him that way. He didn't know if Diane ever had.

He did know that he would never have told his ex-wife what he told Kelly when he picked up his drink and, trading one set of frustrations for another, he explained how the president of Warner-Pico Communications had been offended by Alex's decision not to head their new ad campaign himself. That account had been his father's pride and joy and because it had been so important, Alex had put his two best people on it, one of whom had worked the account for years with his father.

"Why didn't you want to be on it?" she wanted to know.

"For one thing, I wasn't familiar with it. With everything else I've had to do taking over the agency operations, I couldn't possibly give it the attention it needed. The people I put on it were the best. But Warner felt that my not working the account meant it wasn't important enough to the agency. The people I did have working it quit because they were insulted by Warner's insinuation that *they* weren't good enough because their last name wasn't Burke."

"Weren't there other accounts you could have put them on?"

"Nothing high profile enough for their experience. I wasn't about to pull good people off the accounts they were handling just to salve egos."

"So now that you're down two of your top people, the smaller accounts they worked are in jeopardy."

Her conclusion was right on the money. Alex told her that, too, after Ryan came padding toward them wearing his goggles and jumped back into the pool. Alex told her, too, while they both watched the little boy, how he'd tried to soothe Warner-Pico's feathers when he'd come back from London, and how he now had to reschedule all the appointments he'd set up over there so he could get the European operation up and running by the first of the year.

It had been his father's dream to open a London office, and his dad had started the groundwork the year before he'd died. So far, Alex had run with the ball his dad had put into play, but with offices in San Francisco, Phoenix, Chicago and New York to oversee, he didn't see how he'd meet the scheduled target date without benefit of a minor miracle.

"I should be able to do this," he said, his voice tight with the exasperation he felt with himself. "My grandfather did it. My father did it. What's wrong with me that I can't handle what they put together?"

The question was rhetorical. As his fist clenched around his glass, Kelly knew he was only speaking his frustrated thoughts aloud. She chose to answer him anyway.

It seemed his expectations of himself were as lofty as ever, if not just a tad unreasonable. "What's wrong might be that you're twenty years younger than your father was when he took over the company from your grandfather. He worked with your grandfather for years. You had what... five or six years to learn from your dad?"

"About that."

"The Chicago office is new." New since she'd left, anyway. "So the company was also larger when you inherited it than it was when your dad did. If you're trying to expand it more, you're making it larger still."

"It's what Dad wanted."

"That's not my point."

Alex seemed to realize that, only it seemed to Kelly that he chose to overlook the fact that he was up against odds so much greater than either of his predecessors had faced.

"It was his dream, Kelly. He trusted me with it."

"Is it what *you* want, though?"

The way he looked at her made her think he found the question irrelevant. Or, possibly, that she really didn't grasp the situation at all. All she knew for certain was that he was frowning at her when she heard Ryan call her name and she turned to see what he wanted.

Pulling himself from the pool, shivering despite the hundred-plus degree heat because the breeze chilled him, he dripped his way to the table.

"What's the matter?" she asked, draping around his shoulders the towel he'd dropped on his way back to the pool. "Why are you out so soon?"

"I'm getting kind of hungry."

"Hungry, huh? What about you?" she asked Alex, wondering if his perplexed expression still had to do with what they'd been talking about or if something else was now on his mind. "Are you eating with us?"

"Were you going to cook?"

"No," she assured him. "I'm going to have a pizza delivered."

He didn't seem to fully appreciate her humanitarian gesture. His brow still lowered in contemplation, his glance moved from his son's wet face to where Kelly's hand remained on his skinny shoulder. "How long are you staying?"

She hesitated. "Until Monday...after the service. If you don't mind my being here that long."

Alex lifted his chin in acknowledgement of her response, but offered no explanation of his own for why he'd wanted to know. "What kind are you getting?"

Again she paused, shifting mental gears. "Pepperoni?"

"Have them throw some mushrooms on half."

Ryan, catching his dad's wink, grinned.

Chapter Seven

As evenings went, the one by the pool was one of the more relaxed Alex had spent in a very long time—provided he overlooked the strain between him and Kelly. Even with that subtle tension resting just below the surface of nearly every word and glance, he had to admit that spending time with his son and feeling the pride that comes when a parent glimpses unexpected maturity or knowledge, made it worth the occasional moments of uneasiness.

Most of those moments came when Kelly caught him watching her smile while Ryan exhausted himself practicing dives during the hour before the pizza arrived. When Kelly had first returned, the mental block Alex had where she was concerned hadn't allowed him to consider that his son was actually a part of her; that she was anything other than the woman who had betrayed them both. But that block had begun to crumble. Ever since he'd seen Kelly looking more like a mom than his own ever had while she'd sat in a robe with her hair in a towel smiling at Ryan, Alex couldn't seem to help his need to study her for resemblances between her and his—their—son. But other than for the much lighter blue of Ryan's eyes, Alex had to admit that Burke genes had predominated in his progeny. In the physical department, anyway.

He didn't know why that relieved him. Maybe it was just ego. More than likely, it had to do with possessiveness— with the protectiveness he felt toward the child he'd thought of for so long only as his. Ryan *was* his. Still, the similarities he noticed between mother and son, while not so easily detected as any physical feature would be, were definitely there.

It was in Ryan's personality that he took after Kelly. Alex had always tended to take stock of a situation before decisively following through with whatever course of action he chose—a trait that usually left his competition in the dust because his efforts were so much more focused than those of someone who took off half-cocked. But Ryan possessed the same kind of quiet fearlessness Alex remembered in Kelly as a child. Ryan's teachers had always been impressed by how he was never afraid to try anything new. Or, if he was afraid, by how he hid his doubts and forged ahead anyway. In a way, that was exactly what he'd done the other night: masked his fear of the storm by focusing on taking care of someone whom he believed feared it more.

That was very much something the Kelly he'd known years ago would have done. There was something else, too. While Alex would have thought certain traits would be acquired rather than inherited, as he watched Ryan devour two huge pieces of the pizza along with most of the mushrooms, he couldn't help but notice that his son shrugged the same, one-shouldered way Kelly so often did.

It was after nine o'clock when Alex led Ryan up to bed. Kelly, seeming as relieved as she did reluctant to have the evening end, said good-night to both of them in the kitchen, then headed for her aunt's room—which left Alex no choice but to tackle the small matter of fitting London into a schedule already booked with meetings in New York and San Francisco. But having just spent two hours with a woman who moved with the grace of a dancer, whose laugh did impossible things to the nerves at the base of his spine and whose presence threatened to complicate his already frustrating life, he knew he'd only spend the time pacing. So he went to bed himself. He needed the sleep, anyway.

But he didn't rest. At least, not well. Since he hadn't managed a decent night's sleep in a long time, it didn't much matter. He hadn't managed a full weekend off in even longer, but the next morning he figured that didn't matter, either. He'd long ago resigned himself to the treadmill. It was the only way to get ahead, or to stay there. That being the case, he would spend his Saturday doing what he should have done last night and by meeting with his Phoenix manager to go over the accounts being reassigned. Only this Saturday would be different. He would take Ryan with him.

That was the plan, anyway, when he headed into his son's bedroom. Finding the room empty except for the lizard in the jar by the red Ferrari-shaped bed, Alex worked his way through the game room where he'd expected to find the television tuned to the Saturday-morning cartoons he and Ryan had once regularly watched together. The television wasn't even on.

Alex could count on the fingers of one hand the number of times he'd been in the back hallway off the kitchen. The rooms there were for the domestic staff, and there was seldom any reason for him to venture into that part of the house. But when he hadn't found his son in the kitchen, either, that was where he headed.

Of the three doors in the long narrow space, two were open; the one to the laundry room off to his right and the door at the end of the hall. It was from there that he heard voices coming from the room Kelly had once shared with her aunt.

"Are you going to miss her?" Alex heard his son ask as he passed the closed door of Edna's room.

"I don't know that 'miss' is the right word," came Kelly's reply, along with the snap of fabric being shaken free of wrinkles. "It had already been a long time since I'd seen her."

"How come?"

Kelly, in her khaki shorts and blue chambray shirt and with her hair pulled up in a careless topknot, stood folding a yellow blouse beside the farthest of the two twin beds in the room. Atop the rose-patterned bedspread sat a large box partially filled with clothes. Placing the blouse in the box, she disappeared from Alex's view when she walked to the far end of the room just as he reached the threshold.

"I'd moved away," he heard her say. "And we hadn't kept in touch."

An earring lay on the floor next to the doorjamb. Retrieving the shining purple disk, and still preoccupied with work, Alex started inside. His son's observation, however, made him forget completely that he was in a hurry.

"It's hard when people go away. I mean like when they die. Like Grandpa did."

"Do you miss your grandpa?" Kelly gently inquired.

"Yeah. He was nice. I didn't get to see him much, because we didn't come over here a lot. But he used to let me in the study without telling me to be careful and not break anything like Grandma does. We didn't live here when he was alive, though. Was it boring when you lived here?"

"Actually," she said, her lowered tone sounding quite confidential, "it was worse than boring. Most of the time, anyway. The only time it wasn't was when your dad was home. But that was only for holidays and for a couple of months in the summer. The rest of the time, it was pretty awful."

"What did you do?"

"When I was your age, I think I spent a lot of time trying to stay out of the way, but I'd go to school and help the gardener on the days he came. And when I got older, I studied, and I'd do the ironing for Rosalita."

"Who's Rosalita?"

"She was the housekeeper then. Like Edna is now."

"Oh."

"And I read a lot," she added, a smile in her voice.

"Did you have any friends?"

"Your dad was my friend."

"I mean besides him."

"Not really. The kids at school were all from around here, and I didn't fit in with them very well. The ones I did fit in with, I could only see at school."

"How come?"

"Well," she returned, the smile remaining in her voice despite the relentless questioning, "this wasn't my house, so I couldn't invite them over. And since none of us had cars and there was no one to take me anywhere, I couldn't go to their homes. It's probably hard for you to have friends here, too," she went on, compassion in her tone rather than the resentment it could have held. "Since you don't get to go where other kids are, I mean. But I'll bet you have a lot of friends at school in Tucson.''

Ryan said he had a few, but he didn't want to think about having to go back to school. And he certainly didn't want to talk about it. Even if he hadn't said as much, Alex could tell from the expression on his face that all the boy was really interested in, anyway, was in what Kelly had to say.

Alex wasn't really eavesdropping. Not that the technicality would have stopped him even if he had been. As Ryan's father, he felt perfectly justified in knowing what was going on with his son. Yet, had either Ryan or Kelly bothered to look up at the mirror, they'd have seen him leaning against the threshold, watching. They were sitting crossed-legged on the floor by the bed on the opposite side of the room, facing each other in front of a white nightstand. As engrossed as they were in their conversation, neither one had noticed him.

Between them was a stack of papers and correspondence Kelly had apparently taken from the open drawer. She wasn't sorting through the stack at the moment, though. She was watching Ryan study the string of colored beads he pulled through his fingers, his nose wrinkled as if contemplating a matter of considerable weight.

''What's going on up there?'' she asked, touching his temple with her index finger as she ducked her head to make eye contact with the suddenly quiet child.

''I was just wondering.''

''About what?''

Serious as a scientist, he looked up from the beads. ''If you aren't going to miss your aunt, didn't you love her?''

''Oh, I loved her, Ryan,'' she returned, looking uncertain about why he wanted to know, but sure there was a reason. ''And I think she cared about me...as much as she could. But sometimes, even people who love each other are happier apart. In my aunt's case, I was a responsibility she'd never wanted...and I don't think she much cared for children. Some people just don't do well with kids.''

"Yeah," came the muttered agreement. "Like my mom. She didn't want me around, either.''

The softly spoken words put caution in Kelly's expression. At least that was what it looked like to Alex as, stricken by the rejection he hadn't realized his son felt, he watched her slip her arm around Ryan's pajama-clad shoulder.

"Don't say that, sweetie," she urged, her expression suddenly, fiercely protective. "I don't know what happened between your mom and your dad, but I'm sure your mom loves you very much. And she must miss you, too," she added, because he was equating absence with lack of caring. "I'm certainly going to.''

"You are?''

It appeared to Alex as if she were about to smile. Instead, her expression grew pensive, her eyes softening as they moved over the surprise and the hope in Ryan's upturned face.

"Yeah. I am," she told him, and looking as if she couldn't help herself, she pulled him into a hug.

Ryan was apparently going to miss her, too. The way he hugged her back, his arms going around her neck to squeeze hard, made Alex feel as if he'd just been kicked in the gut. Until that moment, he'd never realized what his marriage to Diane had done to his child. Or just how terribly, incredibly complicated were his feelings about his child's mother.

As quickly as Ryan had reacted to Kelly, he just as quickly drew back. The tips of his ears had turned pink and his smile was caught between embarrassment and pleasure. As endearing as she seemed to find the child's sheepish expression, it was the stricken expression on the face of the man in the mirror that had her hand protectively covering her heart.

Glancing from the image, she turned to where Alex stood frozen in the doorway.

"What's wrong?"

At her hesitant question, Ryan, curious, looked up, too.

Old roses. That was the scent Alex noticed when he took a deep breath, then slowly released it. "Nothing's wrong," he told her, loath to betray how shaken he'd been by the sight of his child in his mother's arms. He smiled, the movement feeling awkward. "I was just looking for Ryan when I heard you two in here talking."

The room not only smelled vaguely of the rose sachets on the dresser; when Alex stepped inside, he found it rather resembled a rose garden, too. Audrey had decorated the L-shaped space with prints and pictures of the blooms in every imaginable shade of pink. Even the pillows on the beds had pink rosebuds woven around the edges, and the small love seat and footstool that comprised the personal "living room" area of the space had needlepoint cabbage roses worked into the fabric covering them.

He hadn't been in the room in years. Not since he used to come looking for Kelly. He'd forgotten how fussy it was. Kelly had once said that it reminded her of a picture she'd once seen of Queen Victoria's antechamber, and she'd sworn that if she ever had a room of her own, there wouldn't be a frill in it. Until now, he'd forgotten that, too.

He looked toward the boy unfolding himself from his position on the floor. "I've got to go to the office for a while. How about coming with me?"

"To your office?"

"Sure. I've got work to do, but I can show you some of the new graphics we're working with. What do you say? You want to come?"

There was definitely interest in Ryan's thickly lashed blue eyes. There was also skepticism, as if he weren't sure why his father was making such an offer.

"I told Kelly I'd help her in here," he told his dad, sounding very aware of how a person needs to keep commitments. "And she was going to help me pack for school."

"Where's Edna? She can do your packing."

Kelly stepped over a large manila envelope lying facedown on the floor. "Edna's packing for her trip." Without thinking, she brushed back the dark hair falling over Ryan's forehead. "I can manage here," she told the child. "And we can still do your packing together later. You go on with your dad. You'd better change first, though. I don't think pajamas are acceptable office attire."

"I gotta shower first."

Alex stuffed his hands into the pockets of his chinos. "I'll wait. I need to talk to Kelly, anyway."

There was a definite lack of enthusiasm on Ryan's part when he headed out the door. That surprised Kelly, for she'd thought the child would be more than eager to spend a little time alone with his father. Especially at his office. Most especially since he would be leaving for school in a few days. But when Alex closed the door after him and turned to face her, it wasn't Ryan's attitude she was considering. It was the distance Alex was so careful to keep between them, and the troubled way he studied the purple earring she must have dropped somewhere.

"I heard what he told you," he said. "I had no idea he felt like that. He's never said anything about Diane to me."

Compassion, quick and telling, moved into her eyes. "I take it he doesn't see her."

"No." The word sliced hard. "He doesn't. And he won't. Like you said, some people just don't care for kids."

Even from halfway across the room, he could see the question in her eyes as she stood with her hands clasped in front of her. As clear as that question was, he knew Kelly wouldn't ask why Diane would have had a child if she didn't like children. He knew why she wouldn't ask, too. She didn't trust him not to turn the question against her somehow.

They'd once trusted each other. Completely. But that trust, something he'd once taken for granted, had been shattered. By her. By him. By circumstance.

He'd once thought her heartless for giving up her child. It had been an easy judgment to make; an opinion easy for many to hold, especially those who'd never been faced with the choice themselves. He was a man who saw things in black-and-white. As good or bad. Right or wrong. What he was beginning to see through Kelly was that between black-and-white lay a thousand shades of gray.

He shook his head, his convictions suffering yet another blow. He'd thought it wrong for a woman to give up her baby. And most people would admire a woman who took on another woman's child to raise. Yet, what Diane had done had been far from altruistic. Diane had used Ryan to get to him, then slowly, ultimately, made it so abundantly clear that she didn't want to be bothered with the boy that an innocent child's sense of self-worth had been jeopardized. Kelly had been thinking of her child. Diane had been thinking of herself.

The marriage had lasted six years. Had he been around enough to see how Ryan was being affected, he would have ended it sooner.

The earring landed on the bed. His own culpability kicking hard at his conscience, Alex turned from the caution Kelly couldn't keep from her expression. The woman had no idea how easy she was to read. Everything was written in her eyes.

"Maybe you should try talking to him. You and your father used to talk all the time. Remember how important that was to you?"

His father had always seemed to have more time than he did, too. "We used to talk. It's just been since Diane left that he's gotten like this." He shoved his fingers through his hair, still damp from his shower. "I get the superficial stuff, but the kid never tells me what's going on with him anymore."

"Maybe it's because he doesn't know you anymore. You know, taking him with you this morning is a wonderful idea."

"He didn't seem to think so."

She heard the hurt in his quietly spoken words; saw that hurt in the beautifully masculine lines of his face. He loved his son. He wanted to do what was right by him. Even now, with the demands of a business that often overwhelmed more experienced men, he was trying to make up for some of the time he had to spend away from Ryan by taking him into the office with him. His absences from his son's life weighed heavily on him, but it was clear from the magnitude of his other responsibilities that what time he had was already spread impossibly thin. Even with the demands of an agency with accounts spread from one coast to the other, she knew he felt duty-bound to keep his father's dream of expansion alive.

How much more responsibility would he accept, she wondered, before it all simply exploded in his face?

He'd remained by the door. Sacrificing the safety physical distance offered, she moved closer. She'd never learned to develop any real defenses where Alex was concerned. She was working on them—mostly by keeping away from him, which was why she'd hightailed it to her aunt's room last night when Ryan had gone to bed. Being alone with Alex simply wasn't wise. But for now, the part of her that responded to the soul-deep weariness in him rode right over the part that knew how badly he could hurt her.

"Is there anyone I can call for you, Alex?"

"What do you mean?"

"Is there anyone who can make all of this easier for you?"

He bore responsibility for so much, for so many people. Those in his employ. His son. Probably even his mother, because Jessica Burke had never impressed Kelly as a woman who knew how to take care of herself. Yet, there didn't seem to be anyone for him to lean on. Or possibly, like her, he just didn't let himself need anyone else.

He must have recognized the question. After all, he'd posed it to her not all that long ago.

"*You're* making it easier, Kelly." His brow furrowed, the tension in his body seeming to change quality as his glance roamed her face. "But you're making it all so much more difficult, too."

The shaft of light coming through the window was tinted pink by the rose-colored sheers. In that soft glow, he watched disquiet shift into her eyes.

"I don't mean to."

"It's not your fault." A strand of hair curled against her neck. Without thinking, he reached over to brush it back, and felt her pulse leap when his thumb skimmed the base of her throat. "I'm not sure it's anyone's."

"What are you talking about?"

He shook his head, marveling at how she so guilelessly allowed his touch. He knew she was still wary of him. But she seemed no more capable than he of denying the bond that had somehow survived what should have destroyed it. Even as he soothed that erratic pulse, he was struggling with convictions that had been so radically altered in just a few short days.

He'd had no idea how she'd felt growing up in this house; how lonely it must have been for her. She'd alluded to that loneliness when she'd defended Ryan's little trip to the bus stop the other day, and she'd mentioned it again while she and Ryan were talking a while ago. Coming on top of the discussion they'd had a couple of days ago, the one that had started in the library and ended in the rain, he felt even worse than he already had.

Until Kelly had tried to make him understand why she'd given up her baby, he'd forgotten about what had happened to her mother. He'd also forgotten that her parents hadn't been married and that her father had, according to what she'd been told by Audrey, walked out on her mother before Kelly was born. Kelly had never known the kind of support he'd had while they'd been growing up—the security of a stable family and people who loved her. And when she'd had to make the decisions she'd faced, she'd had no one to turn to but an aunt who'd already witnessed her sister's struggles to raise a child alone. In his young, immature and astoundingly selfish mind, Kelly had simply always been part of his life—the niece of the cook—and he'd taken his life and his life-style very much for granted.

He had the feeling that Kelly took nothing for granted. Ever.

"Alex?"

"I'm sorry, Kelly."

Completely baffled by his torment, she could only whisper, "For what?"

He was sorry for a lot of things. But all he could do was shake his head because he knew she was already confused and his response would only confuse her more. "Thanks for listening to Ryan," he said, needing distance. Needing time. There was none now; Ryan would be back soon. "You always did have a sympathetic ear."

"I still do."

He tried to smile. "Is that an offer?"

"If you want to talk, I'd be happy to listen."

His thumb inched upward, tracing the line of her jaw. If she had looked the least bit hesitant, he would have let her go. He should, anyway. He had no business wanting her. But her eyes held only concern, and there was something almost forgiving in her soft, sympathetic smile.

The knock on the other side of the door had Alex reluctantly easing his hand from her neck.

"Maybe I'll take you up on that offer later."

"Anytime."

"Dad?"

She tipped her head toward the door. "Your son's ready."

Turning away, Kelly covered the spot where Alex's thumb had altered her heartbeat. A moment later, convinced her only defense against him was to go home, she heard the door open and Ryan quietly ask, "Is this okay?"

He was talking about his outfit. Seeing it, Kelly couldn't help her smile. The pleated cotton pants, polo shirt and boaters, other than color, nearly matched what his father wore.

Alex seemed to notice that, too.

"He has good taste," Kelly wryly observed, wondering if it was surprise or pleasure softening Alex's expression.

She'd just decided it was pleasure, rather liking the way it relieved the severity in his features, when his attention turned back to her.

"I'll see you later."

"I'll be here."

"Can you come with us?" Ryan asked.

"Oh, I don't think so," she told him, catching the swift pinch of Alex's brow. "I have to get this room packed up, and I need to call my neighbor and make sure everything is still all right with the nursery."

"The lady with the horse?"

"The lady with the horse," she confirmed, remembering how enthralled he'd been with the description of the view of her neighbor's pasture outside her kitchen window. "You have a good time. Okay?"

Ryan's only response was a nod, which was accompanied by the slight twist of his mouth before he turned into the hall. If his expression was any indication, he was more than a little disappointed that she was staying behind.

The look his father gave her in the six seconds before he joined him, revealed far less. But that was because his father's feelings weren't quite so easy to pin down. As Alex let Ryan lead them out to the garage, telling his son he could start the car for him because he'd always thought it was kind of cool when his dad let him do stuff like that, Alex felt totally torn.

The family's little secret was safe from Kelly. With Audrey gone, there was no one to tell her that Ryan was her child. Yet there was no relief in that fact. He'd seen the look in Ryan's eyes when they'd left her room; the disappointment. It was a look that was all too familiar where the boy was concerned. His son deserved so much better than he was giving him.

He deserved to know his mother.

The problems with that conclusion were legion. And the thought of adding more hassles to everything else he was dealing with made his stomach clench. Still, as he handed the grinning boy his keys and double-checked to make sure the emergency brake was on when Ryan slid behind the wheel, he couldn't help thinking that he had absolutely no idea what Kelly would do if she did know—or even how to tell her. The implications of having her in his life, in their life—if she even wanted to be—were simply too complicated to analyze at the moment.

Time, he told himself. He just needed a little time.

Time was the one thing he didn't have.

Kelly heard the car pull out as she sat on the edge of her old bed in her aunt's room, sorting through the stack of papers she'd picked up from the floor. It had only taken a minute to finish packing up the last drawer of the dresser, so she'd returned to the task she really hadn't wanted to do, anyway: going through her aunt's personal papers. Though the job had to be tackled, it still made her feel as if she were invading the woman's privacy.

That feeling subsided a bit as she finished up the first drawer's contents, for Audrey kept nothing that revealed anything startling about herself. There were envelopes from the church she attended for Sunday offerings, a blood donor card, and a copy of her mother's death certificate. Kelly also found receipts for subscription stubs to cooking and needlecraft magazines, as well as several of the magazines themselves, and a savings-account passbook showing a modest balance. Edna had told her just yesterday that Audrey scrupulously saved her money and when she took her two weeks of vacation each year, she always went on a cruise. It was Audrey who'd recommended the cruise Edna was taking next week.

For some reason Kelly couldn't explain, it pleased her to know her aunt had done something fun, for a cruise would truly be a busman's holiday for a cook. But even as she set the passbook aside, wondering where her aunt had planned to go this year, a strange sense of foreboding forced the thought away.

She'd come to the manila envelope that had been on the dresser. Because it was so large, she'd stacked everything else on it before she'd begun sorting. Now, as she picked it up to pull out its contents, she glimpsed the return label.

"Winthrop Ames, Esq." was printed in bold black ink. The name was familiar. But, for a moment, Kelly couldn't place it. At least she couldn't until she read the short transmittal letter inside. The letter was addressed to Ms. Audrey Shaw, legal guardian of Kelly Lynn Shaw, and stated simply that Mr. Ames had passed away and that his files were being returned to his clients.

As the letter indicated, the envelope contained a legal file.

Kelly's heart felt as if it had stopped beating when she opened it.

Inside that innocent-looking folder was a copy of a document showing Kelly's signature on a Consent to Adopt. Another copy was of that same form of consent prepared for signature by Alexander Ryan Burke IV, but which had, apparently, never been signed. There were copies of birth certificates. One reading "Baby Boy

Shaw''; another, bearing the same dates and the same parents, and reading "Alexander Ryan Burke V."

The names leapt off the pages.

Kelly Lynn Shaw.

Baby Boy Shaw

Baby boy.

She'd had a son.

Ryan.

Kelly was no longer looking at the file. It had slid to the floor.

Chapter Eight

It was midafternoon before Alex and Ryan returned to the house. Alex didn't stay, though. He didn't even get out of his car. He just let Ryan out at the front door and left again because the boy had tired of playing the Solitaire game on a secretary's computer and there hadn't been anything else for him to do while his dad talked and the man he was talking to paced.

At least that was what Ryan told Kelly when he found her in the little herb garden off the kitchen.

The explanation took no more than thirty seconds and was offered by Ryan while he squinted against the hot, bright sun. Pausing for breath, the squint screwed into a contemplative frown when he looked up from the sprig of thyme she twirled between her fingers. "What're you doing out here?" he wanted to know.

She wasn't sure. Actually, Kelly thought, she really wasn't sure of anything at the moment, except that her throat felt tight as she hungrily searched the child's face, starved for details she might have missed before. Starved, too, for details she *had* noticed, such as how the color of his eyes was identical to hers, but had dismissed because the thought that Ryan could be her baby had seemed too fantastic to consider. From the moment she'd first spoken with the boy, she'd felt a connection to him; one she hadn't been able to explain. Now that she could explain it, she wanted desperately to touch him, to run her hands over his shiny, breeze-blown hair and smooth, pink cheeks. She wanted to pull him to her and hug him and hold him and fold his hand in hers and never, ever let go. He was her baby. Her son. And the reality of that fact was as wondrous as it was frightening. Instead, she smiled, jamming down all the feelings welling inside while she memorized the pattern of the dozen pale freckles scattered across his nose and cheeks.

Clearing the knot in her throat, she glanced back to the intricate curves of verdant foliage that glistened beneath a rainbow of mist from the automatic sprinkler.

"I wanted to see the garden," she told him, though it had been the calming effects of poking around in the soil she'd actually been seeking. "I guess I miss mine."

"You have one like this?"

Hers was a little different, she told him, wondering if he'd be so interested in her if he knew who she was—and what she'd done. Would he still want anything to do with her if he knew she had given him up? Or would he feel that she had abandoned him and hate her for leaving him to someone else; to Diane, a woman who hadn't wanted him around.

The thought made the tightness in her throat so much worse, but she kept her tone even as she explained that her herb gardens surrounded her house and the little building where she made and stored the herbed vinegars and oils she sold to local shops. Ryan thought it was neat having gardens everywhere. He also thought it would be neat to be able to dig in the ground and get dirty without having someone complain about what he was doing to his clothes. Like his grandmother always did.

Little boys should get dirty once in a while. At least it seemed so to Kelly when she pointed out a butterfly cocoon she'd discovered attached to a healthy stem of parsley. But as Ryan got down on his hands and knees, stopping just short of resting his cheek in the dirt to get a better look, it wasn't what he needed right now that fed the knot in her stomach. It was what he'd needed before, what she'd thought she'd assured him of having, but he hadn't received.

She had needed to believe that her child was happy. And certainly Ryan had enjoyed better care than she'd ever have been able to provide for him the first years after he was born. But while he lacked for nothing in a material sense, she ached to know that he hadn't had the kind of stability she'd prayed he would have; the love of two devoted parents. She didn't doubt Alex's love for him. Not for a moment. But her child's life hadn't been the ideal she'd envisioned.

Her aunt had always said she was a dreamer. But if a parent couldn't dream for her child . . .

Her child, she repeated, her thought left unfinished because the enormity of her discovery kept pulling her in so many directions. After years of not knowing who or where her child was—of living with that void in her heart—she was filled with a sense of relief so vast she felt her heart might burst from it.

"Do you want to keep the cocoon so you can watch the butterfly come out?"

"Can I keep it with my lizard?"

"I don't think the butterfly would like that. When it starts to emerge, it could wind up as the lizard's lunch. We'll find another jar in the kitchen. Okay?"

"Okay," Ryan agreed, drawing himself back from the cocoon he'd declared "cool," then promptly announced, "It's hot out here."

"Then, let's go in." Restraining herself, she didn't mention the dirt now on the knees of his pants. "If you want, I can help you start packing now."

She might as well have flipped a switch. One moment, his eyes were animated, alive with interest. The next, they had become as lifeless as dust. "I guess," he muttered.

"What's the matter?"

"Nothing."

"I know something's wrong, sweetie. What is it?"

His mouth drawing down at the corners, he leaned over and gave his knees a lethargic swipe, looking all the while as if he might as well do it now because someone was certain to tell him to do it later, anyway. "I don't want to go back to boarding school. But Dad says I have to."

"You talked to him about it?"

"On the way home." He kicked his toe in the dirt, sending up a puff of dust from the ground the sprinkler didn't reach. "He said it's a good school and that I'll be okay once I get back and get into the routine."

"I thought you said school was better than being around here with nothing to do?"

"It was. But it's different with you and Dad here. It was fun last night."

And the night before, she had a feeling he was thinking, though he obviously, thankfully, hadn't a clue how uptight she and his dad had been while they'd all shared crackers and milk and waited for the storm to pass.

"I'm only a guest here, Ryan," she was compelled to remind him, though she was sure he hadn't forgotten. He was just wishing. Much, she suspected, as she used to wish Alex could stay home for forever. "I have to go back to Colorado soon. And your dad is going to San Francisco next week. The last couple of days aren't what it would always be like."

"New York."

Either he wasn't listening, or she'd missed something. "Excuse me?"

"He's going to New York."

"Last night he said he had to go to San Francisco," she told him, realizing he'd inherited his father's dubiously commendable ability to tune out what he didn't want to hear.

"At the office I heard him on the phone saying that he had to go to New York, then he was going to London."

Ryan's dispirited tone made it clear that it didn't much matter where Alex was going. His dad would be gone, and so would he. Strictly speaking, that was the issue. As far as Ryan was concerned, anyway. But hearing Alex's itinerary drew Kelly to a less obvious point. As she caved in and allowed herself to slide her arm around her son's sagging shoulder, she couldn't help wondering what Alex's priorities were. Or if he had even slowed down long enough to figure them out.

"Forget packing, for now." She gave him a quick hug, the closeness making her heart balloon in her chest. The closeness also made her aware of how warm he was in the hot sun, wearing long pants. She could feel the dampness of his skin through his shirt. "You need to work on your cannonballs, anyway."

"I get to go in the pool?"

He most certainly did. And, with Kelly watching him, that was pretty much where he stayed until the clouds that had been building on the horizon all afternoon finally got serious about an hour before sunset. Since being in a pool during an electrical storm was about as smart as playing Russian roulette, Kelly and Ryan headed inside to fix sandwiches with Edna shortly after the first rumble of thunder.

Alex wouldn't be joining them tonight. According to Edna, he had called earlier to say he was having dinner with the manager of the Phoenix office. So the two women and Ryan ate their supper and watched an old movie on Edna's television while Ryan pretended he wasn't afraid of the thunder and Edna dabbed her eyes at the film Ryan declared "mushy."

Kelly scarcely noticed what was on the screen. As her mind conjured images she'd never allowed before—of her child as a baby, then as a toddler—and she tried to imagine him at four and six and eight and all the years in between, she had to admit that she felt a little numb. She also felt angry and betrayed. She felt joyful and relieved. But mostly what she felt was afraid. Afraid of losing what she'd only just found. Afraid of having to fight when she had no hope of winning.

She'd signed away her rights. And Alex had custody. Alex, with his power, his wealth, and a law firm or two on retainer.

The only thing working in her favor was the fragile truce that had somehow been drawn between them. Grasping that thought like a talisman, Kelly prayed the strength of their old friendship would allow that truce to survive.

The storm that evening didn't amount to much. At least not in Scottsdale. According to the ten o'clock news, the west side of Phoenix had really been dumped on, but where they were on the east side, the cloudburst had lasted only long enough to bring the temperature down and leave the air smelling damp and fresh.

Had it not been for the anxiety filling Kelly when she stepped out the back door, she would been enthralled with the balmy night. She loved the clean feel of the air after a storm; the scents of moist earth and rain. Now, she doubted she'd ever think of storms again without thinking of Alex.

He stood by the pool, his back to the house and his profile illuminated by the eerie blue glow created by the pool's underwater light. Kelly had been in her aunt's room when she'd heard his car pull in a while ago. That was where she would have stayed, too, had he come into the house. But she hadn't heard the back door open, which was the one he'd have used to come in from the garage, and when she'd looked out the kitchen window and seen him standing there alone, she knew what she had to do. Edna and Ryan were in bed. It could easily be another twenty-four hours before she found another opportunity to speak to him without one or both of them around.

With the file hugged against the knot in her stomach, she started across the dimly lit patio. Alex must have heard the faint tap of her sandals. She was still several feet away when she saw him turn and glance over his shoulder.

He had his hands in the pockets of his slacks, his stance unusually relaxed. Either the breeze or his fingers had mussed his hair, for one thick strand tumbled disarmingly over his forehead. Seeing her approach, he tipped the corners of his mouth in a slight, and unexpected, smile.

"It was too nice out here to go in," he said, as if he knew she wondered what he was doing. "I really hate being indoors all the time."

She offered a tentative smile of her own. "I remember."

"Was I complaining about being cooped up that long ago?"

"Not complaining." She hugged the file tighter, watching his glance move over her in the pale light of the pool. "I was just thinking of the house you used to talk about building. You wanted it to have huge walls of windows so you wouldn't feel closed in, and you wanted to build it facing the mountain preserve so your views were only of what grew wild." Alex had talked about that house for years. In a way, it had been a declaration of his independence—a break with the more traditional style in which he'd been raised. A dream, she supposed. "I always thought it sounded like it would be a wonderful place."

Alex's glance skimmed her face once more. She looked troubled. But the impression was only fleeting. The thought that stuck was that, all those years ago, she'd apparently heard so much more than he'd even realized he was saying.

"I built that house."

"You did?"

"Yeah, I did." Inside his pockets, his fists bunched. "Diane got it."

Under any other circumstances, Kelly would have said she was sorry. And she truly was, because what that house had represented had been something he'd wanted for a very long time. But the words would have been inadequate, and he'd just given her a lead she couldn't ignore.

"Is that why you moved back here?"

"That, and to have Mom help with Ryan when he was home for holidays and summers. I never kept a staff the way she does, and there was always someone around here to keep an eye on him."

"Did Audrey help with him?"

It wasn't the question, it was the way she asked it that warned Alex, though he couldn't have said for sure what it was in Kelly's voice that made him think she had anything more than a casual interest in this conversation. Or maybe, he thought, only now noticing it was a file she hugged to herself and not a writing tablet as he'd first thought, it hadn't been her voice at all. He'd merely sensed her disquiet.

"Why?" he asked, uneasily aware of how attuned he was becoming to her.

"I'd just like to know."

His focus shifted to the file. "What's that?"

"Something I need to talk to you about."

Now disturbed himself, he watched her even more closely. "Does this have something to do with Audrey?"

"You're not answering my question."

The reminder didn't cause him to answer, either. It only made his glance narrow as he stepped toward her.

Behind them sat the circular white patio table with its four blue-cushioned chairs neatly pushed in. Edna had collapsed the umbrella early this morning when she'd come out to sweep, and the scalloped edges gathered at the base of the tall spire made it look like an overgrown parasol. All Kelly really noticed was the heat of Alex's hand when it slipped under her elbow and he turned her toward that table.

She walked over with him, but she didn't sit. Apparently he didn't intend to, either. He'd just been heading into better light.

"May I see it?" she heard him ask.

She didn't move. For several very long seconds, she just stood with her arms locked around the file and her thoughts at war. Then she felt Alex's hands on her forearms, his expression a blend of concern and impatience as he gently pried the file from where she had it folded against her shirt.

The light wasn't the greatest, but there was enough filtering out from the kitchen and over from the pool that he could read what was in the file when he opened it. Paper crinkled when he lifted the first page. The sound seemed more cautious when he turned over the next one. It only took seconds, but it seemed an eternity before he went as still as the statuary in the living room.

It sounded as if he swore. Or maybe the words he uttered weren't so much oath as prayer.

"Where did you get this?"

"Is that all you're going to say?"

"Where did you get this?" he repeated.

"It was in Audrey's room."

"Where in the hell did *she* get it?"

"In the mail." As his voice had risen, she deliberately dropped hers. She needed to act calm and rational, even if she didn't feel that way. "According to the postmark on the envelope, it was sent to her from Winthrop Ames's office a couple of weeks ago."

"From Ames's office? Why in heaven's name...?"

"Apparently the man died, Alex. It's there in the transmittal letter. But how I came by it doesn't matter. What does, is that I know who Ryan is. All I want to know right now is if Audrey did."

Without the file as a shield, she felt oddly unprotected. She crossed her arms anyway, lending herself the support she couldn't get anywhere else. "The reason she was so insistent about me giving him up," she prefaced, "was it because you wanted him?"

It was then that Alex recognized it: the pain in her eyes that spoke of betrayal. It was in her voice, too, exposing in its faint tremor the depth of that awful feeling.

"Absolutely not." He faced her, preparing to defend himself even though it was the motives of her guardian she questioned. He'd thought to do this in his own time, his own way. Obviously, the Fates were again of a different mind. "I had no idea what was going on until Ames came to me about signing some sort of consent form. There was never any pressure put on you from my end to give him up. I thought you were keeping the baby. Until Ames showed up, it never occurred to me that you wouldn't."

Refusing to revisit the last argument they'd had, knowing how impossible it would be to stay rational if accusations started flying again, Kelly focused on Audrey. As hard as it was to think of the woman betraying her, it was even harder to think that Alex might have, too. "But she knew, didn't she? Audrey knew all these years that my son was with you."

Of course she did, Alex thought, though he saw no point in going into how the situation had been so neatly swept under the proverbial carpet. "It was never discussed, Kelly. When Ryan was brought here, he was treated only as a Burke. Audrey never had any more to do with him than the rest of the staff, other than Katie."

"Katie?"

"His nanny. She came the day he arrived and we took her with us when he and I moved out of here a few years later. Ryan's relationship to Audrey was never acknowledged, and she never spent any time with him."

"Until you moved back last year."

The implications behind her conclusion couldn't be denied. And the one thing Alex couldn't do was discount the amount of time the cook could have spent with his son during the last round of holidays and over the past summer. Especially the last couple of months.

He raked his fingers through his hair. The gesture—and the frustration and fatigue behind it—were becoming far too familiar.

"The other night at the hospital," he reminded her, uneasily aware that it was defeat rather than anger clouding her lovely features, "you said you would never know what she'd wanted to tell you. Well, I have a feeling this was it. When Ryan and I moved back here last year, she had a chance to get to know him. Maybe that changed her mind about telling you what she knew."

If he wanted to carry his supposition a step further, considering that Audrey had received the file from Ames's office about the same time she'd learned her heart was bad, her conscience could easily have made her decide she couldn't keep quiet any longer. Or, possibly, what it had done was make her regret having kept silent for as long as she had.

"I just can't believe she'd do this."

It wasn't Kelly's disbelief that shook Alex. It was the anguish beneath her quietly spoken words. He could see her struggling, trying to accept that her aunt had concealed the truth about her child from her. Alex knew all too well how devastating it was to be deceived by someone you trusted. What he found ironic about the situation as he set aside his own apprehensions and curved his hand at the side of her neck, was that he'd gained that understanding through the woman he suddenly wished he could shield from that awful pain.

He didn't bother to question his quick and certain feeling of protectiveness. At the moment, as her eyes jerked to his, wary and hurting, it didn't matter. What did, was that another shade of gray had emerged out of the fog of the past.

"It's possible that her silence was all she had to give you," he offered, wondering if Kelly knew what it meant to him that she so unquestioningly accepted his touch. "Maybe she did what she did all those years ago because she was trying to protect you. Maybe," he added, because it was the only theory he could accept and still hold Audrey in any regard, "she wanted you to have the chance your mother didn't."

He brushed his thumb along her jaw, the motion slow and exquisitely gentle. She hadn't known what to expect from him, but she knew it wasn't the comfort he offered simply by touching her. She focused on that contact, caught between the sense of betrayal she couldn't shake, and the need to believe the redeeming motive Alex proposed. That he should defend Audrey with such an opinion was remarkable. It was also enormously revealing.

To form that opinion, he would have had to appreciate the influences that had been at work so long ago. He'd have had to understand why she'd done what she had, too, and that meant more to Kelly than was probably wise to admit. She wasn't thinking of how she was jeopardizing her heart at the moment, though. She was considering only how she'd seen Alex's understanding slowly evolve, the antagonism he'd felt toward her diminishing a little more each time they'd been together. It had taken a couple of days for him to let go of the bitterness, and she wasn't sure even now that it was gone completely, but he'd just needed time to sort through all she'd told him so he could measure it against the ideas and opinions he'd held all those years. Now that he had, she could only hope that he'd forgiven her for the hurt she'd caused him.

There was one way to know for certain if he had. And his answer meant as much to her as her next breath.

"Would you have told me?" she asked, her eyes searching his.

Hope stumbled when his hand went still.

"Until this morning . . . no. I wouldn't have."

Defense shaded his voice. There were hints of it, too, in the hard angles and planes of his face, his features looking all the more formidable in the surreal light from the pool.

"Until this morning?"

Like a scientist studying a specimen to be sure he'd identified it properly, he carefully considered her. A heartbeat later, his expression revealing little beyond indecision, he let his hand slip from her to clamp around the back of his own neck.

He faced the house now, seeming to study the darkened windows of the bedrooms overlooking the terraces as if the words he needed were written on their black surfaces. Long seconds later, he gave up his search. "Until this morning, I had absolutely no intention of telling you Ryan was your son. Even once I'd decided I had to, I wasn't ready to talk about how involved you should be with him. I'm not ready now, either."

The breeze blew a leaf across the damp clay tiles, the skittering sound coming to an abrupt end when the leaf joined a bract of hot-pink bougainvillea floating in the lagoon blue pool. Less abruptly, Alex turned to face her.

"I'm assuming you want to be involved. But I shouldn't do that, should I? I suppose what I should do first is ask if you want Ryan to know who you are."

Kelly's quietly certain, "Oh, yes," came without hesitation. The doubts she'd had before—the fear that her little boy might hate her for what she'd done—weren't nearly so great as her fear of losing the chance to know her son.

"Then, I suppose the best thing to do is to work this out before we say anything to him." His hand clamped around his neck again, kneading the knotted muscles there. "He goes back to school Monday. We can come up with some sort of visitation arrangement over the next few weeks and talk to him when he comes home at Thanksgiving."

"Thanksgiving is three months away, Alex. What will take so long to work out that he can't be told before he goes back? He doesn't want to go back to boarding school to begin with."

"Don't you think I know that?"

"Of course I do," she returned, trying desperately to keep the plea out of her tone. "Maybe it wouldn't be so hard for him if he knows he has a mother who cares about him. I want to be part of my son's life, but more than anything else, I want him to know he's cared about."

"I care about him!"

"I'm not saying you don't." She hadn't meant her remark the way it had sounded. Alex obviously didn't realize that, though. Any more than he seemed to realize how, ever since he'd pulled away from her a moment ago, the tension between them had begun to escalate. When he'd touched her before, it had been almost as if he were grounding her. Or maybe himself. Like electricity, without the connection, the current scattered dangerously.

"I know you care about him," she repeated, wanting desperately to reestablish that connection. "It's just that he feels as if no one wants him around...like he's in the way and no one has any time for him. You remember how you felt being shipped off to school. Don't you?"

The question didn't seem to help her position. "The circumstances with Ryan are different. I was sent because it was a Burke tradition, and it didn't matter if I hated it because it was supposed to build my character. I'm sending Ryan to Lockemore because it's the only way I know to provide the stability you said yourself a child needs. As much as I'm gone, the routine is important to him.''

''More important than being around people who love him?''

''Listen, Kelly,'' he muttered, resenting that he had to defend decisions he'd had little choice but to make, ''you might be his mother, but I've been responsible for him since he was two days old. Under the circumstances, you'll just have to trust that I know what's best for him.''

Had Kelly not felt herself in such a precarious position where Ryan was concerned, she would have argued the point. She would also have marveled that Alex's anger stemmed from the fact that he actually felt threatened by her. Given the escalating heat in his voice, she concentrated only on the way tempers were getting closer to the surface. When emotion got in the way of judgment, what was said wasn't necessarily what was meant.

''I won't argue with you,'' she conceded, frustrated with him, with herself, with the circumstances. ''If you think it's best for Ryan that we wait to tell him, then we will.''

Alex watched her swallow her agitation. It seemed to him that she'd backed down a little too easily, given the heat he'd seen in her eyes. But the part of him that was coming to know how decent she really was, the part that could see how wrongly he'd judged her, made him see beyond that protective defense. As badly as she wanted to be part of Ryan's life, she was willing to set aside what she wanted in order to do what was best for their son.

She'd done that before; when she'd given him up.

A fist of recognition caught Alex squarely in his gut, causing him to overlook the scraping sound that came from somewhere across the patio. A moment ago, he'd felt nothing but resentment at having to defend decisions he was being forced through circumstance to make. He didn't doubt for a moment that Kelly had once felt much the same way.

"We obviously disagree about boarding school," he said, his voice much quieter than it had been moments ago. "But it's the only option there is right now. He's better off at school with other children than he is here with me gone so much. It's not like you live nearby, either," he reminded, the logistics of her living in another state presenting their own particular set of problems. "We just have to keep in mind that we both want what's best for him and come up with something that works for us both."

"It doesn't have to be all that complicated, Alex."

She meant the words as reassurance. Unfortunately, it was reassurance that came too late. "It's already complicated. Most people talking about something like this are going through a divorce."

They weren't going through a dividing process, though. They were becoming part of each other's lives. How significant a part was something Kelly was afraid to wonder. She had no idea how Alex felt about her being part of his son's life. Watching his jaw work, she had the feeling he didn't know how he felt about it, either.

"You said, until this morning, you weren't going to tell me about Ryan." It was a toss-up as to which was harder to keep from her voice—the incredulity or the anger she felt that she'd been here for days and he'd volunteered nothing about her relationship to his son. "What happened to make you change your mind?"

For a moment, Alex did nothing but glance down at the file he still held. But when he looked up, all the defensiveness she'd seen before had dissolved into something she didn't recognize.

He handed the file back to her.

"I saw how much he needed you."

Chapter Nine

Morning was Kelly's favorite time of day. Evening had a special appeal, too, because there was such order to it. Birds nested, shadows slowly lengthened into darkness, the moon rose. But morning was promise. With the rising of the sun came the energy of the new day.

That was how Kelly normally felt when she awoke. The last few mornings, being far from normal, she'd awakened wanting nothing more than for the day to be over. This morning, pulling her hair up into a knot as she headed into the kitchen, she was beginning to wonder if she'd ever feel like a morning person again. Not that she was dreading this day; she'd just slept so little that even her shower hadn't brought her fully awake.

The sound of running water met the clink of glass. Thinking that Edna was putting on the coffee, Kelly slipped her spare barrette into her shorts pocket and glanced up with a smile. The coffee was being prepared. But not by the loquacious housekeeper.

Alex stood at the sink, a pair of wet, Hawaiian-print swim trunks hanging low on his lean hips. Water beaded in the center of his beautifully sculpted back and slicked down the hair on his powerful thighs and calves. It appeared he'd made some attempt to dry himself, judging from the dampness of the turquoise pool towel draped around his neck, but he was still dripping a little on Edna's gleaming tile floor.

Six seconds ago, Kelly had been half asleep. Now, there wasn't a sluggish cell in her system. She remembered Alex as lean and sinewy. He still was. Only . . . bigger.

Quite consciously, she jerked her glance from the arrow of damp hair disappearing into the front of his trunks when he turned toward her.

"Morning," he muttered, catching a drip on his jaw with the towel.

"Where's Edna?"

"Sunday's her day off." Hard muscle moved smoothly when he turned with the filled carafe and dumped the water into the coffeemaker. "She has a friend who picks her up for the day. I heard her leave a few minutes ago." The carafe hit the burner. Facing her again, he took the end of the towel and wiped it over his face. "Did you want her for something?"

He'd obviously been in the pool. Doing laps, Kelly ventured, wondering if that was how he kept the muscles in his abdomen and chest looking as hard as sculpted granite. And his arms, she thought, watching the lean muscles bunch and relax when he ran the towel over his hair. A woman could feel very secure wrapped in arms like that.

Security was not what she felt tugging low in her stomach, however. It hadn't been what she'd felt when she had been wrapped in those arms the other morning, either.

"Does your mother know you run around her house like that?"

"I don't do it when she's here. You want some orange juice?"

What she wanted was for him to put some clothes on. But she settled for being grateful for the opportunity to move, quietly surprised that he'd noticed her morning habit of jump-starting her body with a jolt of natural sugar instead of caffeine.

She headed for the refrigerator. "Do you want some, too?"

Telling her he'd hold out for coffee, Alex watched her cross the room. He liked the way she looked in the morning, her skin fresh, and her eyes soft from sleep. It was the awareness he'd seen in her eyes, however, that had his own glance moving up the shapely length of her legs, much as her glance had moved over his body. He wondered if she had any idea what it did to him when she looked at him as she had; if she felt the same fierce need he sometimes did when he was with her. She wasn't immune to him. He knew that. That was why lying awake at night thinking about how she'd felt in his arms when he'd kissed her, how perfectly she'd fit his body, was pure, unadulterated torture.

Waking up wanting her was pretty miserable, too. Doing laps had helped. But he wasn't doing them now.

He'd have to be dead not to be affected by her, he realized. But she was doing her best to pretend she wasn't affected by him.

"Is Ryan up?"

"Not yet."

"May we talk for a minute, then?"

She turned, pitcher in hand, and found him holding out a glass.

The change in his expression was ever so subtle. "If you want," he said, though, suddenly, he didn't sound nearly as cooperative as he had moments before.

Faintly disheartened, she took the glass with a subdued, "Thanks," then added, "It can wait until later."

"It's okay, Kelly. If you want to talk, we will."

"No. Really." She offered a smile, wishing now that she'd paid a little more attention to his mood and a little less to how easily he unsettled her. "I interrupted you."

"You didn't interrupt. If it's Ryan you're wanting to talk about, now's as good a time as any. It's too early for him to be up and there's no one else around."

She started to tell him again that it could wait. She needed for him to be receptive. But instead, when she opened her mouth, all that came out was a whispered, "I hate this."

She hated the caution between them, but she didn't know what to do about it. They were like two dancers, circling each other, moving closer, then pulling back. Never quite connecting.

Alex felt that caution, too. And he was no crazier about it than Kelly. But he was sure she wanted to talk logistics; the how and when and where she might see their son. "Look," he muttered, making himself stay where he was. "I know we have to talk. I guess, for once, I just wanted a morning where I wasn't having to negotiate something."

"I just wanted to ask a question."

"Then ask."

Next to her the coffeepot sputtered and dripped, filling the room with the rich scent of the brew. Sunlight streamed in the windows, causing the floors and counters to gleam and the brass pots and molds to throw off sparks of reflected light. As attuned as she now was to him, Kelly scarcely noticed anything other than the man leaning with his arms crossed defensively against the counter.

"I just wanted to know what he was like when he was little. I missed watching him grow," she said, apparently thinking she needed to explain herself before he would answer. "I'd just like to know more about him. Like when he cut his first tooth, and if he liked to be rocked. If he came by some things slowly, or if he did things early for his age." Beneath the soft khaki fabric of her shirt, her left shoulder lifted in a shrug. "Anything you're willing to tell me."

He hadn't understood what she'd wanted at all. Considering how he'd never really understood her all the years he'd thought he'd known her so well, he supposed he shouldn't have been surprised by his lack of insight. She'd spoken quietly, her calm tone almost prosaic. But Alex was slowly gaining the understanding he'd lacked, and he was coming to realize there was little that could be considered matter-of-fact about Kelly. Everything she felt, she felt deeply. Probably more deeply than was safe or wise. He knew from the way she held his gaze, how very important it was to her that she learned what she could about her child.

It was because it was so important to her, that a few more of his natural misgivings about the changes that would come by allowing her into their lives receded. It was also because of that importance, that he hated to tell her he'd missed much of what she wanted to know.

"I'm afraid I can't tell you all that much," he confessed. "Not about when he was really small. I was away at school most of the time. Even when I was home and with him, when he was little, Katie took care of him."

Kelly stood facing him from five feet away. Close enough to keep their voices low, but far enough to keep him from reaching out to tip her chin up when she looked down at her bare toes. So he closed that distance by uncrossing his arms and his ankles and walking over to nudge her chin up with his finger.

"If it'll help, I can tell you what he was like from about three on," he offered, and wondered why he didn't feel quite as threatened as he had before to be sharing his son with her when he saw her smile.

"Was he as quiet as he is now?"

"Hardly. Katie called him hell on wheels."

Her smile grew, but she ducked her head again. When she did, he found that he'd trailed his finger down her arm and was tracing the delicate bones of her wrist.

He hadn't realized how badly he'd needed to touch her until he'd found himself doing it. So he kept right on toying with her wrist, not certain what there was about the simple contact that felt so necessary, but not questioning it, either, because Kelly didn't. He simply let his fingers run lightly over her soft skin while he told her how Ryan, shortly after he'd turned three, had started meeting him at the door when he came home from work and how he would drag him off to show him the latest toy his grandmother had bought him or his work of art *du jour* from preschool.

Kelly, her smile now as warm and inviting as a bright spring day, wanted to know if Alex had any of those art treasures stashed away somewhere. And if he did, if she might see them. He thought he could probably find a few, he told her, and found himself fascinated by the way she seemed to cling to his every word.

It was hard to know for certain what her thoughts were as he spoke, lost as he would find himself in the serene blue of her eyes. There was something almost calming about the way she watched him, and "calm" was something he hadn't felt in a very long time. That he should feel any sense of peace at all with her, especially standing close enough to feel the warmth of her body reaching toward his, was extraordinary. Yet, while he told her about Ryan's early fascination with electronic games and how his son would teach them to him, then proceed to beat him nearly every time, he supposed that peace was no more extraordinary than the odd little ache that settled in his chest.

Kelly wasn't the only one who'd been left out. There were things *he'd* missed, too. Not with Ryan, though he had to admit he hadn't realized how much a dad often did miss of his child's early years. But with her.

It was that thought that had his eyes skimming over the soft swells of her breasts to settle on the flatness of her stomach. She was slender, her hips gently curved, her waist narrow. Though the top of her head reached his chin, she wasn't a big girl by any means. It had been so long ago, but he could still remember how Ryan had fit in his hands when he'd first held him; how he'd been worried because, to him, the infant had seemed so small. But when he thought of that child being inside Kelly, as small as she was, he could think only of how he'd missed watching her belly grow, how he could have rubbed her back to ease the ache the weight would surely have caused, and felt their baby kick inside her.

It was the silence in the room that he noticed first. Other than the faint hum of the air-conditioning, no sound could be heard, the sudden quiet making him aware of the heaviness of his heartbeat when he raised his head.

Kelly had gone completely still. For a moment, meeting the intensity of Alex's gaze, she wasn't sure she even breathed. Expression had drained from his face, and that only made what she saw in his glittering eyes more penetrating, more shattering. Especially when his glance slipped to her mouth.

His fingers had curled around her wrist, the heat from them burning like a brand.

"Alex?"

His eyes jerked back to hers when she spoke his name, the look in them one of confusion as he drew a deep, shuddering breath. He seemed shaken, deeply so. But no more shaken than Kelly felt herself. She'd seen his glance move down her body, heard the strange roughness enter his voice in the moments before he'd gone silent. Where his eyes had lingered, heat had flared, warming her, making her heart beat faster.

Her own voice was scarcely above a whisper. "I think I hear Ryan."

His grip on her wrist eased, though he didn't let her go. "I hear him, too."

"He'll probably be down in a minute."

"Yeah," he muttered, and finally, reluctantly, let his hand slip away.

"He has an album in his room," she heard him say, stepping back. "If you want, I can show you his pictures."

She nodded, still shaken and crossing her arms over her quivering stomach. He wouldn't even look at her before he turned to pick up the pot that had finished brewing fifteen minutes go. "Thanks, Alex."

"No problem."

"Are you off today?"

He told her he was; that he'd planned to spend the day with Ryan since he had to leave for school tomorrow. Kelly, in turn, told him she thought that was a nice idea and that, since he still wasn't packed, she'd help him with that task since she didn't have to leave for the funeral home until six o'clock. The rosary for her aunt was this evening. It was interesting, she thought, how she and Alex managed to ease around each other—dancing the little dance they were learning so well.

They were doing it so well in fact, that Ryan seemed quite fascinated by the way she and his father were simply hanging around the kitchen on a Sunday morning discussing plans for the day, when Kelly noticed him standing at the far end of the cooking island.

The child could be as quiet as a church mouse at times. She and Alex had both heard water running earlier so they'd known he was up. How long he'd been standing there, though, she had no idea.

"Morning," she greeted, smiling at his stylishly baggy shorts and T-shirt.

Ryan, his lower lip caught between his teeth, looked from her to his dad, then back again.

"Hi," he muttered, and with both hands on the handle of the refrigerator, he leaned back to pull it open.

"The orange juice is over here if that's what you're looking for."

Without a word, he let the door swing closed.

Alex had a glass out and was pouring the juice by the time Ryan had wandered over to the other side of the room. But the boy said nothing when he took it and slid onto the stool at the end of the cooking island. He just sat watching them. Mostly, he watched Kelly.

"Something wrong?" his dad asked.

"I don't want to go back to school."

Beneath the towel still hanging around his neck, Alex's shoulders slumped. "Come on, Ryan. We've been through this." Abandoning his coffee on the counter, he walked over and pulled out the stool next to his son. "I know it's hard. It's hard for me, too. But you'll feel better about it once you get back down there with your friends.''

Ryan didn't look as if he believed his dad for a minute. At least the part about it being hard on him, too. The child would choke before he said so, though. But even though Ryan wouldn't openly argue with his father, Kelly sensed the beginnings of a bad situation brewing. As hard as it was going to be for Ryan to leave in the morning, it would only be worse if he left with his father upset with him. It wouldn't do anything for Alex's peace of mind, either.

''You know, Ryan,'' she began, not certain whom she felt worse for at the moment, ''we never did get to your packing. I know you don't want to go back to school, but since you have to, let's get you packed now. As soon as that's done, you and your dad can go do something fun together. Maybe you could have him take you to one of the malls and whip him at video games or something.''

There seemed to be some potential to that idea. At least, she assumed there was when Ryan stopped frowning and reached for his juice. He downed it in a half-dozen gulps. Then, after politely declining Kelly's offer of a bowl of cereal, he slid down from the stool and headed off to watch television until she needed him.

''Thank you,'' Alex said to her under his breath as the child disappeared.

Picking up Ryan's empty glass, Kelly simply met Alex's eyes, then looked away. It was hard to be appreciative of someone's thanks when she didn't agree with what he was doing in the first place.

As subdued as she'd seen Ryan before, he was definitely more so that morning. But by the time Alex had returned from changing into his clothes, insisting that he would help Ryan pack, too, and Kelly had coaxed the child up to his room to get on with the task he clearly wanted to avoid, he was at least making eye contact with her. For a while, it seemed that all he'd done was stare at her, as if he felt there was something she ought to be able to do about all this and couldn't understand why she wasn't doing it. Once they were in his room, though, and he was having to make decisions about some of the items he could take or leave behind, he seemed to remember that she was on his side.

"I want to take the cocoon." He stood in front of the built-in book-and-toy shelf, spinning the globe on the stand next to it. "And my lizard."

Both creatures, in their respective jars, resided atop the tire-shaped nightstand next to Ryan's red race-car bed. The little gray-brown lizard was straddling the wall of his jar nearest the cocoon, looking very much as if he were trying to figure out how to escape his confines and get to it.

Kelly's sympathies lay with the butterfly forming in the cocoon.

"Your grandmother will appreciate that," came Alex's muffled comment from inside the walk-in closet. "Do you know what all you need to take from in here?"

"Sort of."

Alex frowned at the rows of drawers and neatly hung clothing. "Didn't the school send a list with your registration confirmation?"

"You gave it to Grandma," Ryan replied, putting another spin on the globe.

"Do you know where it is?"

He did. He just didn't look terribly happy about having to get it, though he was far too obedient to balk for more than a couple of seconds.

From the two tiny holes in the upper corners of the sheet, it appeared that the list had been tacked on a bulletin board. Seeing it now, Kelly thought she remembered seeing it on the corkboard on the back of the door in the laundry room. Not that it mattered. What did was that, while his grandmother had purchased the requisite number of briefs, socks, pajamas, T-shirts and other items of clothing on the list—most of which were still in bags in his closet—the directive typed at the top stating that all clothing must be appropriately labeled had not even been started. Ryan was also missing a few school supplies; namely, notebook paper, one multipocket binder, a package of number two pencils, and a compass.

"For geometry," he explained, when Kelly asked which *kind* of compass.

All Alex wanted to know was, "Why wasn't this all done before?"

Ryan lifted one shoulder in a shrug. Kelly simply handed Alex the bags from the closet and gave Ryan back the list.

"Probably because things didn't go the way everyone expected the past week. I'm sure Edna meant to label his clothes and either she or Audrey had intended to get the rest of his things together. Now, we'll do it."

"*We* will?" the two Burke men chorused.

"Hey." Had all males mastered the combination helpless put-upon look? she wondered. Or only the two she cared about? "You're both capable and I'm sure not doing it alone." She motioned Ryan to the door, forcing herself not to smile at his bewildered expression—or to consider what she'd just admitted to herself. Obviously the Burke men, the youngest one, anyway, had been protected from the more mundane aspects of life. "You, too," she added, eyeing Alex.

With the powerful, silent grace of a panther, Alex crossed to where she stood in the center of the impractical white carpet. She knew Alex was aware of her displeasure with what was going on. She was hoping he'd also gotten the message that, while the two of them might disagree, she was determined they present a united front to Ryan.

Eyeing Ryan's dutifully retreating back, he bent toward her. "I appreciate what you're doing. But there's something you need to know."

"What's that?"

He leaned closer, his nearness disturbing. "You're nowhere near as tough as you sound," he whispered, and walked out ahead of her.

Had it not been for the fact that his cooperation was aiding his departure, Ryan might have enjoyed the activity. While his dad sat at the island in the kitchen neatly printing "Burke, Ryan," on the forty iron-on labels Kelly found in a drawer in the laundry room, Ryan opened packages of underwear, which Kelly added to the wash. According to the directions on the labels, the sizing had to be washed out of everything so the labels would stick, so the three of them headed back upstairs to pack what they could before Kelly came back down to switch loads and Alex prepared to take Ryan to the store.

"You'd better come with us," Alex decided, entering the laundry room alone.

"Why? You have the list."

"I just think it'll be easier."

"For whom?"

"Me. I don't want to get upset with him the day before he leaves. But he's really pushing, Kelly."

It wasn't as difficult as it probably should have been for Alex to ask for her help with Ryan. At least that was the impression Kelly had when she told him she'd be glad to come with them and she saw his relieved smile. He was trying as hard as he knew how to keep the day pleasant for

Ryan. He was trying, too, to let her know he appreciated how she'd backed him up on the school issue by getting Ryan's mind off the possibility that Alex might change his.

She had a solution she would have loved to offer, but since she didn't have a snowball's chance in the Sahara of convincing Alex in the next twenty-four hours to let Ryan come live with her—at least until Alex's schedule eased up and the child could live with him—she kept it to herself. Instead, she simply let herself enjoy being with Ryan—and Alex—and spent the time telling herself she would only be setting herself up for a lot of disappointment if she started thinking about what it would be like to have Ryan live with her. That was the stuff of dreams. The kind of dreams that made her think of Alex and the family they could have been.

Whether she allowed herself to think about it or not, any outsider would have thought they were very much a family as they stopped first for hamburgers and then for the school supplies and the "plastic personal soap holder" that was on the list, but which Ryan couldn't find from last year. He wanted a certain type of binder, too, which just happened to be the same kind every other child in the entire valley wanted. So, naturally, the first store they hit was out. The second one they stopped at had a shipment coming in on Tuesday. The third, to Alex's enormous relief, had one left—which was all Ryan needed and which, finally, made him happy. That made Kelly feel a lot better about leaving them alone when she left for the funeral home after the three of them had finished packing up everything except what Ryan would need in the morning.

The rosary lasted less than an hour. Kelly stayed a while longer, though, to visit with the handful of people who'd come to pay their respects. None seemed to know Audrey particularly well, despite the fact that most of them had been acquainted with her for a number of years. The young priest knew her only by sight, because, while she had attended church regularly, Audrey had never been involved in any church activities.

The silver-haired proprietor of the butcher shop where Audrey had purchased the Burkes' steaks and chops at least had a personal impression of her. He remembered her as being a pleasant, patient woman who knew what she wanted—when it came to choice cuts of meat, anyway—and one of his best customers. The three ladies from Audrey's card club, though they'd spent an entertaining evening with her once a week trying to best each other at canasta, remembered her as being quite opinionated when it came to politics and whatever was in the news that week, and extremely reticent when it came to revealing anything personal.

It was while Kelly drove back to the Burkes' in Alex's car, which he'd insisted she take, that she pondered how little of herself her aunt had actually revealed to anyone, especially when it came to the sensitivity and compassion she'd hidden so very well. Those qualities must have been there, though, buried for whatever reasons. If Alex's interpretation of what Audrey had done for her was at all credible, then Audrey had cared far more for her than Kelly had ever realized.

Even if her aunt hadn't considered Kelly's future and the burdens she would face raising a child alone, just the possibility that she'd had Kelly's best interests at heart while she'd pushed her to give up her baby intensified the sense of loss Kelly felt for the years she and Audrey had spent apart. But Alex's interpretation also brought a kind of solace for which Kelly would be eternally grateful. The more she considered what had happened to her own mother and what Audrey must have seen of her struggle to raise a child on her own, the more sense Alex's rationale made—and the more Kelly believed it could well be so.

A weight of sorts had been lifted by Alex's insights. That was why, when she entered the kitchen, Kelly was thinking only that she needed to thank him for the comfort he'd offered. Until she saw him leaning against the desk near the refrigerator.

He was on the telephone. The moment he saw her walk in, he held up one finger to keep her from leaving the room.

"It's okay, Mom," she heard him say. "I'm sure the flowers will get there on time. No. I didn't have to. Kelly's here. She's taken care of everything."

There must have been a pause on the other end of the line. What followed, Kelly could only guess. She knew only that Alex's jaw went as rigid as plaster and, judging from his expression, that he probably cut his mother off mid-sentence.

"He doesn't know," he said, his tone remarkably mild for the irritation so visible in his expression. "It's not your problem to worry about. I'll take care of it. He goes back in the morning," he added, his jaw unlocking a bit. "The van from the school is supposed to be here around noon."

He said something about Ryan being packed and ready to go. Then his mother must have asked how soon Kelly would be leaving, because Alex was now telling her that she was leaving after the funeral. Kelly didn't stick around to catch any more of the conversation. Alex had obviously wanted to tell—or ask—her something when she'd first come in, but he couldn't talk to her and discuss her with his mother at the same time.

Since she had no desire to stand there considering how her presence was once again complicating their lives, hating the awful surge of insecurity forcing her retreat, she avoided his quick frown and headed for the back hall and her aunt's room. She was twenty-eight years old. She was a mature, reasonable, responsible and relatively confident adult. Yet, it had taken only seconds for her to remember the sense of intimidation and uncertainty she'd experienced when she had been seventeen, and had overheard herself being discussed in much the same way

The past, it seemed, would always cloud the present. In Alex's mind, the situation was still, clearly, a "problem." Heaven only knew what Jessica Burke thought. At least, this time, she and Alex would handle the matter themselves.

Less than a full minute passed between the time she'd closed the door and a knock sounded from the other side. Knowing it was Alex, refusing to give in to the insecurity clawing at her, she straightened her shoulders and pulled it open.

His glance darted over her face, slid over her shoulder to the twin bed with its rose-print coverlet, then snapped back to her eyes.

"Are you all right?" The irritation was gone from his features, his frown now one only of concern. "I had a feeling I should have gone with you tonight."

"I didn't expect you to," she replied, touched that he'd even considered it. It had been enough that he'd offered her the use of his car. "You needed to stay with Ryan. Where is he?"

"In the family room watching a video." His eyes narrowed on her face. "You're sure you're okay? The way you headed in here a minute ago, I thought maybe it had been hard on you, going by yourself."

"I'm fine," she fudged.

"Why don't I believe you?"

"Because you have a suspicious nature?"

She tried to smile. Alex didn't even bother with an attempt. All he did was shake his head at her and reach out to brush back a strand of hair that had loosened itself from the gold-colored clip at her nape. The casualness of the gesture made it seem as natural to him as breathing.

"Mom just got the message Edna left for her yesterday," he told her, letting his hand fall. "She'd been on an excursion to some island and just got back to her hotel. There aren't any flights out until tomorrow, so she wouldn't be able to get back in time for the service. She said to tell you she's sorry about your aunt...and she's sending flowers."

"She's not happy about me being here, is she."

It wasn't a question.

"She's concerned."

"That's understandable."

It *was* perfectly understandable that Jessica would be surprised, concerned and heaven knew what else, upon hearing that she was there. But Kelly allowed that it was probably just as comprehensible for her to feel uneasy, and just a tad disturbed herself. She didn't have to let Alex know that, though.

"So am I," he added.

Her attempted confidence was amazingly short-lived. A knot formed in her chest. "Please, Alex," she began, knowing only one thing he could be concerned about that involved her. "Don't tell me you've changed your mind about letting me see Ryan. Even if it's just a few times a—"

"It's not that," he cut in, reaching out to stop her. His hand curved near her neck, his fingers automatically massaging the smooth muscles of her shoulder. "I'm not even talking about Ryan."

He saw her swallow, her eyes searching his as if she wasn't sure she truly believed him. "Then what are you concerned about?"

He was concerned about them. With whatever it was he was beginning to feel for her, and the fact that he knew she was still, in a very elemental way, afraid of what was happening between them. Telling her that would solve nothing, though. The only thing that would, was time.

"You used to be able to talk to me," she reminded him, not prodding so much as encouraging. "Remember?"

"I remember," he told her, skimming his fingers over her smooth skin. She seemed to accept his touch as easily as she once had, though he honestly couldn't recall if she had always, almost instinctively, turned her cheek into his caress the way she did now. He couldn't begin to describe how it made him feel to know she welcomed his touch that way. "But I don't feel like talking right now."

Her breathing seemed to become more shallow, her eyes, more wary. "This isn't a very good idea, Alex."

"What isn't?"

"What you're doing."

He'd moved closer, the pressure of his hand increasing ever so slightly. "You could always move."

The chide was gentle as he touched again the errant tendril of hair curling against the side of her neck. She could feel the warmth of his hand snake inward where his fingers brushed over her shoulder and down the side of her breast. His touch was feather light, the merest whisper of sensation. In his eyes, fire burned.

He was right. She could move. The fact that she didn't told her far more than she'd been prepared to admit to herself, much less to him.

The lightness vanished, to be replaced by the weight of his hand as it settled at her waist.

"I can't deny that I've thought about what our relationship once was," he admitted, his voice quieter, deeper. "And there are things I still need to know. But, right now, all I keep thinking about is what happened the other morning...and how well we fit together when I kissed you."

The pressure of his fingers at her waist increased, drawing her forward to bring her stomach in contact with the hard ridge in his jeans. His head came down. An inch from her lips, he whispered, "Do you remember?"

She did. Most definitely. And what she felt when his mouth closed over hers was the same quick heat that had darted through her when he'd kissed her before. The same sensation of wax melting under a hot sun. Kelly hadn't been prepared for it then, and she wasn't ready for it now. But the heat flowed over her, through her, even as she told herself it was only the memories, only the past sneaking back to resurrect what she'd felt for him once before.

But it wasn't the past. And what had happened then had little to do with what was happening now. What she felt when he pulled her against his hard body and she opened to him had to do strictly with the present. No amount of rationalization was going to convince her otherwise.

He lifted his head several long, debilitating moments later, then kissed her again, shaping her body with his hands, leaving her breathless.

"Standing out here is not a good idea," she heard him say, his own breathing sounding a little unsteady. "But our only alternative is to close the door, and I'm not sure I trust myself in the same room with you and a bed."

His words, like the feel of his hands skimming her sides and back, turned her insides liquid. What she felt when he drew his hand between her breasts, then let it slip to brush against her stomach, was something far more profound.

He drew back, his eyes glittering intently on her face.

They both seemed to know that there were certain things they couldn't talk about without encroaching on territory neither was prepared to enter. There were words wanting to be said, questions that needed to be asked, but everything felt terribly precarious. It had only been a few days since she'd come back into his life and while the intimacies they'd shared in the past had created a bond that couldn't be denied, it would take time to build the trust that had been lost. That it had become so important to Kelly that the trust be restored, was something she didn't bother to deny.

Today had been a good start, though. Or, so she thought as Alex nudged her down the hall only a minute before Edna's friend dropped her off at the back door. Yet, as good as the day had been, it didn't take long for Kelly to realize that Alex really didn't trust her at all.

Chapter Ten

The blue-and-white van from Tucson's elite Lockemore Hall arrived an hour late. The wait for it had done nothing to alleviate the strain between father and son.

Engine running, it sat in the drive beyond the fountain while the uniformed driver loaded Ryan's luggage, and Ryan and Alex faced off by the vehicle's open doors. In deference to the opinions of his son's peers—the seven other uniformed boys the van had been sent to the valley to collect—Alex offered Ryan a handshake. But either the boy appeared in need of more reassurance than the manly gesture offered, or Alex couldn't let his son go without letting him know how much he'd miss him. The handshake instantly turned into a quick, hard hug. Then Ryan, wearing the school's uniform of tan shorts and white button-down shirt, and carrying his crested, navy blue blazer, his cocoon and his lizard, boarded the van without a backward glance.

From where Kelly stood by the wall of windows in the cool white foyer, she watched the dark-haired child move through the vehicle to the back while the driver climbed inside and slid behind the wheel. Seeing the doors close, her glance shifted back to where Alex now stood with his hands in his pockets. He seemed to be waiting to see if Ryan would look up.

He didn't. He even ignored the other boys leaning over their seats to get a closer look at what was in his jars.

It was hard for Kelly to tell which of the two Burke men felt more miserable. It could easily be weeks before Alex saw his son again. Though Ryan probably wouldn't believe it, sending him away from home would have been difficult enough for his dad under the best of circumstances. Suspecting that Ryan was hating him for what he was doing could only compound Alex's silent misery.

Since Ryan had awakened that morning, he hadn't spoken a word to his father without Alex speaking to him first. It probably hadn't helped the situation that the boy hadn't been nearly so reticent with her.

"Are you going back to Colorado?" Ryan had asked when she'd handed him his pets after transferring them to the plastic "bug jars" she'd bought to transport his budding wildlife collection.

"This afternoon," she'd told the sad-eyed child. "My flight leaves at five o'clock."

"Does it take very long to get there?"

They'd stood at the foot of the stairs in the entry, Alex maintaining his post by the luggage he'd dropped near the door. "Only a couple of hours by air. The plane lands in Durango, then it takes about half an hour for me to get home from there. That's really not too long, do you think?"

She remembered thinking how accepting he'd looked as he told her he guessed not. Or maybe it was more like resigned. Other than for being unusually quiet around his father, he'd been incredibly cooperative with her all morning; certainly more cooperative than she imagined most other children in his situation would have been. There had been no pouting, no tears. It had been almost as if he'd thought that by being really good, he could gain a reprieve.

"If it doesn't take long, then, will you come see me?"

"Sweetheart," she'd whispered, her throat tightening at the plea in his darkly lashed eyes, "you can count on it."

She'd been aware of Alex moving toward them then, but she'd been more concerned about the desperation she'd felt in Ryan's hug when she'd bent down and gathered him to her. The child truly didn't want to go. From the way he held on to her, his eyes squeezed tight, it nearly broke her heart that his father felt he had no alternative but to send him.

Kelly touched her fingers to the glass. It had been less than five minutes since Alex had put his hand on Ryan's shoulder and told him the van was there. Yet, she could still almost feel those strong little arms clinging to her waist before Alex had pulled him away from her—just as she could still feel the ache that had come when she'd whispered, "I'm going to miss you, Ryan," and he'd tried to smile.

She'd had no idea just then if it would have helped him to know who she was, and that she would give anything to take him home with her. But having had a couple of minutes to think about it, she was sure the knowledge would only have caused the child more distress and made his departure that much harder. Not that she would have said anything to him before talking to Alex, anyway.

It was unfortunate that Alex didn't seem to believe that.

"I need to go change," was all she said to Alex when he walked back inside.

"Come on, Kelly. Not you, too." He caught her by the arm as she started to walk away, irritation joining the bleaker emotions shadowing his features. "I'm not the heavy here. You and Ryan are both acting like I'm sending him off on a chain gang."

"I didn't say anything."

"You didn't have to."

She felt his hand slip away, his eyes still holding her in place. It was a little disconcerting to be so transparent, but Alex couldn't read her anywhere near as well as he seemed to think he could. Oh, she was upset, all right. And she didn't agree with what he was doing. But there was more to her disappointment in him than that.

"I didn't say or do anything to give Ryan the impression that I was against your decision. You know that, Alex."

"But you don't agree with it," he muttered, unwittingly conceding both her point and the fact that what she thought mattered. "Damn it, Kelly. I've been gone for weeks at a time this past year. It's only going to be more of the same for I don't know how long. I'd hardly ever be here. My mother's hardly ever here, either. Even when she's home, she's so involved in her charities and lunches and whatever else it is she does that she wouldn't have time for him. I could hire someone to live here and raise him, but that seems ten times worse to me than having him where he's got friends."

"I don't disagree with anything you're saying." Refusing to let him get her as irritated as he seemed to be with her, she kept her voice low, her tone even. She really couldn't disagree with him, anyway. She had no right—

other than what he allowed her. "Under the circumstances, you're doing the best you can."

Skepticism slashed at the shadows. No way was he convinced by her concession. She felt certain of that. But he seemed to realize there was a little more to her tacit disapproval than he'd first thought. "If you believe that, then what's wrong?"

"I wasn't going to tell him I'm his mother, Alex."

There was no accusation in her tone, no irritation. Only the disappointment she felt in him, and in herself for not questioning the ease with which he'd seemed to let her into his son's—*their* son's—life. He wasn't allowing her to make her own way with Ryan. On Alex's turf, playing by his rules, he'd merely given her enough room to allow him to observe—and control. "That's why you stayed home from the office this morning, isn't it? To make sure Ryan and I weren't alone together."

Even before the defensiveness stole over his features, she knew he wasn't going to deny her assumption. It was bad enough that he hadn't trusted her to keep her word. At least he didn't compound matters by pretending he didn't know what she was talking about.

Since Alex had become aware of her knowledge of Ryan, he hadn't left her alone with him for a single moment. Kelly really hadn't noticed his watchfulness yesterday because they'd been so busy. But, this morning, it had been subtly apparent that he had no intention of allowing her an opportunity to be with Ryan without being in the room himself.

Earlier this morning, Alex had wanted to go into the office for a couple of hours before Ryan left. She'd heard him on the phone saying as much and trying to juggle some meeting. So when he'd hung up, she'd told him to go on in and that she'd make sure Ryan got fed and dressed, since

Edna was finishing up her own packing. In the mood Ryan was in, he didn't want to be around anyone anyway, so it wasn't as if Alex would be missing any quality time with him. Yet, despite her offer, Alex had stayed home, spending the time in the study pacing or whatever it was he'd been doing until she'd started up the stairs a while later to see if Ryan needed any help.

Alex, who hadn't set foot out of the study all morning, had been right on her heels—supposedly to help, too.

With her aunt's funeral to begin in a little over an hour, Kelly traded one uneasy set of thoughts for another. She needed to change clothes and get ready to leave herself. "Are you still taking Edna and me to the airport after the service?"

Alex, too, seemed to switch frustrations. "I said I would."

"Then, I'd better get ready."

"We never did get a chance to work anything out."

"No," she said quietly. "We didn't."

"We will."

Needing to mask the hopefulness nudging at her guard, she glanced away from him as she asked, "When?"

There was no time now. There would be no time after the funeral, either. Edna would be with them.

"Leave me your phone number. I'll call you in a couple of days."

When she didn't look up, he stepped forward. It seemed he was about to touch her hair, but his hand only hovered uncertainly for a few moments before he lowered it to her shoulder. Skimming it down her arm and getting no response, he shoved both hands into his pockets.

"Just give me a while to get used to the idea of sharing him. Okay?"

It was a reasonable request. One she could hardly fault. So she whispered a decidedly inadequate, "Okay," and left him staring at her back while she moved past a small marble sculpture on a low table and disappeared through the door beyond the stairs. She really couldn't blame him for wanting to protect his son, if that was what he'd been doing by keeping such a close eye on her. Had their situations been reversed, she didn't doubt for a moment that she'd have done the same thing. But just because she understood it, didn't mean it didn't hurt.

Because Edna was with them, there was no opportunity after the solemn service and interment for Alex and Kelly to talk on the way to the airport. And because they were cutting it short on departure times, Alex didn't escort either one inside. He simply dropped them off outside their respective terminals. Edna, who was finally on her way to Florida for her cruise, was first because she had baggage to check even though her flight was later. Then, he dropped off Kelly.

Alex pulled up in front of the terminal she was leaving from as countdown to her departure time slid just under the fifteen-minute mark.

"You'd never make it if you had to check luggage, too," Alex told her, reaching into the back seat for the small carry-on bag containing the few items of clothing she'd collected and the two small remembrances—other than the tapestry-print bag itself—she'd kept of her aunt. Edna had promised to take care of everything Kelly had packed up for charity when she returned from her vacation. "Do you already have a boarding pass?"

Kelly gave him a nod, taking the bag he handed her as she turned to open the door. The moment he released the bag, though, his hand circled her wrist, his grip forcing her eyes back to him.

"Are you all right?"

"No."

"Kelly..."

"I don't want to miss my plane." Evasion turned into an undisguised plea. "You'll call me, won't you?"

"I told you I would."

He was a man of his word. She knew it with a kind of quiet certainty that should have been reassuring. It would have been, too, had he not also been the man playing utter havoc with her heart—and her life. He'd also said it would take him a while to get used to the idea of sharing his son. The last time he'd mentioned a need for time, it had been eleven years before she'd seen him again.

It seemed a large measure of trust was missing on both sides of the relationship.

With a tug at the hem of the beige linen sheath she'd bought a few days ago, she opened the car door and swung out her legs. Heat from vehicle exhaust and the miserably hot and humid day blasted inside as she glanced back over her shoulder.

She couldn't go without thanking him. It didn't matter that the tension between them had been as thick as the thunderclouds all afternoon. He'd done so much for her, being there for her at the hospital as he had, letting her get to know her son. That was what she'd intended to say to him, too, before she heard his low, succinct curse.

Along with the heat came the honking of horns and the ever-present drone of the taped announcement that the zone was for passenger-unloading only. Kelly scarcely noticed. The moment the terse expletive left Alex's lips, he leaned across the console, snagging her right shoulder with his left hand. In the space of a heartbeat, his hand skimmed up her neck and splayed against the side of her head. With his palm burning against her cheek, he turned her to him.

His mouth came down hard on hers, his scent filling her lungs when she dragged in a startled breath. That breath rushed out an instant later, her body going lax as her mouth softened beneath his. There was hunger in his kiss. Possession, too, and need. A kind of need she would have had no choice but to respond to, had he not raised his head to let her go.

She didn't remember what, if anything, she said to his husky, "Be careful," before she got out of the car and hurried into the terminal. She did know that, as shaken as his kiss had left her, it also fed the hope that insisted on defying her best efforts to ignore it. At least it did for a little while.

She was somewhere over the Grand Canyon when she began to consider how she and Alex were still so carefully dancing around each other. And it was as she pulled into the long, arrow-straight drive leading to her trim little house with its wide gray porch, white wicker rocker and grapevine wreath by the door that she realized the little dance they had choreographed had finally established its own rhythm. But it wasn't until three days later—and she hadn't yet heard a word from Alex—that she conceded how easy the steps had actually been to learn. But then again, there was nothing complicated about one step forward, two steps back.

Alex had said he would call. And he'd intended to, but having spent Tuesday and Wednesday in marathon meetings, the only call he'd made that *didn't* have to do with negotiating television airtime for a major San Francisco client, transferring one of his Bay Area ad execs to the

Phoenix office, or his trip to London the following week, had been to Lockemore Hall to check on Ryan. He'd spoken with both the headmaster and a counselor, and both had assured him that his son was doing just fine. Ryan had immediately hooked up with his friends from last year and was looking forward to the extracurricular activities he'd already picked out for the semester.

The assurances relieved Alex's mind considerably, but he was still concerned about his son. More specifically, about their relationship. He didn't want to think about how Ryan must feel about him. He loved that little guy more than he would ever have thought possible back in the days before he'd become a father. Pulling off his tie while he stood at the window in his spacious San Francisco hotel room, watching white lights follow red lights over the Bay Bridge, he missed him more than he'd once have thought possible, too.

It had been so great watching Ryan laugh while he'd lowered the water level of the pool with his cannonballs. And he'd felt so proud when he'd sat in the kitchen listening to him—at only ten years of age—explain what he understood of the physics behind the generation of lightning. He hadn't realized how smart his little boy was getting. How deftly his mind worked. How much taller he'd grown.

There were other things he'd noticed in those few days they'd been together. But those days were gone; already a part of the past. There was no *present* with his son. No real continuation. He hadn't been around today to see Ryan's excitement, his interest, his irritation—whatever it was he was experiencing. And he wouldn't be there tomorrow. With the plans for the company's expansion over the course of the next year already in play, he had no idea if he'd even see Ryan for more than a couple of days at a time.

His son was growing up without him.

He thinks he's in the way, that no one wants him around.

He needs to be with people who love him.

Alex pulled a pink message slip from his jacket pocket. Kelly had apparently called that afternoon. With the time difference, it would be nearly midnight in Colorado. But if she'd called, she must have had a reason. And he needed to talk to her, if only to hear her voice.

Tossing his jacket on the foot of the king-size bed, he tugged his white shirt free of his trousers. After punching out Kelly's number, he started in on his buttons and sat down on the edge of the bed.

The phone was picked up after the first ring.

"Did I wake you?"

"No. No," came Kelly's soft reply, her recognition of his voice instant. "I was just lying here. Reading," she tacked on, as if what she'd really been doing was trying to sleep and getting nowhere with the effort. "Is Ryan . . . I mean, have you talked to Ryan since he went back?"

For the first time all day, Alex felt the muscles in his shoulders begin to relax. He had no idea why that should be, either, unless it was simply that it felt good to talk to someone as concerned about Ryan as he was himself. It was obvious enough that Kelly was still worried about the way the child had departed. After all, she'd scarcely said hello before she'd asked about him. But it was also apparent by her phrasing that she didn't want to get his father on the defensive again by hinting at the misgivings she undoubtedly still had.

"I haven't talked to him. But I've talked to the school," Alex added, before her concern could compound itself.

"They said he's doing fine. He signed up for a class on bugs."

There was a smile behind her quiet, "Really?" Because of that, Alex found himself smiling, too. He also found himself telling her about the rest of Ryan's curriculum and eventually, because she asked, about how the problem with Warner-Pico seemed to be behind him now that the president of the company realized Alex truly had the company's best interests at heart. It was their conversation about what was going on with the agency that led him to explain why he hadn't called sooner and which, ultimately, got him around to asking why *she* had called.

"I just wanted to know how Ryan was doing," he heard her say, once again minimizing the extent of her concern. "And to get his address, if you wouldn't mind giving it to me. I bought a book I think he'd like and I'd like to send it to him."

"You could have called the school for the address."

"I know. I thought about calling them to see how he was, too, but I didn't think they'd give out information about a student to just anyone. At least, I hope they don't."

She was trying to keep her voice light and the conversation easy. He was sure of it. Just as he felt sure she was trying to let him know she wasn't doing anything where Ryan was concerned without him knowing about it—even if it was simply sending him a book. A book about bugs, she told him when he asked.

It was because she was being so open with him and so careful about her relationship with her son, that Alex was beginning to think she was one of the most honorable people he knew. She didn't deserve to simply be "just anyone" where their son was concerned. Though he tried, he couldn't imagine how that had to make her feel. He did know he couldn't stand the thought of how she might come to feel toward him because of it. Kelly knew it was entirely up to him whether or not she participated in her son's life—at least, until Ryan turned eighteen. Neither had mentioned the power he held, but they both knew it was there. It hung over her head like Damocles' sword, feeding the caution, influencing what she said to him. The last thing in the world he wanted was for her to come to resent him because of it.

It took a minute, but he gave her the address of the school, humbled by the fact that, though his son was now starting his second year there, he had to look it up in his address book. His excuse for not knowing it offhand was that he usually had his secretary mail the cards he occasionally picked up—but those occasions, he had to admit, were too few and far between.

That was going to change. The first letter he dictated in the morning—no, the first letter he *wrote*—would be to his son.

"Listen," he continued, tossing his address book back toward his briefcase. "I'm leaving for London Sunday night. The way my schedule's set now, I won't be back for three weeks, but if you don't have plans, I'd like to see you on my way back."

"You're coming here?"

"I thought it would be better than talking about Ryan over the phone." He wanted to know more about her, too. Everything about her, actually. For his own sake as well as Ryan's. "He'll want to know how often he can see you, and I imagine he'll want to know what happened that he wound up with me. We need to decide how much to tell him . . . and when."

"I thought you said you'd tell him at Thanksgiving."

"We'll see how it goes when I get there, but maybe we won't need to wait quite so long . . . and it might be better if we tell him together."

A moment ago, Alex had been able to hear her moving around; the sound of a drawer opening, the rustle of paper. Now, he heard nothing.

"Kelly?"

It sounded as if she had cleared her throat. "Yes?"

"Did you hear what I said?" he asked, wondering if he'd said something wrong.

"Yes," she softly repeated.

"Is my coming there a problem?"

"Not at all." Her voice sounded strained. Or maybe, how it sounded was . . . restricted. "I'll be here."

"You still want to work this out, don't you?"

"Oh, yes," he heard her whisper. "Very much."

He'd have thought she'd be anxious to talk about Ryan. She was certainly giving the answers that would support that supposition. Yet, she didn't sound terribly happy at all. Wondering if she wasn't as talkative as she'd been before because she was getting tired, thinking that a distinct possibility because it was so late where she was, he told himself he should let her go. He'd kept her long enough.

He'd intended to say something like that, too, but the thought of breaking the connection with that soft, soothing voice, tired as it was, made him grip the phone a little tighter.

"I miss you," he finally admitted.

It seemed an eternity before he heard her quiet, "I miss you, too, Alex." But it wasn't until she'd said, "Good night," and he was listening to the dial tone, that he realized it hadn't been fatigue he'd heard in her voice. What he'd heard was a woman choking back hope. It had been almost as if she were afraid to feel good about getting what she wanted. Or, maybe, as if she were afraid to believe she'd get it at all.

Had he thought for a moment that it would do any good, he would have called her back. But he didn't know what he'd say if he did. So he just contemplated the pink message slip that indicated she had called him, and thought about how very much he hated hotel rooms, impersonal long-distance phone calls, and sleeping alone.

As unsatisfying as that call had been, the call he received exactly one week later made his blood run cold.

This one wasn't from Kelly. It was from Lockemore—which was the only reason he took the call in the first place since he was up to the knot in his necktie in agency accountants, his most trusted executives and one very expensive, absolute-best-in-his-field business consultant. But the people he'd left pacing in his office—most of whom had spent the past four days all but locked up with him in his San Francisco office while he honed the competitive edge on his father's growth plan—were completely forgotten the moment he picked up the phone on the secretary's desk.

"Mr. Burke," Stewart Kerby, the headmaster, began after identifying himself. "This is a most distressing call for me to make, but your son is missing from school. We believe he's run away," he hurried on. "Has he been in contact with you?"

It was odd how having to answer the question forestalled the panic. "I haven't heard from him at all," Alex told the man as the shock hit. "Hold on."

His hand over the mouthpiece, a sick sensation spreading through him, he turned to the smartly professional middle-aged woman at the file cabinet. "Has my son called here today, Denise?"

"No, Mr. Burke. I'd have put him through if he had."

The secretaries in all four offices knew that a call from Ryan was to be put through no matter what Alex was doing, or whom he was with. Those who'd been around long enough knew it was a rule Alex's own father had put into effect with Alex himself, years ago. No one broke it.

"Check with the receptionist and see if she got a call while you were at lunch, will you? Hurry!"

The secretary was already on her way when Alex raised the phone. "I can't believe Ryan would run away. Something else must have happened. How long's he been gone? Have you called the police?"

He wanted to know, too, how Ryan could have left the grounds without anyone knowing, who could have come onto the grounds, and where the staff was that was supposed to be watching out for the kids. But all those were moot points at the moment. Even if the normally unflappable Mr. Kerby had been able to provide satisfactory answers, they wouldn't have done a thing to alleviate the awful sense of helplessness that now had Alex in its grip.

He was a thousand miles away and his son was missing.

It was a sorry sort of consolation that Kerby, whom Alex remembered as being tall, affable and the father of three sons of his own, seemed just as upset as Alex was. Of course he'd called the police, he told Alex. But he hadn't done it until after a thorough search of the grounds, including dorms, classrooms, riding stables, gymnasium, playing fields and utility areas. It sometimes happened when a child didn't show up for a meal—as had been the case with Ryan that morning—that the child had just lost track of time, was dawdling, hiding or, as in the case of a boy who'd been missing for three hours last year and had been found on the wrestling mats stored in the gym loft, had simply been tired and fallen asleep somewhere. The search for Ryan had netted no clue as to his whereabouts, however, although one of the four boys who shared a quad, as they called the dorm rooms, said Ryan had been talking about going to see his mother.

"I understand how difficult it is for children when their parents divorce," Mr. Kirby insisted. "And it's not uncommon for them to talk of going to live with the noncustodial parent. But I assure you, Mrs. Burke never contacted us about Ryan leaving school. You hadn't listed her as a relative or contact party on your son's enrollment forms for this year, but we had her phone number in last year's records. When I called her a while ago, she assured me she hadn't heard from Ryan. She also said she couldn't imagine why she would," he added with undisguised disapproval. "Given her attitude, it didn't seem likely that his quad mate had heard correctly."

Alex froze. Disbelief joined the fear, along with a few other emotions he didn't think it wise to sort through at the moment. "Mrs. Burke isn't his mother."

"I beg your pardon?"

"He didn't go to see Diane. That's not who he was talking about." It was with a sickening sense of certainty that Alex realized where Ryan was going. But the relief he felt knowing what had quite probably happened was canceled by the anxiety waiting in the wings. "He means his birth mother. She's in Colorado. Durango." Dear God, he thought, the fear reasserting itself and turning the plea into a prayer. Ryan was trying to get to Colorado. By himself. He'd never traveled alone in his life.

The thoughts of what could happen to a ten-year-old, alone on a road or heaven only knew where, were something Alex simply couldn't face at the moment.

"Her name's Kelly Shaw." He gave Kerby the number, having memorized it after staring at it so long the other night. "I don't know her address offhand, but she runs an herb farm within a half hour of the Durango airport." She'd told Ryan that the morning he'd left for school, when the boy had been so interested in finding out how long it took to get to her house. "I'll try to call her from here. In the meantime, give that information to the police and have them start looking into anything headed in that direction. I'll call you back in two minutes."

Chapter Eleven

It took a little longer than two minutes for Alex to get back to Kerby. By the time he'd listened to Kelly's telephone ring fifteen times straight, twice, spoken with the Tucson police himself, and listened to Kelly's phone go unanswered yet again, half an hour had passed.

It took the secretary about that long to get him on a flight into Durango. The little town in southwestern Colorado was hardly an air-transportation hub, so there weren't exactly unlimited flights in and out of the place. Still, through the efforts of the agency's travel agent, she was able to hand him a ticket connecting him through Phoenix. Allowing time to pick up the rental car she'd reserved, Alex figured he should be at Kelly's place by around seven o'clock that evening.

Given the fact that Ryan hadn't been seen since bed check late last night, the police had agreed it made more sense for Alex to go to Colorado than Tucson, since that appeared to be Ryan's destination. How Ryan intended to get there was anyone's guess. To the best of Alex's knowledge, the child had very little cash in his possession. Other than to purchase a candy bar or postcard in the student store, Ryan had no need for money. Alex paid his expenses by check. That being the case, Ryan couldn't very well buy an airline or bus ticket, which, technically, he shouldn't be able to do anyway, being a child. And Ryan wasn't a child who looked older than he was. If anything, he tended to look a bit young for his age. But the boy was bright and if he possessed even a fraction of his father's determination, he would find a way to get where he wanted to go—provided nothing happened to him in the process.

There was only one thought that kept Alex sane as he walked back into his office and, without going into detail, explained that he had a family emergency that precluded the present project, asked the senior accountant to finish up the numbers he'd asked for, excused himself to everyone else and headed out the door. He was too pragmatic to overlook how Kelly had called for the school's address last week, and he still remembered the way she'd sounded when he'd hung up. There was also Ryan's obvious attachment to her to consider. Though the thought that Kelly might have decided the situation without him once again did awful things to his insides, Alex truly hoped she'd met the child somewhere and had him with her. At least then, Alex knew he'd be safe.

The only thing Kelly had decided as she sorted through the last of the basil and oregano she'd cut that morning, was that she needed to stop daydreaming and concentrate on what she was doing. She'd tied yet another sheaf of herbs without leaving a hanging loop.

Shaking her head at herself and smiling because dreams of any kind—day or otherwise—were something she hadn't allowed herself in so long, she wrapped another length of string around the gathered stems of basil, formed the loop, then hung the sheaf upside down with the other herbs suspended from the long overhead racks in her drying shed. Ever since Alex had called last week, she'd vacillated between imagining Ryan catching pollywogs in the pond with her neighbors' kids and—daring to move from dream to fantasy—Alex sitting with her on the porch as the moon rose, then taking her by the hand and leading her to her old four-poster bed with its piles of pillows and thick, patchwork quilts. Both scenarios made concentration difficult. But the latter made her more than a little restless.

It was that restlessness that now had her thinking she might as well get a head start on tomorrow's work by typing up the invoices and mailing labels for the orders she would box in the morning, when she heard her name being called. At least she thought she heard someone calling, "Kelly!" as she picked up the basket she'd just emptied. The deep male voice sounded too distant for her to be sure. When she heard it the second time, though, the voice was much clearer.

It was also heart-stoppingly familiar.

Dropping the basket into the stack at the end of the long wooden worktable, she darted out the door and into the beautiful summer afternoon. Cottony clouds hung in a crystalline sky. To the north and east, mountains of gray granite and lush green aspen rose with a majesty that rarely failed to move her. Now, she scarcely noticed them.

She saw Alex before he saw her.

He was coming around the side of her house, the side with the little greenhouse where she started the seedlings now growing lush and full in the fields that stretched out in all directions like a verdant patchwork quilt. He called her name again, his strides radiating a kind of impatience that spoke more of agitation than eagerness as he looked toward the storage barn, then swung his glance toward the shed. It was then that he noticed her hurrying toward him.

"What are you doing here?" she called out, heading across the stretch of green lawn between the long shed and her back porch. "I thought you were in London."

He offered no explanation. No greeting. He just kept coming, his expression mirroring his strides. "Haven't the police contacted you?"

Her step faltered. "The police?" He was in front of her now, stopping with his hands on his hips to watch her frown of incomprehension sweep his face. "Why would they call me? What's—?" She cut herself off, her expression reflecting the confusion Alex himself had felt when he'd first received Kerby's call. "Ryan," she said in a rush. "Something's happened to Ryan."

It was the alarm—no, the fear—that darted through her eyes when she grabbed his arm, that told Alex she had absolutely no idea what was happening. Worse, it told him that she hadn't heard a word from their son.

He felt her small hand tighten around his flesh, seeking assurance he couldn't give. He held himself rigid, torn between instinct, logic and the need to seek that same assurance from her. Part of him had refused all along to believe she'd had anything to do with Ryan's disappearance. Another part couldn't explain how Ryan had found out about her if she hadn't told him herself.

"He's run away from school," he said, hating the way she drew back from him. What he hated even more was the ambivalence that kept him from reaching for her. "He told one of his friends he was going to see his mother. I've tried calling you off and on all afternoon, and the police here were supposed to talk to you, too, to see if you'd heard from him. They have an all-points bulletin out on him in Arizona and Colorado.''

''I haven't even received a letter,'' she told him, too stunned by the news to fully comprehend what Alex had just said. ''I've been here all day...except for a couple of hours around three o'clock when I was over at my neighbor's.'' Mrs. Yakamura had run out of sugar while making blackberry jam. Since her husband had taken the truck and gone fishing, she'd walked over to see if Kelly had a bag she could borrow, but Kelly's supply had been just as low. She'd driven to the store, then, at the elderly woman's insistence, stuck around to bring back a couple of jars when the batch was finished. ''If the police came by it must have been then.''

''If you were here the rest of the time, why weren't you answering your phone?''

''I can't always hear it. Especially when I'm out in the fields or in one of the buildings.'' Crossing her arms against the denim shirt she wore over her cutoff jeans, she tried to focus on her son and not on the fear—or on Alex's strangely accusing attitude. ''We need to be looking for Ryan. You said he's headed here? When did he leave?'' She didn't give him a chance to answer. Her mind racing, she uncrossed her arms and shoved her fingers through her hair. ''What if he's tried to call?'' she asked, more of herself than of the man watching her so closely. ''And why did you come here if you didn't think I was home?''

Her agitation was interfering with her comprehension, and her logic. Alex understood completely.

''I'm here because it's where we think Ryan is headed. I figured one or both of you would have to show up sometime.''

''Both?''

His jaw clenched. "It seemed possible that you might have taken him. Or met him somewhere," he added before he could debate the wisdom of voicing suspicions the police had also found credible. That much he would keep to himself, however. "I don't think I really believed you would, but it had to be considered."

"Alex, I'd never—"

"It doesn't matter now."

Yes, it did. It mattered a great deal—and her stricken expression only proved it.

"Kelly," he said flatly. "I couldn't overlook how close the two of you had become. Part of me even *wanted* you to have taken him. If he'd been with you, I'd at least have known he was safe. But I knew the minute I saw you that you had nothing to do with it. All right?" His back teeth clenched, his jaw relaxing only slightly before he proceeded. "What I'm having trouble figuring out now is how he found out who you are. When the headmaster said Ryan had been talking about going to see his mom, I knew he couldn't possibly have meant Diane. Somehow, he found out you're his mother."

"You think I told him."

The defeat in her tone caught him like a blow to the ribs.

"I'm just trying to figure out how he found out," he called after her when she headed up the steps to the back porch and jerked open the screen door. "We never said anything about you being his mom when he was around." He'd been as careful as he could about that. "And I know he didn't see the file."

She didn't ask how he could be so positive of that as he followed her into her homey little kitchen. She was quite aware that he'd kept a constant eye on both of them since the moment Ryan had come downstairs the morning after she'd dropped that file like a ticking bomb in his hands. Ryan hadn't had a *chance* to see it.

"So I guess it had to come from me, then, didn't it?"

Sarcasm didn't suit her. Or maybe it was the fact that she wasn't particularly good at it that ruined the attempt. So, to keep him from seeing how devastating his accusations were, she kept her back to him while she adjusted the white shutters on the window by the whitewashed trestle table to let in more of the summer-scented air. The faint breeze nudged the leaves of the cheerful, saucer-size sunflowers standing in the foot-high blue vase centered on the table.

Alex stayed just inside the door, watching. "I didn't say that."

"Then what *are* you saying?"

"I'm saying I don't understand how he found out."

She rounded on him, her back straight, though she did a lousy job of keeping the hurt and the anger from her eyes. "I didn't tell him, Alex. Whether you choose to believe that or not is your business. But I've been as aboveboard with you as I know how to be, and I don't appreciate what you're implying."

It was her quiet fury that did it. Alex had always known Kelly to hold her anger back; to bury it to keep the peace. She was too much of a lady to rage at anyone, but she would not have her integrity questioned. As she stood with her chin tipped up, her glare defying him to accuse her of lying, Alex had no choice but to back down. Despite all the evidence that seemed to so clearly indicate otherwise, he believed what she'd said. He had to. She'd never lied to him. Ever.

"I'm sorry, Kelly." He hadn't come right out and accused her of anything. But she was right. The implication had definitely been there. "I'm sorry," he repeated, and hoped that, considering what they were dealing with, she would forgive him. "Since you didn't tell him, how do you suppose he did find out?"

She didn't trust the sudden change in his tone, or the contrition in his expression. Nevertheless, eyeing him with the caution she'd come to expect in their every encounter, some of the starch slipped from her spine.

"I don't know," she said in a tone that clearly indicated she wished she did. "I don't think it even matters right now. All that does is where he is. You never did say how long he's been gone." Fear overrode the hurt. "Just tell me what's happened and what they're doing to find him. Please?"

"Let me use your phone first."

All that mattered right now was Ryan. He was all Kelly allowed herself to consider as she motioned to the wall phone hanging under the kitchen cabinet. Anxious for details, she proceeded to pace the length of her bright, farm-style kitchen while Alex called the sergeant in Tucson who was coordinating the search. From what she overheard of his call, it sounded as if Alex had spoken with the sergeant when he'd landed at the Durango airport a little over an hour ago, and that there were still no leads on Ryan's whereabouts. It also sounded as if someone was to obtain a picture of Ryan from a Mr. Kerby, hopefully in time for the late news broadcasts.

Alex knew she heard everything he said. He seemed to want her to hear, since he was watching her wear the polish off her floor rather than face one of the windows overlooking the fields and the mountains. She supposed it was more efficient than him having to repeat everything, and it was nice to know he appreciated how badly she needed whatever information she could get. But she didn't realize just how much he was willing to let her know until part of the reason he'd had to make the call became clear.

"I'm at her house now," she heard him say. "No. She hasn't had any contact with him. She had no idea what was going on until I got here."

The unexpected certainty in his voice brought her to a halt near the old-fashioned white-enamel stove, a good five feet away from where Alex stood.

"Yes, I believe her." His eyes locked on hers, the look in them as unyielding as his tone. "Implicitly."

Moments later, still watching her, he told the sergeant he'd stay where he was until either Ryan showed up or the police found him, then turned to hang up the phone. Not by so much as the twitch of an eyebrow did he let on that he'd said or done anything extraordinary when he turned back. With his hands jammed in his pockets, he immediately began to recap the parts of the conversation she hadn't heard, then moved on to answer the questions she'd asked before.

It didn't take long for Alex to tell her what had happened. Or for her to agree with his conclusion that Ryan wanted to get to Durango. Ryan had asked more questions than she could remember about where she lived, and when she'd talked about the mountains and the fields and the horses, he'd often watched her so intently that she couldn't help thinking he was filing away every scrap of information she gave him. Kelly couldn't feel the least bit good about her son wanting to be with her so badly, though. Not with him out there somewhere all alone.

"Can I get you anything?" she asked, desperate for something to do other than stand there worrying. Alex had said he'd been in San Francisco when he'd received the call—which obviously meant his London trip had suffered yet another snag somewhere along the line. It also meant he'd been traveling for hours. "Are you hungry?"

It was a fair indicator of how worried Alex was that he let her question go without a gibe, teasing or otherwise, about whether or not she planned to cook whatever it was she was offering. All he said was, "No...thanks," then drew his hand down his face before he pulled a card out of his back pocket. "I need to call the school and let them know I'm here."

She'd seen him tired before. She'd seen him near exhaustion the night she'd run into him in the study when she'd first gone back to Phoenix. Yet, she'd never seen him look the way he did now. The deep lines carved around the downturned corners of his mouth and the spiritlessness in his eyes had little to do with physical fatigue, and everything to do with distress. Alex was desperately worried about his son. She wasn't fooled a bit by the way he muttered something about grounding Ryan for life when this was over. He was far more troubled and upset than angry.

Kelly was simply numb.

At least that was the way she looked to Alex when he found her in the greenhouse a short while later after wandering through her appealingly cozy little house looking for her. The sun had already set behind the mountains, so the views beyond the glass panels comprising the walls and ceiling of the plant-filled space were all obscured. But he had no trouble picturing her in this room with the sunlight pouring in on her as she stood at a table along the far wall, her head bent as she took nips out of a tiny, perfectly shaped cypress tree.

"Did you know that the art of bonsai is over a thousand years old?" she asked without looking up.

His brow furrowing, his glance swept her profile. The question was as incongruous to him as what she was doing. "I don't think I did."

"My neighbor told me that when he brought me my first tree. It's that one over there." With the nippers, she indicated a one-foot-tall maple in full foliage. The exquisite, perfectly formed little tree sat on a ledge a few feet away. "It's called *chokkan* because it's in the formal upright style. This one is *shakan* because it slants, and *sokan* because its has two trunks that form a common root system." There were three other styles, she told him, then looked back at the tiny cypress in front of her to take a snip from a windswept-looking branch.

He thought her voice oddly calm, given how upset she'd looked before she'd disappeared. As she worked, she talked, explaining what Mr. Yakamura, her neighbor, had told her about how the container and the plant must blend in harmony. But it wasn't what she was saying that kept Alex so silent as he breathed in the scent of honeysuckle clinging to her hair and the earthy fragrances of leaves and loam and moss permeating the room. It was what she revealed about herself just then—and what he remembered of her as a girl so many years ago.

He couldn't count the number of times while they'd been growing up that he'd found her behind the garage when she was upset—which was usually just before he'd have to go back to school and always after having, yet again, failed to master her aunt's culinary lesson *du jour*. When he would find her, she'd be talking to whatever sickly plant she was nursing back to health, her voice gentle as she'd coax it to grow and be strong. It had almost been as if she could forget her own troubles by focusing on the hapless specimen. What he remembered most clearly, though, was that when she would see him, she would inevitably smile and drag him over to show him a bit of new growth on her patient, as proud as a new parent.

He'd never understood her affinity for plants, so he really hadn't cared all that much about what she would show him. A green leaf, was a green leaf as far as he'd been concerned. The only difference was that some were served in salads. What he'd cared about was just knowing she was all right.

Watching her now, he was finally beginning to grasp just how important her plants had always been to her. And what these little trees might mean. There were times when she'd had little control in or over her life. Times like now, when she was powerless to change the direction of events taking place around her. But with the little trees, she had control. She could shape and mold and bend. The fact that it took a while to see the results didn't matter all that much. What was important was the distraction.

"Does it help?"

Setting the nippers down, she slowly shook her head. It didn't occur to her to question that he'd known what she was trying to do, or the direction her thoughts had taken.

"All I can see are pictures on milk cartons."

Without a word, he turned her around and pulled her into his arms. They were both scared, both worried, and it made no sense for them to be scared and worried alone. They could sort through the emotional baggage stacked between them later. Right now, Ryan was all that mattered. "He has to be all right. So that's what we're going to believe. Okay?"

He needed to believe it. So did Kelly as she slipped her arms around his waist, welcoming the solid feel of him even as she offered what comfort she could. It had to be so much harder on him, she thought, laying her head on his broad chest. He'd known their son for so much longer. He had so many more memories.

"He must have overheard us talking," she said, because she was still trying to determine how Ryan had known about her. "That's the only way I can think of that he found out."

"I don't know when that would have been. But that had to be it. I can't think of anything else, either."

"I wonder how long he knew?"

"It's hard to say. It couldn't have been too long." Confusion, or maybe it was uncertainty, shaded his voice. "Don't you think he'd have said something to one of us?"

Kelly shook her head, the motion rubbing her cheek against his starched white shirt. She loved the way he smelled. The scents of musk and male and heat. "I don't know. Something like that wouldn't be easy to bring up." More immediate concerns took over. "They haven't seen him since...what did you say? Ten or eleven last night?"

"About then."

"What time is it now?"

She felt his left arm turn against her back and the brush of his chin against her hair. She didn't move. She couldn't. She was in the only place that felt safe.

"Almost nine."

Alex's arm resecured itself across her back and his cheek pressed against the top of her head. There was nothing either of them could say just then that would make the waiting any easier.

The only thing that would help would be to hear that Ryan was all right.

As easily as they had turned to each other earlier, long moments later, they just as reluctantly stepped out of each other's arms. Their eyes met only briefly, but Alex didn't think Kelly felt any more of a need for words than he did just then. So when she turned, he followed her in silence back into the house, then went out to his rental car to bring in his travel bag.

There was no discussion about his staying with her. When he returned with his bag, he simply left it by the deeply cushioned sofa in front of her stone fireplace and wondered if he should turn on a light. There were none on in the living room where Kelly stood with her back to him at one of the wide windows. The only illumination came through the doorway from the kitchen.

In that faint light, he saw her glance toward him with a faltering smile, then turn back to lose herself in the darkness beyond the window.

Thinking he preferred the dimness himself, he wandered toward the loom that took up one corner of her cozy living room and found himself wondering how she managed the size and bulk of it when she pulled it out to work. It was so much easier thinking about Kelly than Ryan—or so he thought. It wasn't long before he realized he couldn't think of one without the other; that thoughts of the two had tangled inexorably in his mind. So he tried not to think of either one of them while he moved about the retreatlike space, taking in the small touches that added the warmth and vitality missing from his mother's house.

The effort was wasted. He found himself thinking about them anyway while he paced and Kelly stood at the window behind the sofa, watching the moon play hide-and-seek with the clouds. Every once in a while, he would join her, wanting see if he could find the solace she did in watching the night sky. But he had no luck. He didn't have her perception, or her inner strength, or whatever it was that allowed her to remain so still when the world outside seemed to be falling apart. He would stay long enough for her to offer him a tremulous smile, then he'd resume his restless pacing again.

That was what he did until the last time he came to the window, anyway. "You're exhausting yourself," she said, curling her fingers around his biceps. "Come on into the kitchen and I'll put on some tea."

The pressure of her fingers was light, but he could feel the warmth of her palm seep through his sleeve. It was her touch that provided the calm he couldn't seem to find in his prowlings. So instead of letting her break the contact when she started to turn away, he reached for her—only to feel her stiffen when the telephone rang. An instant later, she'd bolted for the doorway.

Kelly was passing from the living room into the kitchen when it rang again. It didn't ring a third time. She had the receiver in her grip and was answering with an apprehensive, "Hello?" before it had the chance.

Though his thoughts were masked, the bright lights of the kitchen clearly delineated the strain that had etched itself into Alex's features in the past several hours. She didn't know if it was a good sign or a bad one that his expression didn't change when she held out the phone. "It's for you. Sergeant Trujillo."

Kelly held her breath as she watched him take the phone. But it was only seconds before she saw his eyes close, heard his heartfelt, "Thank God," and her breath whispered out with a prayer of her own.

"Where is he now? No. No. Tell him it's okay," Alex insisted, not seeming aware of the death grip he'd had on her shoulder before he let his hand fall. "Put him on."

It was pretty easy to tell from Alex's end of the conversation that the child was afraid. Not for his physical safety, though Kelly could only guess at where he'd been or what he'd been through, but for what might happen to him once his father got hold of him. It seemed a safe assumption that he was okay, given the fact that he was at the police station—a *Tucson* police station, at that—and not in a hospital somewhere. But Ryan's fears had to be diminished somewhat by the way his father repeated he was so thankful he was all right. He also told Ryan that he was at Kelly's house, and that she was thankful he was all right, too. Then Ryan must have asked if they were mad at him, because Alex said, "I don't know what I am right now, son. And yes, Kelly was upset. We'll talk about all this tomorrow. I'm going to call Mr. Kerby and have him take you back to the school. Give the phone back to the sergeant. And Ryan?" He paused, his grip tightening. "I love you."

It was impossible to tell from Alex's expression what Ryan had said next. Or what Alex was feeling when he spoke with the sergeant again and then with Mr. Kerby when he called him a couple of minutes later. But when he hung up the phone and turned toward her, ten years had dissolved from his face.

A patrolman had found Ryan walking back to the school, he told her. From what the police got out of him, it sounded as if he'd left the school not too long before everyone else got up and had made it as far as the Tucson Mall before it got too hot for him to walk anymore. He'd spent a while there, then taken a cab because he didn't know in which direction the airport was. Why a cabbie didn't think it odd that a child was going alone to the airport from a mall was anyone's guess. But Ryan was still at the airport, waiting for a monitor to show a flight to Durango when an airport employee got suspicious because he'd been hanging around for so long.

"He'd have had to wait forever to see a flight to here listed," Alex concluded, shaking his head. "They're all connections."

Kelly didn't think about what she did. Seeing Alex's relief, feeling her own, she did the only thing she could do. Matching his grin, she moved toward him.

Her arms had barely looped around his neck when his arms locked across her back. An instant later, she felt her feet leave the floor. He didn't swing her around, though she didn't doubt for a moment that he would have, had the wall not been in the way. He simply settled for holding her high against his chest and laughing into the soft cotton collar of her shirt.

His deep chuckle lasted only as long as it took for him to whisper, "He's okay, Kelly." The release of anxiety made his voice thick. "Our son's okay."

Kelly couldn't have imagined anything that could have made her stop smiling just then. But at his last words, her heart slammed against her ribs and her smile started to fade. A moment later, she felt the brush of his surprisingly soft hair against her cheek as he lifted his head. In the fraction of a second in between, the tension in the strong muscles holding her underwent a definite change in quality.

Alex held her with her head slightly above his, her arms resting lightly on his shoulders. As close as she was, she could easily see the little chips of gray in his blue eyes and the first strands of silver near his temple. She could also see that he wasn't smiling anymore, either.

Her heart felt as if it were beating in her throat. "You called him our son."

"That's who he is."

"I've just never heard you say it before."

His eyes held hers, their intensity as he searched her face as enervating as the friction of his chest against her breasts when he slowly lowered her to the floor.

"I've thought of him that way pretty much since you showed up at the house. After all of this, I guess it feels even more like it."

They had so few experiences where Ryan was concerned. And none before today that created the kinds of bonds most parents naturally had where their children were concerned: the bonds born of shared joys, concerns, hopes and worries. Yet the tie had been there. Always.

It wasn't the shared experiences of parenthood that finally had Alex letting Kelly go. It was thoughts of the experiences they should have shared bringing Ryan into the world, and of how very much he would enjoy the prospect of getting her pregnant again. When those thoughts combined with the havoc she'd already so innocently created in his body, the need for a little distance proved mandatory.

That was why he kept his hands to himself and asked for a phone book. He needed to call the airline.

The next flight to Phoenix, which was where they'd have to change planes for Tucson, wasn't until eight o'clock the next morning. Since Kelly had left the room again, he didn't discuss her going with him. He just went ahead and booked the flight for both of them, thinking it would be easier to cancel if she couldn't go than try to get her on later.

That he'd assumed she was going was obviously a surprise to Kelly. But it wasn't her surprise Alex was thinking about when he found her standing just inside the doorway of her bedroom with a pillow and a set of sheets in her arms and he told her what he'd done.

What he was considering was her smile.

"You want me to come with you?"

"Sure. You're who he wanted to see to begin with. Remember?"

It had been years since he'd seen her smile that way. Maybe it had been that long since anyone had. But the expression lighting her face was like sunshine in spring: healing, rejuvenating, inviting. It seemed to seep into his soul, warming him, touching a part of him that he'd thought dead long ago.

Standing there dressed in denim, with her hair pulled back, barefoot now and holding a stack of bedding, she was the antithesis of the perfectly manicured and made-up women he saw every day—the Dianes and Jessicas of the circles in which he moved. Kelly could hold her own in those circles, if she chose. He'd seen her look as at ease in peach silk and beige linen, but he'd never known anyone as natural, as innocently sensual, as Kelly appeared to him at that moment. And he'd never found anyone who appealed to him more. She was truly the loveliest, gentlest woman he had ever known.

"What are you doing?" he asked, nodding to the bedding she held.

"I was going to make up the bed in the other room. I thought you might be getting tired."

He took the step that brought him inside her room. "I'm not."

"You should be. It's been a long day."

There was concern behind her smile now. Wondering if she had any idea what it did to him when she looked at him like that, he held out his hands. "I'll help."

The scent of fresh air drifted upward from the sheets when she handed them to him. Or maybe that was what the room itself smelled like, he thought as he noticed the starched white-eyelet curtains and the four-poster bed covered with a thick white comforter, pillows, and old-fashioned quilts made of the palest bits of cream, white and peach.

"Wait a minute. I think I forgot the pillowcase."

Kelly's head was bent, her shoulder brushing his arm as she lifted first the top sheet, then the bottom from the stack on the pillow. She was trying as hard as she knew how to overlook the way he had so pointedly set her away from him in the kitchen and to just be happy for what she had, without wanting more. But after years of denial, she did want more. She wanted him to hold her, to kiss her the way he had before, and just for a little while pretend that he needed her as badly as she needed him. Alex didn't need her, though. He never had. So she would simply be grateful that she was getting to be part of Ryan's life, enjoy being with Alex when they chanced to be together, and try once again to forget that she was in love with him—and probably had been all of her life.

"Kelly?"

She swallowed. Hard. "It's not here. Just a second and I'll get one."

"Kelly," he repeated, his quiet insistence forcing her to look up. "What if I didn't want to sleep in there?"

The air in the room suddenly seemed too heavy to breathe. "Where else did you have in mind?"

His glance moved to her mouth, then back up to the caution in her eyes. Something that looked very much like disappointment drained the strength from his voice. "You're still afraid of me, aren't you?"

She supposed she should deny it. She even started to. But denying the obvious was a wasted effort. "I'm afraid of what you make me feel, Alex. That's all." She ducked her head. "I'll be right back."

A white wicker rocker sat next to the door. It was there that the bedding landed before Alex caught her by the wrist.

Turning her to face him, he slid his hand up her arm. "What would it take for you not to be afraid anymore?"

Despite the flutter of her pulse when he skimmed his fingers along the side of her neck, her voice was calm, her smile gentle. "A miracle."

"Do you believe in them?"

He was dead serious. Because of that, her smile faltered. "It's hard not to believe in them, since I've already been on the receiving end of one."

The tips of his fingers traced upward behind her ear, his thumb brushing the delicate line of her jaw. "You have?"

"Sure. When I found Ryan." Almost involuntarily, her own glance moved downward, touching on the shape of his beautifully molded mouth before drifting down the buttons on his shirt. "Maybe we even got another one tonight."

"Maybe," she heard him agree, his voice sounding rough. "Maybe we did."

It was the huskiness in his voice that drew her glance back to his face. All the time they'd waited for word about Ryan, Alex had stayed close, yet separate from her as he'd paced. He was accustomed to handling difficulties alone, so she'd understood his need for a little distance. That was why, as self-reliant as he'd always seemed to her, she hadn't considered that once their son had been found, Alex would feel any need for the silent support they had offered each other simply by being in the same room.

She had the feeling he didn't want to be alone tonight. Neither did she. And while she was afraid, she was more afraid of never again experiencing what she'd felt in his arms.

Alex watched Kelly's lashes lower and her mouth part slightly as she drew a deep breath. What he wanted was far more than just to be with her. He wanted her beneath him, to hear her whisper his name, to waken in the morning with her still beside him. But she was afraid, and he'd already hurt her enough.

His fingers slipped into her hair. "I'm going to kiss you good-night, Kelly. Then, I'll go make up that bed."

"You don't have to do that."

"Kiss you?"

"Make up the bed."

The caution he'd seen in her eyes now entered his own. "Then where do I sleep?"

Through the open window he could hear the lulling sound of crickets, and the flutter of leaves from a bush near the screen. Those sounds were calming, peaceful. But he felt no peace. All Alex felt in the moments before Kelly finally spoke, was the dull ache of need.

"I don't want to be afraid, Alex."

There was a wealth of meaning tied up in her simply spoken words.

There was even more in his response.

"You don't have to be."

His mouth covered hers, warm, soft and full. He kissed her once, touching her only with his lips and the fingers that had threaded themselves through her hair. He kissed her again, this time holding her face between his hands, gently, carefully, as if she were infinitely fragile, infinitely precious. And a third time, now coaxing her lips to part, mating with her tongue, and turning the flutter low in her abdomen to a warm, liquid heat. He kept his body back from hers, allowing only the contact of his big hands as he angled her head to linger over the slow, sensual foray.

Craving the contact he denied her, Kelly drew her hands up his chest. Fingers splayed, she felt the smooth fabric slide beneath her palms and the rock-hard muscles beneath. Bunching the fabric in her hands, she sagged toward him.

The groan came from deep within his chest. Or maybe the sound came from her. Kelly wasn't sure—nor did she care when she felt his hands skim down her sides, brushing her breasts before curving around to cup her hips. Yet, he didn't pull her against him. In a motion as fluid as she felt, he bent to scoop her into his arms.

He carried her to the bed, but he didn't lay her on it. Lowering her to the floor, he sat down on the edge and pulled her between his legs. In silence, Kelly watched while he worked at the buttons on her denim shirt, his eyes dark and glittering as his fingers moved deftly from bottom to top. When the last button was undone, he slipped his hands inside, skimming them up to her shoulders, and slid the shirt down her arms to land at her feet. With the flick of a clasp, he did the same with her bra.

Instinctively, Kelly started to cross her arms, embarrassed to be so exposed. Alex caught her by the wrists, the pressure of his fingers as gentle as his tone. "Don't." He met her eyes, his hunger burning into her. "I've seen you before."

"That was a long time ago."

"Not that long." With his hands curved around her rib cage, he drew her forward. "I lay awake remembering how you looked standing in the rain that night. I could see right though that gown you were wearing." He tugged her forward, his voice raw. "You've been driving me crazy, Kelly." His lips whispered over her stomach. "And I want you so badly it hurts."

His words did something strangely freeing to her spirit. She liked the idea of making him a little crazy, and the thought that he fantasized about her did some rather healthy things to her ego, too. But the fact that he wanted her was all that really mattered as he trailed a line of fire over her skin.

Then, nothing mattered at all. She felt his breath feather over the underside of her breast. A moment later, his lips closed over her nipple and his palm slid up her back to bring her closer. She threaded her fingers through his hair, as much to steady herself as to quench her need to touch him. But it was what he did long moments later, after he drew a path of kisses down her stomach and pulled back to unzip her cutoffs that made her nearly forget to breathe.

There were only a few faded stretch marks visible above her waistband. Noticing them, a faint frown touched Alex's forehead. He didn't stop what he was doing, though. He only did it more slowly, more carefully, his brow furrowing farther as he slid the denim over her hips so she could step out of them. With his hands back at her waist, he drew the white lace of her panties down far enough to expose the rest of the thin, silvery lines.

He didn't give her time to feel uneasy. Without saying a word, his fingers splayed around her hips, digging into her bottom to pull her forward. Lowering his head, he kissed the pearly scars, each one in turn, then met her eyes with a look that she couldn't begin to comprehend.

He wouldn't hurt her again. Alex swore that to himself as he shoved aside pillows and quilts and tugged her down onto the bed beside him. He could see questions in her eyes, but he didn't know if he had any answers. So he leaned over her, covering her mouth with his and drinking in the sweetness of her sigh. He cared for this woman in a way that he was only beginning to fully understand, and the need he felt for her was almost frightening.

It was that need that ate at the control he'd been so determined to maintain. He hadn't wanted to rush, to let a biological urge take over the way it undoubtedly had when they were younger. But the feel of her small hands working over his back, tugging his shirt free of his pants, was creating pure havoc with his control. The taste of her, the feel of her, had him as hot and as hard as a teenager in the back seat of a car. He'd been that way since the moment he'd first kissed her and the dull ache in his groin had steadily escalated to full, throbbing arousal. No other woman had ever made him feel that quick slam of need. Only Kelly. Always Kelly.

His heart was pounding in his chest when he reared back to pull off his shirt. It had scarcely hit the floor when he jerked down his zipper, and shoes, slacks, socks, and briefs followed. He thought he would die of wanting when he saw her eyes move up his body to his face and she raised her arms to welcome him. But before he dared to stretch out beside her, before he risked letting himself feel the smoothness of her skin against his harder, rougher body, he leaned down and kissed the silky flesh below her ear.

"Do you have anything in your nightstand?"

He'd felt her hesitation even before he'd posed the question. Now, she drew her head back, her eyes searching his as she shook her head against one of the eyelet pillows. "I was just going to ask if you did. I'm not on anything."

"I'll be right back."

It took less than thirty seconds for Alex to retrieve his shaving kit from his travel bag and tear open the foil packet. It took less time than that for him to soothe away the shadows that had crept over her lovely face. "I'll never be as careless as I was with you before," he whispered, and silenced whatever it was she might have said, with the promise in his kiss.

He was speaking of more than another unplanned pregnancy. Whether or not she understood his meaning, as he shaped her body to him, greedy for her softness, he meant so very much more.

Gentleness turned to hunger; want to raw need. Kelly felt the change in him, her own yearning allowing her to return his caresses with a kind of quiet desperation of her own. She couldn't think. She could only feel. And what she felt for this man when he settled his weight over her, imprinting his body on hers, filled her heart to overflowing.

Alex pushed his hand beneath her hip, drawing it along the back of her thigh to nestle against her. Whispering her name, the sound raw and ragged, he eased himself inside, then all but gritted his teeth at the sweet heat that enveloped him. He couldn't hold back. She wouldn't let him. With her arms curved around his back, she moved beneath him, matching the rhythm of his long, fluid strokes with the same urgency he felt. He'd wanted her too long to make it last. Sensation coiled inside, narrowing time and space until nothing existed but the two of them. Then, it narrowed even more, closing in until he couldn't tell where he left off and she began.

Long minutes passed before space expanded and time registered once more. When it did, it wasn't only the exhaustion of sexual release suffusing Alex's body. It was a kind of deep contentment he wasn't sure he'd ever felt before. But it wasn't until hours later, after they'd turned out the lights and he'd explored every inch of her body by the moonlight pouring in her window, that Alex realized what the feeling was. Lying beneath quilts that smelled of fresh air and sunshine, with Kelly nestled asleep in his arms, he realized that making love with the mother of his son was almost like . . . coming home.

The only problem was that he couldn't stay.

Chapter Twelve

The first rays of the sun had just spilled over the tops of the mountains, fading the night and filling the room with a golden glow when Kelly quietly left Alex sleeping in her bed. She had chores to do before they left. While she would have loved to share the sunrise with Alex, given the stresses he'd been under lately, she thought he could use the extra rest.

Thirty minutes later, having watched the sun come up by herself as she usually did anyway and having completed her chores, she set her watering can by the step and opened the back door.

Even before she entered the kitchen, she knew she would be denied the luxury of waking Alex in bed. She could hear him on the telephone. His deep voice drifted toward her, its rich vibrato singing along her nerves. She'd been telling herself ever since she'd awakened it didn't matter that it could be months before she saw him again. But hearing his voice, and aching to be back in his arms, she knew it mattered very much. At that very moment, he was on the telephone talking about the project in London that would effectively remove him from her life for the next year. If he could scarcely find time for his son, she could hardly expect him to find time for her.

That conclusion was not one she cared to contemplate at the crack of dawn. Especially when she saw him glance toward her. The moment he met her eyes, she saw him hesitate, a quick shadow darting over his freshly shaved face. It was that marked hesitation and the uneasy smile he offered as he pulled his hand from the pocket of his slacks and motioned her over, that warned her. While she'd realized last night that she still loved him, what they had shared in the long hours before dawn had only left him wanting to hide his regret.

Her heart hurting, wanting desperately to believe it was only nerves making her feel so irritatingly insecure, she moved toward him. With his attention divided between her and his call, he drew her against him and pressed his lips to her forehead. Kelly wasn't sure why, but there was something about the gesture that made the dull ache in her heart so much worse. The feeling only compounded itself when she glanced up at him. Something that looked almost like sadness flickered through his eyes. Then, the regret moved back and his expression grew shuttered.

He was already distancing himself from her.

Slipping from beneath his arm, envying him whatever ability he possessed that allowed him to separate his mind from his heart, she told herself that she would think only about Ryan for now. Later, when she was back home and alone, she could start to get over his father. Again.

* * *

Alex was still tethered to the wall by the phone cord when Kelly, showered and dressed herself, returned to the kitchen half an hour later. Doing her best to ignore the way he avoided her glance while he paced and talked, and paced and listened, she opened the fridge for the orange juice. She had no idea who was on the other end of the line now; whether it was the same person, or someone different. She could tell only that the conversation had something to do with some expert and a comparison of European markets to those in the States. From the way he pushed his fingers through his hair, Alex seemed more tired than agitated—and a little less than enthusiastic about whatever it was he was hearing. She was pretty sure part of his fatigue, and his distraction, came from the worry over what his son had done.

Worried about Ryan herself, she handed Alex a glass of orange juice and pointed to her watch.

The dark hair tumbling over his forehead bounced as he nodded in acknowledgement.

"Fax those numbers to the Phoenix office, will you?" she heard him ask whoever was on the other end of the line. His glance running the length of the pale yellow, mid-calf T-shirt dress she'd pulled on, he took the glass she offered. "I'll be there sometime tomorrow morning. I'm not sure where I'll be tonight," he added. "Maybe in Tucson. Just leave any messages in Phoenix."

Thirty seconds later, he'd hung up the phone.

"What time did you book me to come back?" she asked.

"I didn't." Half the juice disappeared. "Your return is open. Are you ready?"

"All I have to do is lock up."

She watched the other half of the juice follow the first, the strong cords in his neck convulsing as he swallowed. A moment later he handed the drained glass back to her with a grateful, "Thanks. But that'll never replace coffee, you know."

The corner of his mouth lifted in a smile, but the strain behind it was still there, robbing it of life.

"Sorry," she returned, as determined as he seemed to be to work around the tension humming in the air. "I thought you were supposed to be in London," she observed, quite casually, on her way to the sink.

Over the sound of running water came a distracted, "I was."

"Did something come up again?"

The dark shadows in his sharply defined features seemed to increase, the weariness that had abated for a while last night taking over once again. "I took another look at Dad's growth plans and saw a couple of things that won't work in the current markets. To keep from burying ourselves the first year out, I hired a consultant to look over the projections and make some recommendations."

He was going to meet the responsibility he felt to the family business, come hell or high water. That was as obvious to Kelly as the vein throbbing in his temple when his jaw hardened. That he was beginning to sound a little resentful of the demand placed on him was something she thought best not to mention. He had enough to deal with right now.

"So when will you be going over?"

"The first of next month, probably."

"Will you be able to spend some time with Ryan before you go?"

With his hand clamped around the back of his neck, he muttered, "I thought I'd spend weekends with him."

"He'll like that."

She meant her smile to be encouraging. Alex thought he would have found it so, too, had he not been so aware of what she wasn't saying. She could have easily pointed out that Ryan probably wouldn't have run away, had he made that sort of time for him before; had he been there for him. But she didn't accuse, and that made him feel even worse than he already did.

When several seconds passed in silence, she looked away. Her tone, quiet before, grew quieter still. "Have you had time to get used to the idea of sharing him yet?"

He hesitated, not sure he trusted the question. "I guess that would depend on what's on your mind."

"I'd just like to make some definite plans. I can wait until after you leave to see him…after today, I mean. But I'd like to have some time with him. Maybe to bring him here for a few days. And to have him for Christmas," she added, thinking Ryan would love the snow. "You could have him for Thanksgiving, but if that doesn't work, we could switch."

For a moment, Alex said nothing. It occurred to him just then that there really wasn't much he could say. Kelly was clearly thinking of them as having separate relationships with their son—which was something he had assumed, too, he supposed. The idea just didn't seem as acceptable as it once had. Yet, as unappealing and unavoidable as he found that thought, it was the one following on its heels that truly gave him pause.

He remembered once thinking that he didn't want Kelly to resent him for the control he had where Ryan was concerned. But she had a power so much greater than any legality. She'd cared about Ryan even before she'd known he was her son, and Ryan had cared enough to run away to get to her. It might have been some sort of maternal bond, if there truly was such a thing, but it didn't much matter what it was or what it was called. The emotional connection was there. And Ryan needed her.

"Sure," he muttered, wishing he could end the tug-of-war going on inside him. But it would be at least a year before that battle could be resolved, for it would take at least that long to fulfill his father's dream. Every time his mother asked when she should plan to go to London for the opening of the new office, that was what he told her. One year. "I don't see where that would be a problem."

It would do little good to consider everything pulling him in the other direction. Feeling more torn than he had in his life, he reached toward Kelly and slowly ran his knuckles down her soft cheek. He'd have given anything to turn the clock back to last night; to hold her and, just for a little while, feel the peace he'd felt with her then. "We'd better go."

The campus of Lockemore Hall, with its beige stuccoed buildings, vast lawns, and hiking trails leading up to the craggy hills, was nestled at the base of the Catalina Mountains in a saguaro-studded valley. In its own unique way, the setting was as beautiful to Kelly as the views beyond her fields; as utterly peaceful and serene. The atmosphere inside the library-like office of Mr. Stewart Kerby, however, was not.

Within seconds of passing through the arched entrance of the administration building, Alex and Kelly were greeted by a matronly secretary. Seconds after that, they were ushered past a wing that, judging from the row of closed doors, contained classrooms and they were then led into the headmaster's office.

The tall, reed-thin and kindly-looking Stewart Kerby was on his feet even as they entered, his hand outstretched as he crossed the sound-muffling carpet to meet them. The man was both nervous about the school's failure to have properly supervised a student and unhappy with the student not only for breaking school rules by leaving the campus without permission, but also for the trouble the child had caused. Alex wasn't interested in listening to the man's apologies, explanations or accusations, though. At least, not now. All he cared about was seeing his son—which was all Kelly was interested in, too.

Mr. Kerby said he understood perfectly, which was a good thing, Kelly concluded, since Alex didn't strike her as being in the mood to be put off. Asking them to follow him, the headmaster led them to a door at the end of the eerily quiet hallway. Kelly assumed classes were in session. That could be the only possible explanation why a building with over one hundred grade school boys in and around it was as silent as a church.

"He's waiting for you in here," Kerby told them, courtesy keeping him from openly staring at her as he opened the door.

Kelly didn't care that the man seemed so obviously curious about her. She supposed he was probably entitled to a little interest, considering he'd always assumed another woman to be his student's mother. Whatever his opinion or conclusions, however, all she cared about was the little boy sitting all alone in the very formal conference room.

From the doorway, she could see Ryan, in his uniform, sitting on one of the red leather chairs lining the walls around a long mahogany conference table. He was slouched down, his bottom lip between his teeth and his feet swinging just above the floor. The moment the door had opened his head snapped up. Now, seeing who was being escorted in, the rest of his body froze.

An instant later, having been schooled to rise when adults entered a room, he was on his feet, his back ramrod straight. A look of pure apprehension clouded his face.

"I'll be in my office," Kerby said to the man staring hard at the miniature version of himself. "I'll be available to you whenever you're ready."

Receiving no reply, he gave Kelly one last glance and a polite nod, then quietly closed the door.

It had no sooner clicked shut than Alex, like a panther moving in on its prey, was crossing the burgundy red carpet. Before Kelly could swallow past the knot that had formed in her throat when Ryan's eyes had widened at seeing that she'd come, too, Alex was bending over the child, wrapping him in a hug that lifted his feet off the floor.

Eyes squeezed shut, tears suddenly leaking out the corners, Ryan hugged him back, his arms tight around his dad's neck.

"Don't you realize what could have happened to you?" she heard Alex growl, his face buried in the shoulder of his son's blue blazer. "Didn't you stop to think how dangerous what you did could be?"

"I didn't mean for anybody to worry."

"Not worry? My God, Ryan. How do you think I wouldn't worry?"

As Kelly cautiously moved toward them, she had the feeling Alex didn't really want that question answered. He knew very well why Ryan might be inclined to think such a thing; his son didn't think he cared.

The muscles in his shoulders flexing beneath his light blue shirt, Alex lowered Ryan to the floor. He didn't let go of him, though. With his hand smoothing Ryan's hair he pressed the boy's head to his hip, watching as Ryan caught a betraying tear with his finger and wiped it off on his uniform shorts. Almost as an afterthought, or so it seemed to Kelly, Alex glanced toward her.

Sucking in a lungful of air that smelled faintly of lemon oil, floor polish and chalk dust, she kept her focus on Ryan and lowered herself to the chair he'd occupied. After dropping her purse on the chair next to it, she reached over to nudge back the dark strands of hair tumbling over his forehead.

"Hi," was all she could think to say.

The look in the darkly lashed eyes blinking back at her was mostly speculation. "Hi."

"Were you coming to see me?" she asked. "Is that why you ran away from here?"

She noticed Alex's hand tighten a bit on the small shoulder.

Ryan nodded.

"Why?" Alex asked from above them both.

He didn't answer his father. When Ryan looked back up, it was to meet the sympathy and affection in the eyes of the woman watching him so carefully.

"Are you really my mom?"

Her voice was as quiet as the halls beyond the door. "Yes, Ryan. I am." She tipped her head, aching to reach for him but contenting herself with studying his sweet little face. "Is that all right with you?"

Beneath his hand, Alex felt the muscles in his son's shoulder shift. He'd kept Ryan at his side to reassure him, and because he'd needed the contact with the skinny little body to assure himself that his son was truly okay. Now, he realized he was holding him back.

He let his hand drop to his side just as he saw the small dark head move in another nod. A moment later, Kelly had drawn him into her arms as easily as if she'd been comforting him forever.

"Why didn't you just call me?" he heard her ask, when Ryan drew back a few moments later. Tenderly, she smoothed back the hair again covering his forehead. "I would have come here, sweetie. All you had to do was call."

"I didn't have your phone number."

"You could have called directory assistance."

One shoulder lifted in a shrug. "I guess I didn't think about it."

"Then how were you going to find me when you got to Durango? There are hundreds of farms around there."

"I had your address." Another tear escaped. He swiped away that one, too, clearly considering himself too big to be doing something so childish as crying—even though he hadn't been quite big enough to handle the complexities of being out on his own. "It was on the package you sent me."

She considered that for a moment, looking up at Alex to see how he was taking this. Just as she did, the strident sound of a bell jarred the sudden silence in the room. A moment later, muffled voices underscored with laughter and a stampede of footsteps filled the hallways beyond the door.

The sounds had yet to fade when Alex pulled out a chair for Ryan and, after moving Kelly's purse, sat down himself in the empty chair next to her. All he seemed interested in was getting a few answers of his own.

Leaning forward, he planted his elbows on his thighs and clasped his hands between his knees. After contemplating his son's apprehensive expression for as long as it took the child to stop fidgeting, he calmly asked, "How did you find out about Kelly, son?"

The answer wasn't immediately forthcoming. In fact it wasn't until Alex had assured Ryan that he wasn't going to get into trouble for anything he said, that he and Kelly learned Ryan had overheard their argument the evening Kelly had confronted Alex on the patio with the file she'd found in Audrey's room. Ryan didn't know the part about the file. All he knew was that he'd been lining up his Ninjas on his windowsill, instead of sleeping as he was supposed to be doing, when he'd seen them by the pool. It had looked to him like they were "fighting or something," so he'd opened the window to hear what they were saying.

He told them he hadn't heard all of what they'd said, however, because their voices would get louder, then they would drop. He knew his dad had said something about having no intention of telling him that Kelly was his mother, and that Kelly had said she wanted him to know she was. He'd also heard Kelly say that she cared about him.

It quickly became apparent from the other little bits and pieces Ryan mentioned overhearing, that he'd heard enough to convince him not only that Kelly was his real mother, but also that his father wanted to keep him away from her. This, Kelly didn't doubt for a moment, had everything to do with the way Ryan had acted toward his dad the following couple of days.

Alex apparently came to that same conclusion. His eyes closed as he dropped his head, his breath rushing out in utter disbelief while the muscle in his jaw worked.

"Why didn't you talk to one of us?" he asked when he finally looked back at his wide-eyed son. "You completely misunderstood what was going on. One of the reasons it's wrong to listen to someone else's private conversation is because you don't always get the whole picture. It's not only rude, it's dangerous." He immediately backed down. He had no one to blame here but himself for what Ryan had been left to assume, and a lecture wasn't going to help a thing. "I wasn't going to keep you from Kelly. Is that why you ran away to be with her? Because you thought I wasn't going to let you see her?"

"Sort of."

"What does 'sort of' mean?"

Having found himself in no further trouble so far, Ryan studied his thumbnail for only a moment before adding another weight to his father's broad, but already overburdened shoulders.

"I kind of thought you wouldn't be so unhappy if I lived with Kelly. Then you wouldn't have to worry about what to do with me. And when you came to see me," he hurried on, staring back at his thumb, "then we could be like we were."

"I'm not sure I understand," came Alex's quiet reply, the slug of distress over his son's admission not nearly as well-hidden as he'd probably have liked. "What do you mean, we could be 'like we were'?"

"Like when we were all together at Grandma's house. You and me and Kelly. You know." His little mouth twisted, his voice dropping. "Like a family."

Like a family.

The phrase hung suspended for several very long seconds. At least it seemed that way to Kelly before she saw Alex drag his hand down his face.

Feeling for him, for both of them, she reached over and touched Alex's arm. Beneath her fingers, she felt strong muscles tense, then relax as he met the compassion in her eyes.

"Maybe you should tell Ryan about the time you're going to spend with him."

Alex seemed to appreciate the rescue, even if it did feel to Kelly as if she'd offered it at her own expense. He also seemed oddly reluctant to let her pull her hand away. He didn't stop her when she did. He just moved closer to her, keeping his hip in contact with hers when he leaned forward to tell Ryan about his plans for the next month, and about how Ryan would get to spend some time in Colorado with his mom.

"Can I call you that?" Ryan wanted to know, his eyes lighting at the news that he'd get to go to her house. "Mom, I mean?"

Kelly opened her mouth, but the sudden tightness in her throat at knowing she'd now be known as "Mom" made speaking risky. So she was left with nothing to do but give him a quick nod, while Alex covered her sudden inarticulateness with the news that Ryan could go to Kelly's for Christmas, too.

As thankful as she was to Alex for his quick sensitivity, it was the pressure of his hip that proved truly preoccupying. The contact was barely noticeable. But as with so many other times when he'd touched her, she could almost feel a little more of the tension coiled in his body drain away with every moment he stayed close to her.

Ryan's spirits had improved considerably. He wasn't what Kelly would call overjoyed by any means, but when she and Alex left the administration building two hours later, he was as happy as he could be, given that he still had to stay at Lockemore. They had spoken with Mr. Kerby, who had agreed that the circumstances didn't warrant expulsion, though a little light detention would be in order since Ryan had broken one of the school's strictest rules. The boy would, therefore, be raking leaves.

If Kelly had her way, Ryan could rake leaves all day, but he wouldn't be spending one more night at Lockemore Hall. He'd be living with her while his father juggled the other priorities in his life. She planned on telling Alex that, too.

Now didn't seem to be the time to mention her alternative, however. If Alex's silence as they headed down the steps was any indication, he wanted only to be left alone.

That wasn't necessarily what Alex wanted at all. But as they walked beneath the cottonwood trees shading the block-long walkway to the parking lot, pods crunching beneath their feet, the one thing he knew he didn't want was the status quo.

He'd been thinking about his situation ever since this morning. Longer than that, if he wanted to be honest with himself. His first real doubts had taken root in a San Francisco hotel room while he'd been on the phone to his son's mother in Colorado with their son tucked away in Tucson. But he hadn't realized how long past due the decision was until his little boy had told him he'd thought his father would be happier without him.

He couldn't afford another year away from Ryan. Now, walking away from him once again, he knew beyond the shadow of a doubt that if he left this time he would regret it for the rest of his life. He *had* no life. All he had were responsibilities. And Ryan, as Kelly had not-so-subtly tried to tell him, was the most important one he would ever have.

"I'm not going through with it. The London operation," he added, shoving his fingers through his hair as he came to a halt. "It's costing too damn much."

As she stopped beside him, puzzlement swept over Kelly's look of concentration.

"Is that what your consultant told you this morning? About the European market?"

For a moment, his expression mirrored hers. Realizing what she was referring to, and not at all surprised she should think him preoccupied with business, he shook his head. "That report hasn't been completed yet. Not that it matters," he muttered, wondering if he hadn't subconsciously sabotaged himself. It was entirely possible, he supposed, that when he'd hired that consultant, he hadn't been looking for a way to compete. He'd been looking for a way out. "I'm not talking about the agency. I'm talking about Ryan."

And you, he added to himself, but he had no idea how she'd take such an admission, given the skepticism so evident in her eyes. Last night, she'd said she was afraid of what he made her feel. She still was. He could see it. She hadn't believed then that he wouldn't hurt her somehow, and he could tell she was no closer to trusting him now than she'd been twenty-four hours ago.

Able to cross only one bridge at a time, he muttered, "I can't do this to him."

"What about the company?" she asked, as stunned and pleased as she was curious. "About what your father wanted? Your family—"

"My family," he cut in, "has always been very big on the business and loyalty to each other. But Ryan is my family, too."

He turned away, his agitation growing. His family had always demanded, and received, everything from him. But it wasn't until Kelly had come back that he'd begun to see just how expensive that loyalty was. "I'm not blaming them for anything," he explained, refusing to abdicate responsibility for his own actions. "I was the one who got so caught up in their expectations that I couldn't see what really mattered. I'm not my father. Being the biggest name in advertising doesn't mean a thing to me. All I care about is the integrity of the company, not the size. But since being the biggest meant so much to him, and because I respected him, I felt I'd be failing somehow if I didn't see his plans through.

"I was always being told what they wanted, Kelly. What they expected. Not once did anyone ever ask what *I* wanted." His tone was as fierce as it was quiet when he stopped in front of her. But then the fierceness faded. "No one but you."

His eyes roamed her face, seeking something Kelly wasn't sure she understood.

"What do you want, Alex?"

"I want a lot of things," he said, his voice husky. "Some I'm not sure I can have. Or deserve. But if I had just one wish, I'd wish my son could have his mother. He needs you, Kelly. To be with you."

With the same caution he saw enter her eyes, he lifted his hand to catch the strand of hair the breeze blew across her cheek. He'd wanted to marry her all those years ago. But being young, being influenced much as she had been by the adults in their lives, he'd hesitated and waited too long to let her know. Whether that was an excuse or a reason didn't matter. What did matter was that having let her down so badly before, he couldn't help but wonder why she should be interested in marriage to him now. She didn't have to have him around to be with her son.

"I need you, too," he told her. "Badly." He heard her breath catch, the sound as soft as the feel of her skin beneath his fingers. "I lost you once before. I don't want to do it again."

Even when he'd felt as if everything were about to come crashing down around him, there had always been something about being with her that loosened the perpetual knot in his gut. She was hearth and home and family. The very essence of what had been missing for the past eleven years of his life.

"Say something," he urged, finding her silence far too unnerving.

"I think I'm afraid to."

"Why?"

"Because I want it too badly."

The admission was absolutely all the encouragement he needed. Alex moved closer, not caring that they were standing in clear view of half the buildings on campus—or that the bell had just rung and a hundred little boys were swarming over the walkways to the dorms and the playing fields beyond them. At least none of them should be heading for the parking lot.

His fingers curling over her shoulder, he searched the clear blue of her eyes. "What is it you want so badly?"

"What Ryan was talking about before."

"Me, too."

Hope, bright and strong, bloomed in her chest. "Are we talking about the same thing?"

"I don't know about you, but I'm talking about making us the family we should have been all along. I can think of about a dozen details we'll need to work out, but not one of them matters to me more than you and Ryan." For once, he didn't need time to weigh options. There was no option, other than this. Being with her, being part of her, *felt* right. "I love you, Kelly. If you think you could ever feel that way about me, then I really think we ought to do what we can to give that little boy his mom and dad."

Her smile soft, her eyes suspiciously bright, Kelly curved her arms around his neck. A touch of mischief, long missing, danced over her delicate features. "What about a brother or sister?"

She felt him go still. "Yeah," he whispered, his eyes glittering. "A brother and a sister."

She'd said "or." But she wasn't given the opportunity to clarify herself. Alex pulled her against him, his mouth covering hers in a kiss that stole the very breath from her lungs. She didn't care. She kissed him back just as hard, just as feverishly. He loved her. And she loved him. She always had.

She told him that, too, when he drew back. Then he made her repeat it after he'd turned her insides to warm mush once more.

The sound of laughter drifted toward them.

"I think we're being watched," she heard him whisper in her ear.

"I think so, too." She smiled up at him, feeling her heart squeeze at how the years had melted from his beautiful face. "Shall we go see what our son thinks about this?"

They didn't have to go very far.

When the other children had been dismissed to play, Ryan had been handed a rake. He hadn't disturbed many of the leaves covering the lawn, though. Standing in his shirtsleeves beneath a sprawling cottonwood with the rake held loosely in his hand, he was carefully watching what was going on about halfway down the sidewalk. He wasn't giggling—or gagging—like the half-dozen other boys eyeing his parents. He was grinning.

That grin, so like his father's, was still in place when, having dropped the rake, he ran down the sidewalk and launched himself into his parents' outstretched arms.

Epilogue

The house Alex and Kelly built overlooked the mountains north of Scottsdale. It had a huge greenhouse on one side, a pool in the back and views that went on forever. Jessica Burke—who had told Alex shortly after he announced the consolidation of the agency's offices that she and his father truly had never realized how they'd held him back—had offered the use of her decorator. Alex and Kelly had both, politely, declined. While they were sure a professional could decorate with children in mind, they wanted to design everything themselves. So they had— which was why the "kids' wing" had so much room in it.

They could have used a little more space in the children's bathroom, though.

"When's Dad coming home?"

"He should be here any time, sweetie. His flight was due in at seven o'clock."

"I sure hope he doesn't have to leave again," came the muttered reply.

"I'm not going anywhere."

The deep-voiced statement had all eyes swinging toward the bathroom door. Within seconds Ryan's relieved, "Hi, Dad," was followed by a squealed "Daddy!" and a feminine smile that made Alex forget he'd just spent two days in New York in a snowstorm. Because he'd consolidated the Chicago office with the one in New York, and San Francisco with Phoenix, he now only had to travel three or four days a month.

"I think Ryan's glad your home," Kelly returned, ruffling her oldest son's hair as she passed where he was kneeling next to the bathtub. Slipping beneath her husband's arm, she welcomed him home with a quick kiss. "He's had to bathe Jeffy two nights in a row and he's tired of getting soaked."

"There is a lot of water in here," Alex mumbled, unable to avoid grinning at the eighteen-month-old bundle of energy presently chanting, "Daddy home, Daddy home," while he slapped his little palms into the shallow water."

"Cut it out, Jeffy," Ryan muttered in exasperation—then tried not to grin at the way his little brother's bottom lip poked out because he suddenly thought his adored brother was upset with him. "Let's get you out of there."

"I'll do it, son."

Jacket and tie were hung over the doorknob. Watching his dad, Ryan shook his head when Alex started to roll up his sleeves. "You might as well take it off," Ryan told him, turning to pull at his own very damp T-shirt. "He's just going to get you wet."

Kelly took his shirt. She liked very much the way he looked without it. He must have realized that, too, when he caught her glance skimming over his broad chest. "Did you miss me?'' he whispered as she curled his shirt in her fingers.

"Always."

His breath feathered warm against her ear. "I think I'd like to discuss this later."

Talking wasn't what he had in mind. She knew that from the familiar heat in his eyes. "Much later," she teased. "I've got one more for you when you're done there."

"You want me to bathe the baby, too?"

He didn't look anywhere near as pained as he tried to sound, though he did give it his best effort. He'd been out of town for two days, cramming a week's worth of work into forty-eight hours. But as he watched his wife disappear, then return with the tiny pink bundle they'd named Chelsey Dawn, he knew he wouldn't have changed a thing. He was still exhausted at times. But he loved it. And he loved Kelly for allowing him the chance they'd missed the first time. He had every wish he could ever hope for.

And she had every dream.

* * * * *

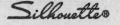

Silhouette

SPECIAL EDITION™

FATHER IN TRAINING
by Susan Mallery

HOMETOWN HEARTBREAKERS

Hometown Heartbreakers: Those heartstoppin' hunks
are rugged, ready and able to steal your heart....

For sixteen years, Kyle Haynes had never been able to
forget Sandy Walker. So the sexy deputy couldn't
believe his eyes when she moved in next door with her
three kids. Kyle immediately fell for the ready-made
family, yet Sandy kept insisting he wasn't the father
type. But didn't she realize he'd been in training for
this all of his life?

Find out what Sandy's real plans are for Kyle in
FATHER IN TRAINING, the next story in
Susan Mallery's Hometown Heartbreakers series,
coming to you in July...only from
Silhouette Special Edition.

Silhouette

SPECIAL EDITION™

MAN & Woman & CHILD

Three provocative family tales...three wonderful
writers...all come together in a series destined to win
your heart!

MOTHER AT HEART
by Robin Elliott
SE #968, July

Raising her sister's son as her own had been a
joy for Tessa Russell. But now her happiness was
threatened by the appearance of the boy's father,
Dominic Bonelli—and the surprising but
overwhelming desire she suddenly felt
for him....

Coming in July, MOTHER AT HEART by Robin Elliott,
Book Two of MAN, WOMAN AND CHILD.
And don't miss one minute of this innovative
series as it continues with:

NOBODY'S CHILD
by Pat Warren
SE #974, August

Only from Silhouette Special Edition!

MWC-2

He's Too Hot To Handle...but she can take a little heat.

SILHOUETTE

Summer Sizzlers

This summer don't be left in the cold, join Silhouette for the hottest Summer Sizzlers collection. The perfect summer read, on the beach or while vacationing, Summer Sizzlers features sexy heroes who are "Too Hot To Handle." This collection of three new stories is written by bestselling authors Mary Lynn Baxter, Ann Major and Laura Parker.

Available this July wherever Silhouette books are sold.

ANNOUNCING THE

PRIZE SURPRISE SWEEPSTAKES!

This month's prize:

L-A-R-G-E—SCREEN PANASONIC TV!

This month, as a special surprise, we're giving away a fabulous FREE TV!

Imagine how delighted you and your family will be to own this brand-new 31" Panasonic** television! It comes with all the latest high-tech features, like a SuperFlat picture tube for a clear, crisp picture...unified remote control...closed-caption decoder...clock and sleep timer, and much more!

The facing page contains two Entry Coupons (as does every book you received this shipment). Complete and return *all* the entry coupons; **the more times you enter, the better your chances of winning the TV!**

Then keep your fingers crossed, because you'll find out by July 15, 1995 if you're the winner!

Remember: The more times you enter, the better your chances of winning!*

PRIZE SURPRISE
SWEEPSTAKES
OFFICIAL ENTRY COUPON

This entry must be received by: JUNE 30, 1995
This month's winner will be notified by: JULY 15, 1995

YES, I want to win the Panasonic 31" TV! Please enter me in the drawing and let me know if I've won!

Name_____

Address _____ Apt. _____

City   State/Prov.   Zip/Postal Code

Account #_____

Return entry with invoice in reply envelope.

© 1995 HARLEQUIN ENTERPRISES LTD.   CTV KAL

PRIZE SURPRISE
SWEEPSTAKES
OFFICIAL ENTRY COUPON

This entry must be received by: JUNE 30, 1995
This month's winner will be notified by: JULY 15, 1995

YES, I want to win the Panasonic 31" TV! Please enter me in the drawing and let me know if I've won!

Name_____

Address _____ Apt. _____

City   State/Prov.   Zip/Postal Code

Account #_____

Return entry with invoice in reply envelope.

© 1995 HARLEQUIN ENTERPRISES LTD.   CTV KAL

OFFICIAL RULES

PRIZE SURPRISE SWEEPSTAKES 3448

NO PURCHASE OR OBLIGATION NECESSARY

Three Harlequin Reader Service 1995 shipments will contain respectively, coupons for entry into three different prize drawings, one for a Panasonic 31" wide-screen TV, another for a 5-piece Wedgwood china service for eight and the third for a Sharp ViewCam camcorder. To enter any drawing using an Entry Coupon, simply complete and mail according to directions.

There is no obligation to continue using the Reader Service to enter and be eligible for any prize drawing. You may also enter any drawing by hand printing the words "Prize Surprise," your name and address on a 3"x5" card and the name of the prize you wish that entry to be considered for (i.e., Panasonic wide-screen TV, Wedgwood china or Sharp ViewCam). Send your 3"x5" entries via first-class mail (limit: one per envelope) to: Prize Surprise Sweepstakes 3448, c/o the prize you wish that entry to be considered for, P.O. Box 1315, Buffalo, NY 14269-1315, USA or P.O. Box 610, Fort Erie, Ontario L2A 5X3, Canada.

To be eligible for the Panasonic wide-screen TV, entries must be received by 6/30/95; for the Wedgwood china, 8/30/95; and for the Sharp ViewCam, 10/30/95.

Winners will be determined in random drawings conducted under the supervision of D.L. Blair, Inc., an independent judging organization whose decisions are final, from among all eligible entries received for that drawing. Approximate prize values are as follows: Panasonic wide-screen TV ($1,800); Wedgwood china ($840) and Sharp ViewCam ($2,000). Sweepstakes open to residents of the U.S. (except Puerto Rico) and Canada, 18 years of age or older. Employees and immediate family members of Harlequin Enterprises, Ltd., D.L. Blair, Inc., their affiliates, subsidiaries and all other agencies, entities and persons connected with the use, marketing or conduct of this sweepstakes are not eligible. Odds of winning a prize are dependent upon the number of eligible entries received for that drawing. Prize drawing and winner notification for each drawing will occur no later than 15 days after deadline for entry eligibility for that drawing. Limit: one prize to an individual, family or organization. All applicable laws and regulations apply. Sweepstakes offer void wherever prohibited by law. Any litigation within the province of Quebec respecting the conduct and awarding of the prizes in this sweepstakes must be submitted to the Regies des loteries et Courses du Quebec. In order to win a prize, residents of Canada will be required to correctly answer a time-limited arithmetical skill-testing question. Value of prizes are in U.S. currency.

Winners will be obligated to sign and return an Affidavit of Eligibility within 30 days of notification. In the event of noncompliance within this time period, prize may not be awarded. If any prize or prize notification is returned as undeliverable, that prize will not be awarded. By acceptance of a prize, winner consents to use of his/her name, photograph or other likeness for purposes of advertising, trade and promotion on behalf of Harlequin Enterprises, Ltd., without further compensation, unless prohibited by law.

For the names of prizewinners (available after 12/31/95), send a self-addressed, stamped envelope to: Prize Surprise Sweepstakes 3448 Winners, P.O. Box 4200, Blair, NE 68009.

RPZ KAL